THE NAMELESS DAY

THE
SEAGULL
LIBRARY OF
GERMAN
LITERATURE

# THE NAMELESS DAY

## *A Case for Jakob Franck*

### FRIEDRICH ANI

TRANSLATED BY ALEXANDER BOOTH

LONDON NEW YORK CALCUTTA

This publication has been supported by a grant
from the Goethe-Institut India

**Seagull Books, 2022**

First published in German as *Der namenlose Tag* by Friedrich Ani
© Suhrkamp Verlag, Berlin, 2015

First published in English translation by Seagull Books, 2018
English translation © Alexander Booth, 2018

Published as part of the Seagull Library of German Literature, 2022

ISBN   978 0 8574 2 999 5

**British Library Cataloguing-in-Publication Data**
A catalogue record for this book is available from the British Library

Typeset by Seagull Books, Calcutta, India
Printed and bound by WordsWorth India, New Delhi, India

*Close to belief, from*
*Earth far, forever within*
*This life one dark star*

# CHAPTER ONE

# The Wave from Behind the Wall, I

A woman kept calling out my name, but it wasn't me she really meant.

How rude.

I never saw her, there were too many people; they were all yelling at once, and I got dizzy. I couldn't look away; every time I turned my head I saw my mother lying there—everything silent.

Not even Willy made a sound; puffed up and stiff, perched on top of his cage as if he was stuffed.

'Where are you?' the woman called, I pressed my lips together out of pure fear. A single word and I'd have been dead. So I kept on hiding behind the sofa. The TV was running, everyone was happy and full of life but not my mother or the world around her.

A voice inside my head, I swear, said: Your mother's never coming back.

Although she was lying right there, almost next to me. I could've crawled over and touched her. The voice said: You can forget about all that. I cringed and continued to listen to that other woman calling out my name.

And without wanting to, I raised my hand a little and waved.

I waved to the sofa—how stupid is that?

That I was a kid is no excuse, I should've stood up, showed myself and done something.

Why didn't I do anything?

The voice inside my head relentlessly asked: Why didn't you do anything, why did you just stay there, dumb and afraid? I wanted to say that that wasn't true at all; my mouth was closed, but deep down inside me it was clear: the voice was right.

As a kid, and I've known it till today, I spoke to myself more than to other people. I probably even spoke to Willy more than my father. And my father for his part probably spoke more to his clients than to me and my mother. That's just how it was.

He didn't speak, he yelled. And that day my mother yelled back, louder than I'd ever heard her before. Until that night, I didn't even know she had that strong a voice. She was just Low-Voiced Liese. Everyone called her that, the neighbours, all the people in the shops; my father called her Liese, just like his brother and everybody who knew us. But when no one was listening, my mother really was Low-Voiced Liese. Because she liked to whisper and most happily wouldn't have spoken at all. To me it was beautiful, at least to the degree I can remember.

That was the day my memory just stopped. More than anything else I wanted her to say something, to yell like she had before, loudly, viciously, and flap her arms about like waving to the good Lord.

But she just lay there; I cowered behind the sofa; nothing made sense any more; the woman on the TV kept calling out my name, and I hated her for it. She was the fake one and she didn't mean me at all, just someone I could see as little as she could.

That was the day when people in East Berlin made it through the Wall, and I disappeared behind one because I didn't trust myself enough to walk over to her as she called out my name.

I was just two metres away from her, I held my arms over my head and, small and thin as I was, cowered between the sofa and the wall because I finally wanted to find my Porsche Carrera 6 and nothing else.

And nothing else.

How was I supposed to know what it sounds like when someone dies?

CHAPTER TWO

# When the Dead Come to Visit, I

The dead, for their part, never stuck to the day of the dead. They came whenever they wanted and stayed overnight, sometimes even in twos—though most of the time alone—as if they had agreed to steal neither space nor time from each other, or out of respect for the other's dignity.

Jakob Franck had been contemplating these things for years but did not expect any answer. The dead's presence explained enough. His thoughts were only supposed to distract him from himself, and sometimes they actually did. He would sit at the living-room table and—silently, his hands wandering—hold a conversation about his guests' motives and intentions, occasionally take a butter cookie from the plate in the centre, rock his head, put on his glasses and take them back off, then eventually lean back and nod deliberately as if after intense examination of all the arguments he agreed with his own opinion.

He was aware of how detached he seemed, but in all the years he had not found any other way to confront the ghosts from his past without making himself ridiculous by indulging his fears with little mind games, like a child stuck down in a dark basement.

He had simply had the small hope that after his retirement his visitors might begin to spare him.

Today, however, two months later, he just shook his head thinking about it. In retrospect, it all seemed so abstruse.

The dead had always been a part of his present; it made no difference that he had once been a part of the squad in Department 11 and responsible for notifying family members of a relative's death or that recently, as a divorced homemaker without any partner, he could halfway handle his interior monologues. His professional and personal status did not matter to the dead. Back when starting out with the higher services, he had opted for their world and no one came back from that world unscathed or dreamless. Jakob Franck had known this from the beginning—or had at least suspected it—and, until now, did not regret his decision whatsoever.

He only wished they would not spook him to death every time.

The thirty-two-year-old woman had thrown herself in front of the long-distance train to Budapest. The crime scene was forty metres long; her left hand lay on the other side of the rails, which is where a co-worker from forensics had found it and waved over to the inspector with it.

For weeks, Jakob Franck had not been able to get that wave out of his head.

Whenever he saw his colleague dressed in his protective suit in his mind, he was tortured by the thought of whether or not the young woman had also raised her arm—seconds before the train took hold of her and transformed her hand into a grotesque, weightless wave, far away from the rest of her limbs. Her face extinguished.

For one whole day and night the woman had remained nameless, then her mother reported her missing and gave the police a photo. An absent person, Franck had thought, and was ashamed of himself. What the investigators had been able to learn was not enough to reconstruct a biography—the conversation with her mother was halting, from time to time Franck had had to raise his voice in order to tear the fifty-two-year-old woman out of her lethargy or shake her out of her internal flight for a couple of minutes. In his estimation, Lore Balan had simply not wanted to know about her daughter's tragedy; she condemned her suicide and settled into the idea that from then on she would bear the mark of Cain, that for the rest of her days she would have to carry around other people's contempt.

'It's true!' she said and repeated herself whenever she showed up to see Franck as if she was a welcome guest. The inspector disagreed with her emphatically—even today, on the last day in October. He spoke into the emptiness, just like he had back then.

Paulus Landwehr was there too. He was not bleeding. He never bled. He always arrived in the same grey-white, paint-spotted dungarees and the green, no-less-tattered sweatshirt and would ask for schnapps, cherry brandy if possible. The detectives had discovered eleven unopened and nineteen empty cherry-brandy bottles in the Landwehr's apartment; beer crates were stacked in the hall and the kitchen, three half-full bottles of egg liqueur had rolled out from under the blood-soaked and red feather-strewn bed. After splitting open his wife's head, Paulus Landwehr had killed himself with nine stabs of a knife. The trail of blood led from the kitchen down the hall and into the sitting room where he had collapsed. When Franck arrived at the crime scene, the master painter was still alive, and, as if he had recognized the detective, reached for his hand and whispered, 'The woman was completely right.' He died on his way to hospital.

'The woman was completely right,' Landwehr said to Lore Balan. Franck opened the balcony door in his room and inhaled the cool, damp air in the hope that when he turned around, he would once again be free.

But the two were still there, deep in conversation, a conversation Franck could not hear; their sentences simply continued to echo through his head. And so he bent over the table, took a biscuit, chewed as loud as his teeth would let him, smacked his lips when he swallowed, grabbed a second one and repeated the process six times.

After that he slumped down in the chair, closed his eyes and let his thoughts wander through the empty city park: the gravel crunched under his soles, the wind practised a melody with the branches and leaves. A great feeling of security enveloped the ex-inspector and he wanted to enjoy it. And maybe he would even have been able to if the telephone had not rung and, thanks to a professional reflex, he had not jumped up and hurried out into the hall.

On his way, he did not have to turn around once to understand whether both of his guests were still at the table: Lore Balan—divorced, kitchen help at the Ibis Hotel, mother of a daughter suffering from depression who in her suicide note begged for forgiveness for doing what she did and for her entire life. Paulus Landwehr— husband to Pia Landwehr for twenty-nine years, once a sought-after craftsman, an alcoholic like his wife who, as neighbours and relatives testified, he constantly hit up for money until she gave in and handed him another few cents.

In the hallway, Franck heard him say, 'You're tot'ly right, your daughter shouldna' done that.'

With a quick motion, Franck grabbed the receiver and held it up to his ear.

'Franck.'

'Winther.'

Then: silence. The caller hung up. For a few minutes Franck stood in the hall with the receiver in his hand, looking at the front door as if waiting for the bell to ring and ready to open it for a guest whose arrival would not careen into his present like a meteor.

'Please forgive me for yesterday,' the man at the door said before mentioning his name for the third time.

'That's quite all right.' Franck stuck out his hand. The two men looked at each other for a while without saying a word, their eyes full of a certain awkwardness.

The day before, the telephone rang again after an hour; Franck toyed with the idea of letting the answering machine get it, which was unlike him. He always took calls at home—a habit that could be blamed on the precision police work required, like his cursive handwriting, legible down to the very last comma, or his use of the word cursive—as opposed to printing —to begin with, when not to mention copy versus duplicate.

On the other end of the line was a man whose voice he recognized immediately though he only said a word and Franck had last spoken with him around twenty years ago.

He was also able to place the name right away— receiver in his right hand, eyes on the door—after not moving an inch from where he stood. At his back, the ghosts from his past; in the air, the drawn-out sound of the telephone became a whistling and, at the moment the world behind the name Winther became clear, the ex-inspector knew that soon a third guest would be sitting in his living room.

He hung up and, after the telephone did not ring again, only turned around, perplexed, an hour later.

Then he went and sat in the kitchen, drank a glass of beer and sifted through the paper but was unable to concentrate; instead, he thought about that evening just over twenty years ago when he had met the woman in the blazing darkness of a humble house in the eastern half of the city.

Winther, he thought. Winther.

He could no longer remember the woman's first name, it made him so mad that he even considered going through the cartons with all the old files. Growing steadily angrier and in a spiral of increasing self-accusations and fanatic ruminations, he jumped up, rushed into the hall and—as if having a panic attack—would have collapsed in the adjacent room had the telephone not rung one more time, causing him to stop abruptly.

Short of breath, he picked up the receiver, and the man at the other end of the line almost hung up out of shock.


'Just along here,' Franck said. He led his stooping guest into the sitting room and had him sit at the narrow end of the table, the one facing the window, with his back to the corridor—where for reasons known only to themselves the ghosts never sat down—he poured his guest a cup of coffee and held out the dish with the cookies to him. With an imperceptibly shaking hand, Ludwig Winther took one and carefully placed it on the saucer. He did not care for any sugar or milk—as opposed to Franck who, once he was sitting, was not shy with either.

Franck sat at the long end of the table across from the painting with the forest motif, the one that his wife, as she had put it, had 'gladly' left him after the separation; she had always found the picture 'borderline'. Franck had bought the oil painting at a flea market, to him it was like the 'gateway to a better time', an explanation Marion had neither understood nor wanted to understand—so that, until she moved out, the picture had hung in Franck's office next to the wardrobe with the copies of those files that, like the dark and shadowy piece of art, had a similarly chilling effect on her.

'This painting,' Ludwig Winther said, after a silence he had mostly filled with observing his coffee, 'speaks to me.'

Although Franck thought that the man would now turn to look at the picture even more intensely, he continued to listen patiently. 'As soon as I came in, I thought that this painting fit you. It corresponds to you, if I may say so. Thank you for taking the time. Thank you.'

Franck simply sat there, alert, hands folded in his lap, as if conducting an interrogation against his will; he had even placed his pen and notepad next to his plate. He squinted his eyes and concentrated on the hands of the man in the black suit. Experience had taught him to mistrust words as much as gestures and silence almost by default, and he paid no attention whatsoever to a deliberately friendly demeanour. Five out of ten people he had sat in front of as an investigator had tried to warm him up with clumsily-knitted-together lies; two of them had dumped theirs on the table as if naked facts, one had uttered complete nonsense, one had been the culprit and thus temporarily entitled to telling lies, and only one out of the ten had actually said what they knew and it corresponded to reality. His personal statistics had never let Franck down, not a single time.

Without noticing, within seconds he had reverted into the role of an on-duty clerk.

Even throughout the hour to come his behaviour remained the same; he never noticed that he had occasionally scribbled down a word or a sentence—as if in passing or by mistake—while nodding at the same time but without looking away, thereby encouraging his counterpart to continue.

And indeed Winther felt encouraged; he enjoyed his host's receptive proximity in a way he would not have thought possible. Out in front of the door, he had still been gasping for air because of the uncertainty and anxiety and had needed a while before he could actually ring the bell; when he heard a crackling in the intercom and the buzzer rang, he was unable to even utter his name.

In the meantime—just like Franck—he seemed to be another person, if possible a 'better one' than he had been that morning, that day of the dead.

'If only I'd been there, and as close as I am to you right now. Where you can reach out and hold someone. Esther. No one held her tight, the little girl. Well, the word "little" isn't all that accurate; she was already seventeen. Sometimes I walk around my flat and can't get the number 17 out of my head. Seventeen, seventeen—it's a constant din, and I walk over to the window hoping to see something in the garden just so my head will quieten down.

'But nothing ever happens; the police would've had nothing to do if they'd been on Ellinger Way. Seventeen, seventeen. Then I drink a beer, two bottles at the most. I really don't like beer. I don't remember the last time I was drunk. But back then, during the dark time, I was drunk every day, that goes without saying. But that was a long time ago, seems like an eternity. That was something else, my life was broken and when life breaks, you break too—it's a law of nature. If you're lucky and life goes back to normal and picks you up again then you don't need to hide any more bottles from yourself, isn't that right? You know that as a police officer, you know people, you cast one glance at us and: done. Continuously walking away makes us nasty and ill.

'That's a really nice picture you have hanging there; it seems familiar. Not because I've spent a lot of time in the woods, mind you. What would I be looking for there? I'd just get lost. I get lost all over the place.

'I'm always racing to get somewhere I don't want to be. But here with you I'm well aware of where I am, and it's an honour for me to be here, I know you have better things to do than listen to old stories.

'I would've just died had you turned me away. Please, as far as yesterday is concerned, I have to say it once more—I'm really very sorry that I just hung up like that. You shouldn't do such things and I myself have never done something like that before, I can assure you.

'As soon as you said, "Franck!" I got spooked and the receiver fell out of my hand, you have to believe me, please. But can you imagine? The receiver falling out of a grown man's hand! After that, I was so upset I punched the wall with my fist. Fancy that! With my fist. You can see the scrapes on my knuckles here, all fresh and embarrassing. In the past, I would have cursed the good Lord or Jesus.

'Thank you for allowing me to be here.

'I'll stop talking in a moment. It's not all that often that someone sits and listens like you. Most people just act like they're interested but, in the end, no one's interested, not even me. Where was I when I should've been there? In Salzburg. Salzburg, where's that? In no man's land. I still remember getting off at the train station, there was an icy wind, and I thought: It'll snow soon, maybe even tonight. Do you know what day that was? February the fourteenth.

'I don't let the fourteenth of February appear in my calendar any more. I tear it out at the beginning of the year, and not only on my desktop calendar but in my daily planner too, though I don't have any appointments to keep. I used to buy myself little bound calendars with maps of European cities in the back and tables with distances. So that you knew how long you'd have to travel if you wanted to go to a particular city, Amsterdam or Madrid or Budapest. It's nice to read and to see the colourful maps with their tiny writing and the blue sea and the countries surrounding it. I used to spend hours looking at them as a child. Of course, as a child you don't know what a country is or how far away from home it is or what all the connections are, you just look at it and think: It's a big world. But it's really only printed paper. No, no, I'm not that childish any more. I only tear out that one page, I wouldn't be able to make it otherwise. It's got to go, that page, and then the little book becomes lighter, isn't that right?

'Well, as I was saying, on the fourteenth of February I was in Salzburg, for the company had decided to pay for a training course. Sales strategies, psychological interaction with clients, argumentative discussions on various pieces of clothing. There were eleven of us. I sat in the meeting room of the hotel and shivered, cold as clay; and yet, strangely, the heat was on. All the men taking off their sport jackets and the women undoing the top buttons of their blouses but not me. I was shivering inside and thought I'd become ill and need to take some medicine.

'A sign from God. That's what I thought after returning to the room my girl had left behind.

'There was nothing left. She was lying in the autopsy room for more detailed examination. I visited her there at the hand of my wife. Hello, Esther, I said to her. I was so dumb and embarrassing that day and all the days after that and I still am. Dear God, I said, listen to me just this once and let her breathe again. There has to be some breath left in Heaven, I said out loud in our daughter's room. My mind came up with such things and I spoke them out loud. Doris, my wife, was at the kitchen table crying. I didn't cry. Or I did, but only much later, but that's not important.

'We didn't know anything. Sandra was the first one to tell us that Esther had wanted to do something to herself. Lies! My God. She actually stood in front of us in our living room and said such things. Just a couple of hours after we'd got back from the autopsy room. I didn't believe it at first but my wife did. Imagine that, Inspector, Doris took Sandra seriously. I've never forgiven her for it, not then and not later. Apparently, our daughter had some kind of melancholia inside of her and that's why she hung herself. I ended the discussion right then and there and went back into the room and prayed again to the dear Lord to make another breath and to give it to Esther.

'I'm admitting all of this to you because you're listening to me. And believe me, I can see that. Other than you, I've never confessed this to anyone.

'I am now sixty-four years old and back then I was forty-four, an experienced man—in other words, an employee with a well-known clothier and the owner of a little house in Ramersdorf with a nice yard. That kind of man doesn't kneel down in a room and say: Dear God, make my child breathe again. Even the walls laughed, but nothing could tear me away from my child-like behaviour. I was one hundred per cent certain our daughter had not committed suicide.

'Then the police officer came to us, a colleague of yours, and said that the forensic doctors could not *completely* rule out unknown perpetrators. Not completely.

'That a phrase like that even existed was new to me but I understood and believed it immediately. Unknown perpetrators. And so I yelled at my wife, in front of the well-dressed detective—dark tie, dark jacket, calm demeanour, none of it could stop me from yelling at my wife, because she'd earned it. Because she'd believed Sandra's every word, because she hadn't called me in Salzburg, it'd been the police instead at the hotel. All the others in the group already had mobiles at the time except me. But that's no excuse. My wife could've reached me. She didn't want to. She couldn't, that's what she maintained later. I didn't believe a single word.

'"Unknown perpetrators" means that someone was there and had the rope. And tied it around our daughter's neck. And hung her to the tree in the park around Bad

16

Dürkheimer Straße. The police ruled this out in spite of what the forensic doctors believed.

'They asked all the school kids and investigated all the leads and they swore that they'd tried everything. Isn't that right? No witnesses, no evidence.

'There was no trace of melancholy in my daughter's heart. She was the victim of a murderer. And you have to find him, *Herr* Franck, I'm begging you on my knees.'

# CHAPTER THREE

## When the Dead Come to Visit, II

His eyes moved from the small, still, clean-shaven face of his host back to his own pale and hairy hands which, for whatever reason, he had laid on the table. The sight was as oppressive as the silence, and he felt just as responsible for it.

'I mean . . . ,' he began, paused, and with a rough gesture tore his hands away from the table and stuck them into the pockets of his suit jacket. However, this struck him as being terribly rude, so he immediately took them back out but then, mortified, let his arms dangle by his sides. By the time he raised his head again, Franck's smile was gone.

Ludwig Winther just could not sit still. He sipped his by-then-cold coffee and made sure that the cookie did not slip off the saucer while putting it down.

'I'll bring you a fresh cup of hot coffee,' Franck said.

'It tastes fine, please don't make any fuss.'

'Thank you for coming,' Franck said.

This remark confused the former salesman completely. All the things he had said had not unburdened him but put him into some kind of shock. He was overwhelmed and the inspector's patience just exacerbated the feeling.

Winther wondered what he had expected from his visit and why in God's name he had not been more careful than to dump his dirty laundry at the feet of a total stranger. And, on top of it, in the stranger's home, on a holiday, just two short months after the inspector's retirement from such professional obligations. The man was no longer responsible for other people's pain, and certainly not for a crime that lay twenty years in the past.

But it was indeed a crime, Winther thought.

He awkwardly fingered a blue cloth handkerchief out of his trouser pocket, dabbed at the corners of his mouth and held it in his hand until he noticed the inspector watching him. Then he stuck the little piece of cloth back into his jacket pocket and tried to reach once more for his cup, but his hand was trembling too much.

'I remember it well.' Continuing to concentrate on listening and observing, thumb and index finger ready to take notes with the pen, seemingly unfazed, Franck compelled the man across from him into being fully present.

'Yes, yes, yes,' Winther would have preferred to get up and run. He felt he had stuttered, stammered and said things that were untrue and vain and that had nothing to do with anyone. He began to feel afraid. The inspector's gaze made him feel timid. His palms became damp. He wanted to ask for forgiveness but did not know for what.

'Shall we have a schnapps?' Franck asked.

'Oh yes!' the five letters sprang out of his mouth; before he realized that he had forgotten to say 'please', Franck had already stood up and gone to the cabinet. From out of a wide, curved bottle he poured the fruit schnapps into two glasses, sat down and held out one of them to his guest.

'Cheers, *Herr* Winther.'

The salesman did not say a word. He had not had a schnapps in two or three years, he had not had any occasion for it. At home, he always had a few bottles of beer and at the weekends he allowed himself one or two other glasses. As soon as he began to feel a little bit drunk, he would stop. At the beginning, he was proud of his discipline but, in the meantime, had come to find it exaggerated and immature.

He was not an alcoholic, not even a drinker. He had made it through the darkness and overcome his compulsive drinking; he was clean, he thought, whose business was it if he wanted to lay drunk on his couch or wander through the streets of Berg am Laim?

The schnapps was velvety. Winther licked his lips all the way to the corners; its warmth electrified and softened him at the same time. At ease, he let out a sigh and the inspector's glance no longer made him feel shy.

'Noble drops,' he said. 'That was a good idea. Now I have something else to tell you, please do not get angry, please. I no longer knew your name. I racked my brain and went through all my files. I have so many pages, hundreds, about the results, photos, articles, a diary from my wife. But your name was nowhere to be found.'

After a quick glance at his notepad, Franck turned back to his guest. His face was suddenly covered by a red gleam, and his hand no longer trembled.

'And then a film came on the television.' Winther's voice sounded almost lively. 'It was about Anne Frank in Amsterdam, and something clicked. It immediately occurred to me that yours was spelled with a "ck" and so I called information, it all went very smoothly. I can't explain why I couldn't find your name anywhere.'

'Now here you are, and we are drinking a schnapps together.'

'Yes, we are.'

'Twenty-one years have passed since the death of your daughter,' Franck said. 'And your wife Doris . . .'

'How do you know that so well?'

'Excuse me?'

'The number of years.'

'You mentioned it yourself.'

'Oh, right. Sorry.'

'And your wife Doris died one year thereafter.'

'She didn't die, she committed suicide. Hung herself, just like our daughter had been hung. By a murderer.'

'Do you have any new clues that point to a crime, *Herr* Winther?'

'I stand by it. Full stop.'

'By what exactly?'

'My conviction.'

'Who killed your daughter? Who do you suspect?'

'No suspicion, conviction. Would you like to offer me another schnapps? Only if you'll have another.'

'Of course.' Franck poured two more, stuck the cork into the bottle, raised his glass and paused. Amazed, he looked at the notepad with its scribbled words and for a moment could not remember when he had written them down. He drank his fruit schnapps and observed the widower as he once again licked his lips and carefully, or awkwardly, put his glass back down on the table.

Franck waited for Winther to feel comfortable again with his stare. 'What reason could someone have had to kill your daughter?'

'I have no idea. Stupidity?'

'At the time, my colleagues found no motive, but they did find evidence of your daughter's intention to kill herself.'

'It's all in my files. Nevertheless, it isn't true.' For a while, Ludwig Winther put up with the silence; the inspector clearly refused to agree with him. Then he took out his handkerchief, dabbed again at his mouth and put it back away. 'Why, *Herr* Inspector? Do you know how old Esther was? Do you?'

'She was seventeen.'

'That's correct, seventeen, and she was a cheerful soul and had a nice home and good marks at school. That kind of young person doesn't leave her parents' home to go hang herself in the park. That's absurd. The detectives left us alone with our doubts, and with the truth as well.' Winther hung his head, stretched his back, and seemed to be pulled downward by an interior force of gravity. Again, his arms dangled from his sides and his breath grew heavy.

'Would you like a glass of water?' Franck asked.

Winther shook his head tiredly.

Franck wondered if he should take a break, open the balcony door, make some fresh coffee and talk with his guest about something else in order to distract him a little. Experience had taught him to take advantage of a witness' tense, agitated state to force them into giving an irreversible statement even if there was always the risk that they would later try to take it back.

Once again Franck caught himself thinking like an interrogator with only the admissible conclusion of an investigation in mind. But the man sitting in front of him, broken and bent by the leaden emptiness of his life, was no witness, he was a relative, a surviving dependent, the father of a daughter, the husband of a woman who had also hung herself and left behind a man who ever since had been wandering through the cages of his questions.

The black bird of loneliness is nesting in this man's eyes, Franck thought; he knew it well from his innumerable encounters with people whose souls had been disfigured by fate.

He said, 'Tell me about your daughter Esther.'

'I already did,' Winther confusedly lifted his head. 'I already tried. She was beautiful; she had long, dark hair, and she was affectionate—there wasn't anyone who didn't like being around her. I know that what's in the files is wrong. She did not voluntarily step out of life. No, never ever.'

'After all these years,' Franck said, speaking slowly but forcefully and with an undertone allowing for no contradiction, 'you make the effort to find my name which you'd forgotten. You call me, although you nearly don't have the courage. You ask to meet. You overcome your inhibition and come to my flat. You implore me to look for your daughter's murderer, although Esther's death was declared a suicide in accordance with the available evidence.

'Please do not interrupt me, *Herr* Winther. You maintain that you do not have a suspect and that your daughter was a happy child, that she wasn't depressed at all, that she was cheerful and would never have entertained any dark thoughts. I don't believe you.

'Back then, I wasn't one of the investigating officials, you know that, but I visited your wife while you were taking part in the training course in Salzburg, I'm familiar with what happened. We don't know whether there were unknown perpetrators involved in your daughter's death. You don't either, *Herr* Winther. The doctor's supposition, if I'm not mistaken, was based on the traces found on the rope and, in addition, that there were temporary doubts as to the manner in which your daughter was able to climb up the tree and hang herself. As far as I know, these doubts were eliminated. As you yourself have said, the investigators found no concrete traces or indications of unknown perpetrators.

'On the other hand, some students made statements that, already some time before her death, Esther had begun to act differently, had become withdrawn, had seemed depressed, I don't know the particulars any more. In any event, all of a sudden she was no longer a happy-go-lucky teenager, but closed up and silent.

'And there were conflicts within the family which, however, my colleagues were unable to verify as neither you nor your wife wanted to share your views. Tell me if I'm wrong. Tell me if you're of a different opinion.

'And, above all, tell me who you suspect of having killed your daughter and made it look like a suicide. Who could that have been?'

'Jordan, who else!' Winther cried out in a quivering voice. The two men were standing on the balcony smoking but neither Jakob Franck, the former investigator, nor Ludwig Winther, the former salesman, found any particular pleasure in it; however, when the host had asked his guest whether he wanted a cigarette to relax, without any further ado he had answered: 'Yes, please.'

Franck had got the pack out of the drawer where he kept it in order to trick himself; after a few, even if in the end harmless, problems with his lungs and stomach, he had given up smoking fifteen years earlier, something that from day one had caused him more stress than any doctor's visit. He had bought himself running shoes in order to go jogging regularly; he began to take the stairs instead of the lift; he had a go at eating different kinds of salads and other variously praised foods; he changed from sweet coffee to un-sugared tea, poured litres of mineral water into himself and lost six kilos, a fact that for him—as opposed to his doctor—did not have the slightest point. Not even a year later, rather modestly and without any particular fervour, he went back to coffee and cigarettes, started to walk calmly through the neighbourhood again, confined his vitamin intake to bananas and never touched another piece of lettuce. Since then, he had felt better than ever, above all, because he almost never drank and had forgotten his cigarettes, sometimes even for days.

As a young man, Winther had rolled his own cigarettes and never used a lighter, only matches, most of the time the short plastic stubs that at the beginning burnt his fingers but, in his eyes, made the ritual perfect. Although his wife had asked him for some consideration while she was pregnant, he continued to smoke in secret, after Esther's birth too, though not in her presence. After Esther's death, he had given up for a while until his wife's death robbed him of any discipline whatsoever. Drinking and smoking became one. Self-disgust and the stench of the bar hung about him like a cloak. For a long time, he did not notice the gradual disappearance of his friends. Of all things, on a night when the darkness outside seemed almost a clearing compared to the black nothing in his head, the bartender at the pub brought an advertisement to his attention: a beverage shop was looking for a driver. To this day, Winther had never discovered why Micha, the bartender, had given him the tip and no one else.

Winther had not been the only one in that room who had lost his job and for whom the outside world basically continued to exist mainly as an object of hatred. Within just a few weeks, he became a fixed part of the tribe of workers at the Giebl beverage shop on Schwanseestraße. For almost a whole year, he did not touch any alcohol and enjoyed a cigarette only on weekends. And despite all the years that had not changed much.

Thanks to the schnapps and the fresh air on the balcony, he had become a little dizzy, but he inhaled the nicotine into his lungs as deep as he could.

'Are you okay?' Franck asked.

'Quite fine. It's nice here. At first, I thought the Industriestraße would be louder and further away than it is, but it's right in the middle of Aubing. I've never been here before.'

'This is the first flat we ever shared, my wife and I.'

'What happened to your wife?'

'We got divorced.'

For a few seconds, Winther was no longer a part of the present. The cool air and the biting smoke of the cigarette chased off the thoughts whirling through his head; he stamped out the butt in the ashtray which Franck had placed in an empty flower box. 'You haven't got remarried?'

'No. Like you.'

'Yes, you're right. May I admit something to you? For years it didn't even occur to me that I *could* remarry. As if I'd forgotten it was even possible. Do you have a new partner?'

'No.'

'Neither do I. Have you had one over the last few years?'

'No.'

'Neither have I. It sure is strange, we don't know each other but have so many important things in common.'

'Maybe they weren't so important to us—the things.'

'I don't know, *Herr* . . . Franck. Please excuse me . . . I know your name, I'm just a bit confused. Because of everything. And that you live here in a big flat, alone, just like me in my hole over on Ellinger Way. You can become addicted to solitude, I've learnt that much. At first you need it in order to survive and get free from all that's happened. Every morning you're happy you're still here. Isn't that right? What do you think, *Herr* Franck?'

'Whether I'm happy to still be here?'

'Yes, that can indeed be a realization, you make it through the grief and find life to be pleasant, something possible, manageable even. Or is thinking like that a sin against one's fate? My wife died, my daughter was murdered, and one morning I woke up and understood: I'm alive and still have some life left. Are you allowed to think like that?'

'You have to, otherwise you're done for.' Franck shivered and wondered if it only had to do with the growing cold.

'Well, why shouldn't you be? Why am I still here but not my loved ones? Why did my daughter have to die, and my wife follow her? Who determines something like that? Or . . . or . . . '

'Shall we go back inside?'

'Yes, in a moment.' Under his suit Winther was wearing a roll-neck sweater; he did not notice the icy wind, to him it was a welcome and unexpected breath of air for his embalmed words. 'But that's not what I wanted to say. Solitude's like alcohol, it's good for you, we can't get enough. We get drunk the whole time and think what we're doing is normal. Or do you think your solitude is abnormal?'

'Of course not.'

'Of course not. You say so too. It's an experience, and we delight in it. We think that that's what life's about, but it's only the basement of life. Because we're so far down and there isn't a soul around. Isn't that right? That's how it is, I see it in you, and I myself couldn't get back out. Out of the basement, out of alcohol, out of solitude. You live here at the edge of town or already somewhat outside it; I'm almost in the outskirts. It doesn't matter whether we have one room, or three or four, we reside in solitude, and that can't be good. It makes us old and morose. Every day we ask ourselves why we're still here but the others aren't. Every day of the year. Don't you?'

'No.'

'Then you're lying to yourself. Pardon me, that just came out so quickly. I didn't mean to offend you what-soever, I don't know why I'm talking so much, I never do, never.'

'Talk, that's why you came here,' Franck said.

While he busied himself dabbing the edges of his mouth with the blue handkerchief, Winther nodded and seemed, as before in the flat, to be free from his burden for a few moments. 'You're still listening to me, and I'm stealing even more of your time. I had to come, you have to believe me.'

Franck could no longer handle the sight of goose-flesh on his arms—he had rolled up the sleeves of his shirt after the second glass of schnapps—and made his way past Winther to the balcony door. 'I know that and now I'd like to go back inside where it's warm.'

'Would it bother you if I continued to stand here while you stood inside?'

Winther had asked the question in such a serious and purposeful way that Franck turned around and looked at him. 'Three minutes,' he said. Then he crossed his hands behind his back; rolling his sleeves back down would have been vain.

The salesman had stuck the cloth back into his jacket pocket and taken a step closer to the door. Apparently, the situation did not strike him as odd at all. 'You tell me, how could I have forgotten to get involved again? It didn't occur to me, not for three or four years. I had overcome my drinking and had the good position at the beverage shop. Every day I got up at six and came back home around six. Still do. I can work a few more years as long as my eyes collaborate and my nerves manage to handle the city traffic. But one day I woke up and thought: I'm alone, there's no one there any more. Sure, a handful of friends who understood I wasn't a drunk any longer and had re-established contact. But beyond that? No one. My needs were gone, too. Bodily needs, I mean, you understand. Do you think something like that's possible?'

'Well, in any event, it's uncommon.'

'It is. Very. I'm not going to ask you how you take care of your bodily needs; that's a private issue. I tried to get to know a woman. After I recognized my solitude-addiction. I didn't want to become addicted again. But I already was. Over it, I mean. I thought, I'm not that ugly and some woman will have pity on me.

'And that's how it came about too. We were together for a quarter of a year; then I left her.' After a pause, he said, 'I'll tell you why it didn't work out. One morning I cried. I woke up and the tears were running down my face, that's not good. The woman lay there, and I liked her, she had a supple body and was interested in me and genuinely committed; we had volcanic hours, believe me; but my daughter cried out from within me. It was so embarrassing that I had to tell the woman to go and go for good. And she did. There's no coming back from solitude. If you're not careful, you'll come to a dreadful end there, just like you will with drinking.'

In the middle of the night, in the warm glow of the desk lamp, Franck finally stopped wondering why hours before the idea had come to him to walk back outside on the balcony, wrap his arms around the beverage delivery man and hold on to him for a few minutes in the horrible atmosphere of All Saints' Day.

# CHAPTER FOUR

# When the Dead Come to Visit, III

The name, Ludwig Winther explained, came up again and again in the files and in his own notes as well. Until then, he had not noticed because it had had to do with an all-round beloved neighbour. Dr Paul Jordan—Winther could no longer remember the first name of the man's convict brother, but swore to have written it down somewhere—was a dentist and worked in a group practice next to the East Station. Back then, it was rumoured throughout the neighbourhood that Jordan liked to go after young girls and that he had even had some success.

As per usual, Franck scribbled down further names. 'People believed he was having affairs with schoolgirls,' he said.

Having come back to the table, they both drank another schnapps. Franck gradually felt the need for quiet, and it was only with effort that he was able to get rid of idea that his guest, in all his urgency and painful candour, had in some way invaded his space and burdened him with the unbelievable misery of his life.

Maybe, Franck thought, the schnapps was making him impatient. Maybe the man belonged to that group of preordained guests that came to visit him some days—with the difference that Ludwig Winther was still alive, even though he evidently was no less exposed to the onslaught of his past than Franck.

How she had clung to him.

Franck had not thought of it in a long time, but just now it came to him so unexpectedly and powerfully that he was driven to do what he did: he went back on the balcony and forced his guest into speechlessness through that spontaneous embrace, a speechlessness Winther was only able to escape after another fruit schnapps.

Winther said, 'I didn't believe it then. Today I not only believe it, I know it's the truth. That he had relationships with underage girls, I mean, and that his wife knew it and that he also seduced my Esther. This is why I came to see you. Because this is proof and the man cannot be allowed to walk away unpunished, you must prevent that from happening.'

'Did your daughter make any hints to that effect?'

'Of course. But we, my wife and I, were too dumb to understand what she meant. What she really wanted to say but didn't dare to. I mean, it was left between the lines.'

'Do you remember any of these suggestions?'

'She said that there was someone she didn't like but who was friendly and kind. Those were her words—I wrote them down. I'm so stupid, I should've brought my notes with me so that you'd believe me. I didn't want to jump the gun, so to speak, I wanted to speak with you first, and I thank you for giving me the opportunity.'

Franck said, 'You don't have to thank me. You never found out who your daughter meant.'

'I did. Dr Jordan.'

'Did you speak to him about it?'

'No.'

'Did you speak with your wife about the dentist?'

'No, she didn't want to.'

'Why didn't she want to?'

'She was one of his patients and despised me for accusing him.'

Franck waited for Winther to dab at his mouth and put his handkerchief away. 'From the very beginning, your wife was convinced that your daughter committed suicide for other reasons.'

'Yes.'

'Then she had to have been aware of what those reasons were.'

'She didn't have any reasons, she just made something up in her head.'

He's lying, Franck thought for the first time but did not know what to do with the suspicion.

Families in which someone had committed suicide rarely disclosed their secrets, their everyday apathy, their ideas and fears of failure. They lied to themselves, to their doctors and to police officers; and this was day-to-day life on the death notification squad. In all his years in the department, Franck had only rarely reproached the bereaved and only if they were clearly hindering the investigation.

Conceivably this is what Doris and Ludwig Winther had hoped to achieve twenty-one years ago: to get the police to believe in a false image of their family life so that the background events leading up to the event would simply disappear. However, Franck thought, the tentacles of guilt had never let Ludwig Winther go; two decades later he felt he was suffocating and the only thing left to do was make a clean break which he could not do for himself. That one old lie was the coat Winther continued to wear. Franck did not want to rule out that that very coat had been a gift from Winther's wife and that it would hold together through thick and thin right through the end.

'Let's stay with you,' Franck said. 'You're convinced that your daughter had a relationship with the dentist. Why would he have wanted to kill her?'

'Because she wanted to out him.'

'She could have done that.'

'But she didn't have the courage!' His voice grew louder then immediately broke again. 'I'm sorry. It's . . . I'm not used to talking like this, with someone, I mean, so directly, face to face. She wanted to, believe me, but before she could find the courage, she had to die. And the guy is clever, he doesn't do a thing without thinking. He picked up on the rumours at school and thought, That's what I'll do and no one will ever get wise to me. What else?'

'The rumours about your daughter's depression,' Franck said.

'The rumours and who knows what else. Then he went with her to the park, as they most likely often did, and tied her up and hung her—just like a cold-blooded murderer. He's an animal, a violator of children, rubbish and scum.' Spit trickled out of the right side of his mouth. He licked it away with his tongue, looked completely horrified and hastily reached for his handkerchief.

Franck let a few minutes pass. 'I'll have another look at the report but I'm certain my colleagues did not find any trace of any kind of bindings on your daughter. Or am I mistaken?'

'Whether you are mistaken or not, I cannot say. The fact that no traces were found does not mean that there were none. There surely were, it's that no one paid any attention because they all just saw a damn suicide. Nothing else. The damned suicide of a girl who had been used and abused—that's what they talked about at the school and the dentist was off the hook, but people pointed their fingers at me. This man, Dr Paul Jordan, is guilty of my Esther's death; he is guilty of my wife's death; he is guilty of me having lost my job and almost coming to a terrible end. And he continues to hang around his practice at East Station making a million a year and has a house in the country and goes for a walk every day in the park where he hung my daughter from a tree.'

Winther uttered these last words in the direction of the picture on the wall, into the dark woods. Franck quickly noted the remark that everyone had pointed a finger at Winther, lay his pen straight across his notepad and, to his guest's surprise, stood up. 'That's enough for today,' he said. 'You were unusually honest with me, and I thank you for that.'

'But . . . ' As Franck did not make any movements to either sit back down or give further explanation, Winther raised himself up heavily and a bit unsteadily.

'I'll accompany you to the door.'

On their way, Winther paused once more. 'I really didn't want to disturb you,' he said in a pale voice. 'The sudden break just came as a surprise, you understand.'

'We'll see each other again,' Franck said.

Stooped and sluggish Winther stepped back into the hall, took his jacket, which was the same grey-black colour as his roll-neck sweater, from the wardrobe, pulled it on with a practised spin and extended his hand. 'Thank you for the schnapps and the cigarette and every-thing. Will you do anything?'

Franck had already opened the door. 'I will study the files and have a think. Then I will make other decisions.'

'You cannot let the man walk free, not after all these years.'

'The body of evidence is scarce, but I won't let you down,' Franck said, for he once again had to think of Doris Winther and then the image of their first encounter came to mind: there she was in the half-light while he stood in the door in civilian clothes, a tie, polished shoes; she was wearing a blue smock with pink-coloured flowers; the smell of freshly baked apple cake hung in the air. At the sight of her, his words had simply died upon his lips.

Knowing he was from the Criminal Investigation Department and that his silence was akin to a declaration, she walked up to him, wrapped her arms around him and remained that way for hours.

For seven long hours.

'See you soon,' Winther said.

Franck noticed his guest's dusty shoes and added, 'Get home safely.' Then he closed the door, locked it and went back to his office and to the files, back to the patient ghosts.

In that room which had never become a child's room, Franck played a number of rounds of online poker with Rubem43, GinaRella, Toby8115, Firegreen and Bella-Xroma. Ever since retiring, a number of times a week he logged in as 'Hannes7' and gambled for two to three hours before going to bed relaxed. In about half a year, he thought, he would have enough experience to trust himself to play for real money. But, until then, the play-money table would do just fine.

Earlier—outside of work-related operations in illegal clubs or professional curiosity—he had hardly had any interest in poker or card games in general, just like his wife, and the two of them spent entire weekends watching movies on their videocassette recorder. After the divorce, his enjoyment of films dwindled; if he went to the cinema at all, it was out of boredom or not knowing what else to do.

He had become aware of poker thanks to an advertisement. He had got himself a pack of cards and a book of rules and began to play against himself; it looked—and he knew it—even sillier than playing roulette or Monopoly against himself. But, in the end, he had found a website where he could play against others, and from that moment on he had a new hobby—his very first, if he really thought about it.

At the beginning, he would get angry whenever he lost; in the meantime, however, he could see through his opponents' strategies after a few rounds and was able to measure out his bets dispassionately.

That night he turned the volume on his laptop up, louder than usual; the sound of the cards being dealt out by the computer, the tapping of the waiting players, the jarring ringtone when someone took too long managed for a moment to drown out the incessant whimper of a woman who had fallen out of time and into the inspector's arms.

He had grabbed her as soon as she began to tip over; she straightened herself up a little, put her arms around him and then stopped moving.

It was not right.

An unknown pain began to flood through her body; Franck knew its effects from other similarly tragic encounters, and so he also put his arms around her shoulders, the provocative smell of the cake, which no doubt had just been taken out of the oven, allowing a closeness that exceeded every professional boundary. He had missed the right moment to pull away and lead her into the living room, carefully have her sit down in a chair and then attempt to put the incomprehensible into some kind of suitable words.

And that was where Franck was among the most experienced. Whenever the news of someone's death had to be delivered, his colleagues called on him first. One day he simply became the ultimate point of contact, the ever-changing excuse for all those police officers who in their dealings with blood and bodies and sneering culprits never lost their professional demeanour but who in the presence of a victim's relatives stumbled into clumsy detachment or false compassion and useless words of consolation.

Indeed, there were no words in any guide on how to deliver the news of someone's death. What there was to say, Franck speculated, could maybe be found in the echoes of one's own childhood when in boundless heartache you shed tears bigger than your pupils and your parents reacted with understanding, love and gentleness and, until the very last sob finally slipped off with sleep, would stay sitting next to you at the side of your bed.

Franck simply did not think about it. He had accepted the role and had never held it against any one of his colleagues. Whenever he rang at a door, he only said a single, complete sentence and it was always the same. Any further words would develop out of the situation and in front of a stranger who, in just one second to the next, had had to leave the world as they once understood it for ever.

'I have terrible news. May I come in?'

'Please do. What kind of news?'

'May I shut the door?'

'What kind of news?'

'Shall we go into the living room and sit down?'

'We can do that, I just finished baking a cake, but it's still too hot to eat.'

'Would you like to go on ahead?'

'What kind of news?'

'Shouldn't we go into the living room first?'

'I would rather hear the news right here.'

'Here in the hall?'

'Yes.'

He told her what had happened. She swayed back and forth, took a step towards him and reached out her arms.


He continued to hold her.

He had never done something like that before.

In the past, he had only given the slight hint that embraces were acceptable. To those he informed he was a person of respect; even under the weight of an unforeseen flood of fear, no one sought to come into physical contact with a state official. Until then, no man or woman—not even those abandoned by God—had ever stepped over the line and treated him like someone who was just as needy as they were.

Doris Winther had not hesitated for a second.

As he sat in his office, which had never been a child's room, he saw her once again standing in front of him in her apron, her arms around him, her body shaking and heard that whimpering which did not seem to bring out her voice but the blood in her veins and the suddenly dark chambers of her heart.

More and more the monotonous sound that came from her mouth, that streaming wail of pain, seemed to Franck like the song of the very last person on earth, a person who no longer cast any shadow and could not remember anything but the taste of gooseberries on a moonless night thousands of years in the past.

He continued to hold her.

At eight thirty that fourteenth of February Franck had come into the Winthers' home, and till three thirty the next morning he continued to hold Doris Winther in his arms.

In the meantime, she had said the same thing three times and three times he had not answered; he knew that it was unnecessary.

Twenty-one years later, he was sitting in his office, which he continued to refer to as such even though he was retired, sifting through accurately-filed papers; he looked at newspaper photos, overcame his desire to continue playing poker, took off his reading glasses then put them on and could not escape the smell of freshly baked dough.

At one point, he jumped up from the chair, pulled open the window and bent outside. When he sat back down at the table, the smell of cake caused him to lick his lips, something he found distasteful, almost like disturbing the dead by blowing his nose.

He had never told a single person about it, not even his ex-wife.

He figured he had owed Doris Winther that much. No one would have understood his behaviour; they would have said he had stepped over the line and lost every bit of professional stature.

I simply could not let her go, he answered, interrupting the discussion with himself, I would have continued holding her till dawn if she'd wanted me to. Naturally, André Block, his former colleague from Team 112 who had asked Franck to take over the duty of informing her, had wondered how the meeting with the dead girl's mother had gone.

'She was very quiet,' Franck had said. They were standing in the hallway smoking and no one cared.

'Then you were lucky.'

Franck gave an experienced nod. In his position as an informer of death he had had more than enough of such conversations; he had the necessary sentences at his disposal, and even a few inescapable lies. 'Any new findings?'

In addition to suicides, the death notification squad, which Block led, handled cases concerning deadly industrial accidents, involuntary manslaughter, unexplained terminations of pregnancy and, as the police called them, unnatural deaths. If any evidence of a crime came up, Team 111 took over. Franck and his colleagues were responsible for deliberate homicides and other crimes, blackmail and abduction, harmful injury, hostage crises and police officers' use of firearms resulting in injury or death.

'Everything points to suicide,' said Chief Inspector Block. 'I'm about to go to forensics. The parents didn't suspect anything?'

Franck said, 'I haven't spoken with the father, he just got back this morning from a conference in Salzburg.'

'His wife didn't call him immediately?'

'She couldn't get hold of him.' What else was he supposed to say, Franck wondered. He had spent the night and early hours with Doris Winther, and she had not mentioned her husband even once. Only when they were in the kitchen and he asked her why Ludwig Winther had not come home did she mention the conference. In any event, she had hesitated—Franck could not get any explanation out of her—calling her husband; instead, she had begged the inspector, who handed the task to a colleague with the explicit instructions not to mention any details, to merely ask the man to come home immediately.

Block stubbed out his cigarette in the sand-filled ashtray. 'This is the second suicide of a young girl this year,' he said, 'and it's only February. What do you think were the reasons this time?'

'I don't know.'

'What kind of impression does the mother give?'

'She collapsed.'

'It seems strange to me that she didn't call her husband. Who does something like that? We'll speak with the two of them later today. Even if we can't change anything,

I'd still like to understand, just a little. Over the last year in Germany there has been one student suicide a day, which is just crazy. And if you add attempted suicides, you arrive at numbers no one wants to know anything about. Adults are even worse. Sometimes I'm happy I don't have any kids of my own. Just imagine, you don't notice that your daughter—yes, most of the time they're girls—suddenly begins to drift away and only pretends she's still sitting with you at the table. And then she takes a handful of pills or jumps off a bridge or hangs herself, and then a police officer rings your doorbell and asks you why you didn't notice the signs. The responsibility as parents is ours. Be happy that you don't have any kids either.'

'I'm not so sure,' Franck said.

'To hang yourself at seventeen! How's it possible no one's there to stop it?'

After that they walked away from each other, each into their respective offices, and despite some doubts from the forensic doctor, Chief Inspector Block's final report was unambiguous.

Franck had a copy of the report in front of him on his desk. He turned the folder over, took off his reading glasses, closed his eyes and went back into the Winthers' hallway, back into the embrace of the woman in the smock. And he heard her whisper that single sentence, three times over throughout the course of the night.

'Tell me it isn't true.'

CHAPTER FIVE

## Tell Me It Isn't True, I

Four, maybe five, hours had passed before she moved her head, which had been resting upon his shoulder, and mumbled the sentence a second time. Franck continued holding her without uttering a word. As before, she nestled her head below the collar of his shirt; her whimpering became softer and, after another hour, finally ceased.

Franck had no idea how late it was; nor did he notice the smell of the cake any longer, only the vague smell of a perfume which at first had not appealed to him and made the woman, he had thought upon meeting her, seem older. Much later, during the period of the heaviest silence in his entire professional life, he remembered it and sniffed softly, the smell was still there.

With a cautious step backwards which the woman willingly and silently followed without changing the position of her hands, he leant up against the wall next to the mirror in order to sustain her weight.

After his colleague Block had called him, he had taken down some information about the Winthers, which is why he at least he knew how old they were and what the husband did for a living. Esther had not had any identification on her but the woman who was walking through the park with her dachshund and had discovered the corpse did not express the slightest doubt to police as to who it was. Chief Inspector Block, whose unit had been informed by the patrol officers, checked the name and then turned to his colleagues in homicide.

'Tell me it isn't true.'

Franck had almost not heard the voice. For a few seconds, he increased the pressure of his hands on the woman's back, which seemed to please her; she emitted a soft sound and briefly rubbed her head against his throat.

As always, Franck had undone the zipper of his leather jacket before ringing at the door in order to make it clear—above all, to himself—that he was unarmed and to not give the impression that he was in a hurry and just doing his duty.

Before his encounter with Doris Winther, however, he would never have ascribed such a meaning to his ritual; he was sure the woman would not dare to have touched him if he had come in completely buttoned-up. The forty-one-year-old woman did not embrace him; she clung to him, if without desperately pressing him to herself. It seemed to Franck that she had had little experience embracing anyone and was overwhelmed by the strength of her desire.

Little by little, he thought, and risked looking over her shoulders at his wristwatch, she had begun to trust the reactions of her body and no longer thought about her unheard-of abandon. She wanted the stranger's instantaneous closeness; the longer she stood in front of him, silently forbidding him to speak, the terrible piece of news he had delivered in a soft voice somehow became less terrible for having been named.

As of late, Doris Winther had been familiar with the terrible. She saw the man at the door and immediately wiped her hands on her smock. She suspected that she would soon need her hands; for what, however, was not yet clear, but she would be ready. And so, as soon as he delivered his one sentence it seemed natural to her: she claimed her right to his care immediately.

'I must inform you that your daughter is dead.'

At first, she looked the man, whose name she had forgotten, in the face without believing him; but then, in the next moment, she did.

She knew that her daughter was still alive; she knew that her husband was not there, the coward. She knew that the visitor was an inspector from the Criminal Investigation Department; and that when one of them came to visit, death came along with them.

She knew all of that but as all that knowledge was not worth a thing, she collapsed and robbed, as in her opinion was her right, the well-dressed inspector's dignity. Furthermore, he smelt nice; he did not have to wonder what to do with his arms. He pulled her to himself, and Doris Winther would have kissed him on the cheek had she not been at least one head shorter.

Her mind grew full of gossip just like in the Café Luitpold on a Saturday afternoon; everybody talking over everybody else and knowing everything better. Esther's dead which can't be true because she's only seventeen. Esther's not dead, there must be some mistake . . . the police have failed all the way down the line . . . What kind of cologne is the man wearing who's suddenly standing in your home and no longer moving because you're holding on to him just like a lover . . . I don't have any lovers. Why are you pressing yourself against him so he can no longer breathe? He can breathe, he's a criminal investigator . . . What's a criminal investigator doing in your house after 8 p.m., especially considering the fact that your husband's not at home? My husband's in Salzburg. What's he doing there? Training. Ah ha, training. What's that supposed to mean? Nothing, nothing. What does the stranger want from you? He wants to tell me something that's untrue . . . Why don't you send him away? I can't. I can't, I can't let go of him, or I'll fall off the side of the earth.

She would have preferred death to continuing to hug the man like a long-lost soldier returning home from the war, that man who from the very first glance she knew was telling the truth.

She knew that there was no escape no matter how far she plunged into his arms. If he let her go, she would fall out of the world but that was reasonable, for she was the accomplice to a murderer and could not evade justice. Doris Winther took this decision before she let go of the man's arms and struggled for breath and looked up into his face marked by hours of being awake.

Once they were in the kitchen, Doris Winther turned on the coffee machine, waited until it was done and then poured each of them a cup.

'Let's finally sit down,' Doris Winther said. She held the white cup in front of her mouth with both hands and sniffled; her eyes filled with tears.

'Would you like me to call a doctor?' If Franck correctly understood the symptoms, his terrible muscle pains were due to having stood for so long.

Doris Winther put the cup down and covered her mouth with the hands she had warmed on it. 'How did she die?'

'She hung herself,' Franck said, officially relieved of finally being able to get the statement out. He did not let the woman out of his sight.

She showed no reaction. 'Hung herself. Yes.'

One minute passed, then another. 'I know Esther, I know how she can be, pitiless towards others at times, and towards herself too. Hung herself. If it's really my daughter you found, then there's a murderer guilty of her death. She could not have done something like that on her own. Do you understand?'

'Yes,' Franck said. 'My colleagues will discover the truth.'

'You won't?'

'I'm not responsible for investigations.'

'But you're here.' New shadows, a sudden thought darkened her mood. 'They sent you. Because the others didn't trust themselves.'

'I am here voluntarily. It just happened this way over the course of the years.'

'That you became the one to deliver terrible news.'

'Yes.'

'That you hold on to people.'

'I've never done that before.'

'Is that really true?'

'My sincere condolences, *Frau* Winther.'

She bit into her lower lip and listened into the silence. 'How long did we stand there?'

He told her.

Then she began to cry. Franck reached across the table for her hand, and she let him.

As Doris Winther let out a loud, hoarse scream, he went on holding her hand, her fingernails digging fine weals into his skin.


The light on his desk continued to burn; files and loose sheets of paper lay scattered about; the confused handwriting scribbled here and there disappeared before his eyes; the silence full with the voices of the dead.

Too sluggish to stand up, Franck reached for the bottle of beer on the ground, drank what was left, placed it back on the table but kept his hands around it as if someone wanted to steal it.

In the cartons in the wardrobe he had found less material about Esther Winther's case than he had hoped. As far as he could determine, the majority of his files contained copies, photos and newspaper clippings from straightforward and solved criminal cases or murders involving a principal suspect who the investigators brought to court but, in the end, was not convicted.

Two other boxes contained reports on suicides he had saved just because he had been the one to deliver the news of their deaths to their families.

After the night between the fourteenth and fifteenth of February, he had only had contact with the Winthers two more times—once in a talk with Esther's father and again at Esther's funeral in the East Cemetery. He had not learnt anything from Ludwig Winther that he had not already learnt from his wife. Furthermore, his colleague Block had affirmed that any indication of unknown perpetrators was far too vague for a capital offence and the reports from classmates and two teachers as to her psychological struggles and changes in personality far too clear.

As to the events and possible causes for Esther's change within the family, both Franck's and Chief Inspector Block's enquiries were fruitless thanks to her parent's measured resistance; supported by relatives and neighbours, they only asked for the appropriate time to mourn.

In the end, Franck had thought, like most parents in that kind of situation, they would not be able to escape the endless emptiness of their child's room. So long as they did not want to designate their beloved's grave a black, incomprehensible, fear-provoking planet at the end of the universe, they would have to confront the silent questions of every single stuffed animal.

But until today, the thought that Doris Winther had refused that dialogue with her daughter's room and had instead made an irreversible decision plunged Franck into an abyss of bewilderment and self-reproach; and he began to understand just why it was that he had listened to his unexpected guest for so long that afternoon.

André Block did not want to be bothered by an over-twenty-year-old and, on top of it, closed case. As, however, for some months he had taken up the habit of going every afternoon to a little cafe near the headquarters, he agreed to meeting his former colleague and even allowed himself to be talked into doing a little bit of research.

To Franck's surprise, he ordered a ham, pineapple and cheese sandwich, a salad and a small beer. During his time on the force, alcohol, even during breaks, had been strictly forbidden. He ordered two pairs of Vienna sausages with bread and a mineral water.

They sat at a window table. On the other side of the Hansastraße prostitutes wrapped up against the cold were piloting their clients into the by-the-hour hotel, the bar next door was being cleaned, its doors and windows wide open. In spite of a new building, thanks to the lack of space in the inner city, many departments—homicide, missing persons and others —had been moved to a building complex in the West End surrounded by similarly plain offices, gaming halls and red-light clubs, and directly on one of the longest and most heavily trafficked link roads in the city. Block had liked the area from the very beginning while until his very last day Franck had never got used to it.

Once the waitress had delivered the sandwich, sausages and salad and wished them to 'enjoy', Franck began to wonder about what he had ordered. The sausages were a strange colour, as was the slice of bread and the dab of mustard which a notable Austrian writer Franck had once read passionately likely would have called 'a different kind of yellow'.

'And this is where you eat every day,' the former inspector said.

'It relaxes me.' Block really did seem to be blessed with a good appetite; he dug into the indefinable rectangular mass together with the slice of pineapple sunk into the cheese, folded each piece of lettuce into a bite-sized bit and gave off the impression of being, on the whole, quite happy.

In order not to seem pretentious or rude, Franck ate three of his sausages, though without bread or mustard; he emptied half his water and wondered how to free his palate from the dubious taste. He decided on a large beer.

Just like when growing up in the country, the two ate in silence, which made Franck unhappy; not because he was in a hurry or because he felt uncomfortable—he simply did not like the food—but because the case they wanted to discuss had been bothering him for three days and he did not have anyone else he could discuss it with.

'Was everything all right?' the waitress asked as she took away their plates.

'Very good,' Block said.

'A bit too much for me,' Franck said, looking at the remaining sausages. Then he toasted Block and picked up the files, which he had laid next to himself on the chair. He opened them, glancing at the top sheet with the notes he had begun after Winther's visit. He looked at Block. 'Did you find the name Jordan anywhere?'

'No. We definitely did not speak with him. He even lived on Bernauer Straße, like the Winthers, and we made enquiries in the neighbourhood, naturally; however, there is nothing about the dentist anywhere. How'd the father come up with the idea that his name's in the files, and how is it he suddenly considers him to be a suspect?'

'Apparently Jordan had regular relationships with young women, with students, they say, possibly with Winther's daughter too.'

'Did he say that?'

'He believes Jordan killed his daughter in order to get rid of her as a witness.'

'Back then he didn't say a single word.'

'His wife hung herself one year after her daughter's death,' Franck said and looked out to the street, seeking distraction.

'I hadn't forgotten. What are you thinking about?' Block asked. He waved to the waitress and ordered a double espresso. Franck could feel the alcohol; he was gripped by restlessness—all of a sudden, he thought of the conversation he had with André Block twenty years before, the day after Doris Winther's funeral when they returned to the homicide department on the Löwen-grube, still under the influence of the terrific emptiness he had felt in front of the open grave.

Doris Winther died on her forty-second birthday. Four days later, she was placed into a grave next to her daughter in the East Cemetery.

Much sooner than necessary, the girl's final resting place had become a family tomb.

Throughout the ceremony, Franck had worried about passing out, thoughts were rushing so wildly through his head. He could not stop pressing his colleagues as to whether they had painstakingly followed up every lead from various points of view and whether they had given their absolute attention to each and every one of them.

The forensic doctor had not one hundred per cent excluded unknown perpetrators, even if he and the other technicians in the criminal laboratory could not demonstrate that someone else had tied the rope and placed Esther's head inside of it.

No signs of struggle or resistance; no abnormal wounds or injuries. The investigators did find other footprints nearby, as well as fingerprints on a plastic bag under the tree, neither of which belonged to Esther. In theory, someone else could have been there and, with great skill, brought about her death.

Classmates' statements about Esther's change in behaviour were not taken seriously, nor did they force her parents into offering any definitive explanations.

Within a single day, everyone had simply agreed it was a suicide. No suicide note, no final call to her best friend. No particular events at the weekend. The same old waking up on Monday morning to go to school. And from two o'clock onwards: nothing.

Where the seventeen-year-old had spent the afternoon remained a mystery to investigators. According to her best friend Sandra Horn, Esther had wanted 'to go to town' to meet someone. She did not know who that might have been and she stuck by her statement. The police did not get any names from other students or Esther's parents. Esther did not have a steady boyfriend; she was considered a loner.

At seven o'clock, Linda Schelling discovered the young girl's corpse in the park. The specialist in forensic medicine established the window of death at fifteen minutes. That meant that Esther had died between six fifteen and six thirty; in other words, shortly before Linda Schelling came into the park with her dachshund.

No one had seen a thing.

The perpetrator would have had time to escape. On the afternoon of that grey, frigid fourteenth of February there had hardly been any walkers in the park.

And over and over again the doctor's conjecture that the multiple-knotted noose with unknown fingerprints could have been completed somewhere else.

'That's ridiculous,' Chief Inspector Block said. 'We found clear traces of microfiber on the girl's hands. She hung herself.'

'What about the traces the doctor is referring to?' Franck's hand trembled as he stuck a cigarette into his mouth in the inspector's office. He was still wearing the black suit with his black tie and had walked back into the inner city from the East Cemetery in order to calm himself down and to get rid of the smell of incense, which as a child had always made him feel ill.

'One year later and you're starting up with that business again. There were foreign traces, true. We could not match them, true. They most likely came from the salesman. The girl had to have bought the rope somewhere, we already talked about this.'

'At the funeral, I couldn't think about anything else,' Franck said. 'It bothers me that you didn't find out where the rope came from.'

'We had two home improvement stores to choose from. No, we still don't know today and we're not going to know. Everything points to suicide, and her parents accepted the final report. What are you talking about, Jakob?'

'About the voices in the night.'

'Oh, give it a rest. The best thing for you would be not to deliver any more death notices for a while. Let your colleagues take care of it. It's great that you took on the job for all of us but it's not good for you. And you shouldn't have gone to the mother's funeral.'

In the meantime, Franck had told him about the seven hours they had spent in the hallway. 'Can I have another cigarette?'

Block held out the pack to him. 'How's the husband?'

'Not speaking a word. His sister-in-law is taking care of him. Have you all had any contact with her?'

'Winnie, my colleague, spoke with her briefly—the two sisters don't seem to have been very close. She's been living in Berlin since the end of the sixties.'

On the table, a machine which Franck had not noticed until then, gave off a strange noise. 'We're all getting these now,' Block said, reaching for his mobile. 'You will, too.' He held the phone to his ear.

Franck crushed out his cigarette in the ashtray, buttoned his suit jacket, sniffed his sleeve. His suit, he thought, smelled on incense. He would have to change immediately; nevertheless, in spite of it being his day off, he had taken it upon himself to ask his colleagues about the state of the murder investigations underway.

Block finished his conversation. 'A body was found in a rubbish-strewn flat on Hansastraße, looks like drugs, the guy from patrol said. And the prostitution strip is right around the corner. I wouldn't want to live in that area, or work there either. What's wrong with you? Are you still thinking about the funeral?'

'I'm thinking about the woman's farewell letter.'

'It's kind of tough to call that note a letter.'

Neither detective had forgotten Doris Winther's final words.

*I'm leaving. I never want to see you again.*

'I had to think about what Esther's mother left behind,' Franck said. 'There's a photocopy here in my files. How can a husband go on living after getting a message like that? And how come he never told us the reasons why?

What did his wife blame him for and what drove her to kill herself? Do you remember the words?'

'No.'

'She never wanted to see her husband again.'

'No matter how long we've done this job, there are just some people we'll never understand.'

'Thanks again for taking the time to look through the old files.'

'What do you plan to do with the name Jordan now?'

'I'm going to speak with the man.'

'I can tell you how that's going to play out.'

'I know, I'm going to consult with a few other people beforehand.'

'Don't you have anything else to do?' Block seemed truly worried about his former colleague. 'What do you do all day long? You look pale and thin. Any female points of light on the horizon?'

'This case occupies me day and night.'

'Do you have Alzheimer's? You're retired, you should be taking walks in the English Garden and enjoying your life.'

'I can't do that,' Franck said.

Block nodded. He had known his colleague for many years, and they had worked together on a series of difficult, not to mention nightmarish and tragic deaths; he could not remember having ever seen him lively or even slightly letting loose after work or at the annual outing.

In his opinion, Franck was not troubled by any particularly excessive zeal for work, nor did the often-horrifying details of a murder case give him nightmares; he was simply, Block thought, a man who by nature did not get sidetracked. He appreciated that about him. And Franck's marriage had not fallen apart because of too much overtime or the constant studying of files at home, but because Marion had remained an adventurous spirit, full of curiosity while somewhere around his fortieth birthday Jakob had lost the joy of seeing Spring. When he was not at work, he was sunk in books; when friends came to visit, he let his wife do the talking. Franck had begun to live beyond the seasons and simple things of life. As such, perhaps the love between him and Marion had not ended immediately but their everyday life together lost all its meaning and soon they were divorced.

'Do you visit Marion sometimes?'

'What does she have to do with anything?' Franck asked. 'We talk on the phone.'

'How often?'

'Why are you asking me these questions?' Squinting his eyes, Franck decoded the sum on the bill. In a moment of vanity, he had left his reading glasses behind. As the waitress took the money and gushingly thanked him for the tip, he let a smile escape, which amused his former workmate.

'It's fine,' Block said.

'What do you mean?'

'Thanks for the invitation.'

After looking through the window over to the red-lit building across the street, Franck ran his hand across the grey files. 'I'm giving myself a week, and if there's nothing to Winther's accusations, the carton is going into the basement, and it's going to stay there.'

'You're still blaming yourself for that woman's death, even after so much time.'

Franck noticed the waitress looking over at him from the bar. He guessed her to be around twenty; in her green jeans and orange jumper, with her blonde mane and her bright, make-up-free face with bright blue eyes she seemed like an emissary from a world outside of time: it was as if he would only have to get close to her in order to receive a new skin. His yearning to hold her for just five seconds unsettled him immensely.

Out on the street, both men looked over to the by-the-hour hotel where with chaotic gestures and clumsy steps a man was trying to defend himself from the caresses of an overweight hooker. Wherever it was she had managed to pick him up, he had followed and now did not stand a chance. With practised decisiveness, she manoeuvred him to the entrance and threw the door shut behind her.

'And now the fun begins,' Block said.

In front of the locked glass door of the office building, he offered his colleague his hand. 'One week, and not a day more, I'm going to go through it, you can count on it.'

'No worries, I'll be in touch.'

After Block entered the numeric code next to the door and disappeared into the entrance hall, Franck was on his way to the parking lot of the pub where he had left his car. Just two months had passed since he had retired, but the area seemed different somehow and even more repellent than before; and in all those years he had never once been in the cafe.

Once behind the wheel, he sank into the observation of his hands. He thought about the young girl in the green jeans, her unobtrusive presence, her glance over from the bar directly into his absence. He had no idea what to do with such thoughts, but was in no hurry to get rid of them.

He leant back and carried on looking at the unreal colour of his fingers as they lay there on the wheel, one next to the other, still, cartilaginous witnesses to a love story from time immemorial.

# CHAPTER SIX

# The Man at the Window, I

On his way to the suburban rail station he had exited earlier in the day, Ludwig Winther wandered confusedly through the outskirts of the city. In his left hand the brown briefcase with all his crucial papers, in his right his black umbrella. Earlier that afternoon as he looked through the window of his flat he was convinced it would rain. With a childlike reserve, he was even happy about it. Later, while walking through the streets and then in the train, he had forgotten those thoughts and had concentrated instead on his awkwardly announced visit and the things that, at all costs, he wanted to speak about in addition to those that had nothing to do with anyone—not even the inspector—and that in his daughter's name he had to keep to himself.

He did not trust himself to ask anyone for directions.

His talk with the inspector had intimidated him and that angered him a little. Now and then he had had the feeling that Franck did not believe a single word and was instead subjecting him to an extremely subtle kind of interrogation.

'Walk!' an older woman grumbled to him at the green traffic light before hurrying on past and across the street.

'Excuse me.' He followed behind her. When he reached the kerb on the other side of the street, he once again came to a stop and turned around. No, he thought, the inspector had not embarrassed him; there had not been a single word about the nasty allegations that had destroyed his wife's life as well as his own, those things played no role in the search for truth and, therefore, he was not lying just because he did not say them out loud.

He looked around. That part of town looked like a village —crouched houses, small shops, a church, historic building fronts.

'Are you looking for something?' A man in a uniform had appeared next to him. Only at second glance did he realize it was a policeman. He had not considered running into someone like that at all.

'No,' he said. The next moment, however, he felt caught somehow and added, 'Well, actually I'm looking for the suburban rail station.'

'Well, actually I'm looking for the suburban rail station,' the policeman repeated, a man about Winther's age, sixty or thereabouts, a grey moustache hanging over his lips. 'Well, the best way is to take this street here to the next crossing, then turn right and go straight on to the underpass . . . '

Winther thanked him. As he crossed the street for the second time, he figured that the policeman would call out after him. When he did not, Winther, relieved, quickened his step, vaguely followed the directions and after a quarter of an hour finally found the sign for the railway.

Clearly, he had made a wrong turn again somewhere. His steps began to trouble him more than he had feared.

For months his back had been hurting him; at most, he slept four hours a night. When going shopping he often had to stop for breath. The reason he now wore unpolished shoes—in stark contrast to his not simply work-related but lifelong conviction that a man's character could not only be seen in the care he took of his fingernails but in his entire appearance—had to do with his impaired ability to walk. Each and every movement required an effort.

The only time he had been able to relax as of late had been two hours before when drinking schnapps and smoking at the inspector's home. At such moments, he thought once he was finally in the train watching the barren, holiday-still landscape of the outskirts blur, he was only a breath away from collapsing under the weight of the truth. Earlier, he had almost begged his patient listener to forgive him for all the silence and the closed windows he had entrenched himself behind, as otherwise he would have to have followed his wife; though for that, so much he knew, he was still not man enough.

Whenever someone walked past down on the street below, he would take a step away from the window, careful not to brush the curtains; would catch himself holding his breath. His behaviour was shameful, but for days he had been tortured by an inexplicable tension that drove him out of bed at night and over to stare out the tiny attic window, as if someone were following or observing him; as if he were a man on the run who had holed up in a two-room attic flat near an arterial road, under a false name, with a light bag, ready to disappear any minute.

There was, of course, no truth to any of that but when Ludwig Winther thought about it—something that he inevitably did in the hermetic darkness of his sleepless nights—he came to the conclusion that he really was not too sure about anything.

Until then, it was quite possible that he had simply failed to notice his pursuer, had mistaken the new guest in Micha's pub for a regular neighbour just recently moved in to the area and had not recognized him for who he really was: an undercover hitman out to lure the murderer of seventeen-year-old Esther W., the one who had got away, into a trap and kill him.

I'm already half dead, he said to the fogged-over windowpane and was startled by the sound his voice made in the silence.

It had been four hours since he had come back from Aubing, and since then he had been fighting his hunger, his compulsion to look out the window, his self-disgust. That morning when he looked in the mirror after his shower, he almost vomited into the sink. His face looked bloated and as grey as a cleaning rag; his hair clung greasily to his skull, his colourless eyes were runny, his dark mouth a drooling grimace, skin a hairy shroud.

So this, he had thought, is what's become of me: just a dead widower in a hole of world.

He was thinking the same thing again at the window at that moment, around ten o'clock on All Saints' after his little holiday trip to the other end of town, his plea to the inspector, his brutal life outside of home wrung from the weight of his shadow.

The trip, the talk, the shared drinking and smoking had planted the feeling of a different, lost life within him, and it nourished him. Maybe, he thought and breathed cheerfully at his counterpart in the glass, after work it would be good to go have a few a bit more often—not at Micha's, he would immediately ask him useless questions—at some bar or other close to the beverage shop, one where you did not have to sit down but could get your beer at the counter or at a bar table and when you asked for a cigarette a stranger would pull one out without any long discussions and the two of you would go outside, exchange a word or two out of politeness and belong for a while to the world of everyday humanity.

The image appealed to Winther, he tried to remember if he had left a previously opened package of tobacco lying around in a drawer. Then it dawned on him that he did not have a balcony and did not have the slightest interest in going down to the garden to smoke.

He had never liked the garden—the miserable apple tree, the hopeless Thuja shrub, the gnawed bit of grass, the two camping chairs and the folding table on the terrace—the whole filthy cosiness of stressed-out and smug homeowners who had long lacked the money for any renovations but who therefore exploited their tenants with the grotesque lie that they would not find a quieter street around.

Every time he ran into the owners, a married couple living on the first floor, he thought their voices sounded like leaf blowers and that their eyes looked like weeds. Winther was convinced they were proud of themselves for doing him, that beverage-shop driver who was just scraping by, the favour of giving him a place to stay and, even after eight years, not raising the rent one cent.

Bent over and with a painful movement, he turned away from the window; the fleeting ease of the afternoon completely disappeared. The sight of his room oppressed him; it was as if every measly object—the beige, eternally empty vase; the grey, threadbare couch; the low, scratched glass table; the dark, high-backed wicker chair where he had thrown his brown briefcase; the tube TV with the stitched, ridiculous little cover on top—everything was proof of his guilt, the expression of his ruined existence which exhaled failure and cowardice out of every pore.

At that moment, Winther asked himself if he had ever shown any resolve even once in his life or had only ever told people what they wanted to hear, without them noticing, just like all the years he had spent in the men's department.

He asked himself if his daughter had died because she thought he was a pushover.

He asked himself if his wife had loathed him because she believed more in Esther's tombstone than she did in him.

He asked himself why he was still alive.

He asked himself what it was that kept him from ending it all.

The answer to the last question seemed so obvious that he grinned. He dabbed at the corner of his mouth with the blue handkerchief, folded it up, looked at it and, with a gesture he considered lively, put it away in the pocket of his suit jacket. Then he took a step away from the window, let his glance wander for a second time and, as if speaking to someone else, said, 'But that's something old Luggi doesn't trust himself to do. That's something Luggi just won't do.'

In order to prove it to himself, for a while he just shook his head, looked into the tidy insignificance of the room, and then made a decision. Which did not mean that he immediately acted upon it; for a moment, he just delighted in the idea.

He knew the condition well; he would think about something, weigh the different possibilities, do the final calculations, stretch his arms, turn his hands, stand there without moving an inch and silently talk to himself or the people he imagined were there—his daughter, the bartender Micha Talhoff, his daughter's murderer Dr Paul Jordan. In this way, sometimes an hour would pass and when it had, he would sink exhaustedly on to the couch and once again accept how wretched he was.

That night, however, he did not sit down. He forced himself to ignore his back pain, the voice that wanted to stop him from leaving his flat again, the customary torpor and tire he carried around like a suit of chain mail almost as soon as he opened his eyes in the morning.

To his surprise the cheerless and damp darkness outside made him happy; he did not care about the rattle of the gate, the sound his shoes made on the asphalt, his coughing fit on Virgilstraße.

As he pushed open the door to the Enzianstüberl, the sound of easy-listening music and the voice of the bartender slammed into him; he discreetly caught his breath so as not to break into tears.

'I've never seen you here before,' Ludwig Winther said. He had already silently had a beer with his back to the table in the corner where the guest was sunk into himself, having surrendered to the bartender's chatter which, as always, did not really pertain to anyone, or maybe just his wife who had not yet arrived.

'Sorry?' The man raised his head without turning it in Winther's direction. He was looking at the yellowed wall with its tin schnapps advertisement.

'Excuse me,' Winther said and regretted having turned around, even if it was only because he had thought about going to the toilet. To do so, in any event, he would not have had to continue holding on to his beer glass; once again, he had deceived himself.

As already so often, he admitted, in the end he wanted to speak to the man he thought was following him or, at least in that place, watching him.

He drank, pressed his lips together, placed the glass on the counter and dabbed at his mouth with his handkerchief. In the toilet, he thought, he would be distracted for a few minutes. The old tunes playing endlessly on the radio caused him to remember things that exposed him, but he would not have wanted to be anywhere else.

Where would that have been anyway? In his silent flat? In the presence of a person he could trust?

For the second time that day—and perhaps that year—his lips curled into a grin: there was no such thing as a trusted person! He was alone. Outside was the world, and he was here. The ether sent him voices and melodies from out of the same, godforsaken universe in which the light of long-extinguished stars unsuccessfully tried to trick him. He was the one indeed, he thought, picking up his glass and taking a step towards the table, in whose veins the more than twenty-year-old detonated times still beat, bringing him to his knees.

'Would you like to sit down?' the man in the corner asked.

'I would, thank you,' Winther said. He slid down below the tin sign, groaning quietly, for he had no interest in talking about his bodily pain. But he doubted if he really wanted to speak at all; all the same, lending an ear, he thought, might be pleasant.

The man was older than he was, well over seventy; his grey, thin hair fell like a veil across the back of his head and ended raggedly on the collar of his black shirt; a life of alcohol, cigarettes and insomnia was reflected on his face; his voice was raw and hard, his glances always seemed to double back about halfway across the table, something Winther found very comforting. The stranger's unexpected closeness dispelled the weight of Winther's emotions in a way he had not experienced in a long time.

'Enver,' the man said.

'Sorry?'

'The name's Enver.'

Winther had still not understood the man's name but did not trust himself to ask again.

'Ludwig.'

'Like my brother.'

Winther nodded, but did not know why. He drank from his beer and realized that his hand was jittery; he laid it next to the glass on the wooden tabletop, stared at his fingers, felt the man's eyes, lifted his head and was happy when he noticed the man's glance no longer took him in.

'I've only lived in this area for a little while,' Enver said. 'Right over there in that dump, one and a half rooms, more than I had before.' Without being asked, Micha, the bartender, brought him a fresh lager and then walked away without paying any attention to Winther.

'To your health.' Enver toasted Winther quickly, took a gulp and crossed his arms over the table; beneath the left arm of his shirt, the tail ends of a tattoo were visible, blue-black lines criss-crossing into one another.

'I've lived in this area for quite some time,' Winther said in a light tone.

'That's obvious.' Enver turned his head towards the bar and cast a quick glance at the three guests. 'Who would travel across the city to come to this kind of bar? I feel comfortable here, that's how it should be when you don't have anything else to do. You still get up, that much works. You drink your coffee, look out the window;

depending on your mood, for a longer time, or you go and do something else. Are you someone who stands at the window often?'

'No.' Winther had not intended to lie; his reaction took him by surprise.

'Really?'

'Sorry?'

'Everything okay? Do you have to go?'

'Why do you ask?'

'You keep looking at the clock.'

'I . . . ' While he was still answering, Winther looked towards the yellow, moon-like clock behind the bar.

Enver took a long drink from his beer. 'I've been observing you for a while now. Last week, for instance, you were somewhat nervous, sweat was pouring down your face, you constantly had to dry yourself off. Do you have problems? Can I give you a suggestion?'

'Me?'

'Has something gone wrong in your life?'

'What could possibly have gone wrong?'

'A relationship, some kind of deal.'

'I don't make deals.'

'I'm only asking because, in my opinion, you're not inclined to talk with people. But it can help. You understand?'

'Yes.'

'You don't have to.'

'No.'

'Married?'

'Sorry?' Little by little, Winther fell into a state of uncontrollable confusion, he felt the sweat break out on his forehead, his breath grew heavy; he would have liked to have jumped up and run out of the bar. At the same time, the way he felt inside struck him as extremely shameful. Out of embarrassment, he looked at the clock again. He should, he thought, go home and get into bed and beg for sleep to come for him, just like he did every night. He judged himself for having bothered the man in the corner. And on top of it, he had been right: the man was gathering impressions about him, had been studying his habits, had probably talked to Micha about him and was now just testing him with questions he already knew the answers to.

'I'm not married,' Winther said.

'But you're wearing a ring.'

Winther had not thought about that. The ring belonged to his finger like his fingernail and the scar from being bitten by a dog; he could not remember the last time he had taken the ring off. So that is how closely the man with the strange name, which he had already forgotten again, had been watching him.

I shouldn't drink any more, he thought, those days are over; all the same, he had knocked back a few schnapps, and in broad daylight too, which was completely out of character; and he had smoked; and talked a lot. And then he had even left his flat once more but, at that moment, the reason why was a great mystery to him.

Enver said, 'Can I offer you a schnapps?'

'Why?'

'Seems like a good idea.'

Winther helplessly rummaged through his reserve of politeness to find an answer. Not finding one, he said, 'Well, then, please.'

Micha brought two fruit schnapps filled to the rim.

'To your health,' Enver said again. Winther thanked him for the invitation, the schnapps did not taste half as good as at Inspector Franck's, but the burning it set loose in his stomach distracted him, he washed it down with beer . . . Nancy Sinatra sang 'These Boots Are Made for Walkin'' and he . . .

He was sixteen years old and in Marlies' naked arms so drunk he did not know what to do with his mouth. He drooled, she giggled and ran her hand across his stomach; he was dizzy; he should not have drank any egg liquor, or, in any event, not five glasses. Nancy sang out of the speakers down in the party-room, which stank of cigarette smoke, beer and old wood, no one else was left but him and the girl—there on the creaking sofa they would later have to scrub clean, he was ashamed of himself, she laughed with or was it at him, naked still and he bent down into her smell which would later always come back to him but then disappear, like a comet.

Together with Enver he drank another schnapps, then a third, and once he was back at the window in his silent flat looking down onto the street, he leant his head against the pane and said in a pitiful voice, 'Many happy returns, Ludwig'—just like he had the year before and

the years before that. Down below there still was not a
soul on the street.

He considered the fact that earlier he had had to
think of Marlies as a kind of sixty-fifth-birthday gift
from his memory; later, in bed, awake and shivering, he
waved to her, his extinguished star from aeons ago.

CHAPTER SEVEN

## The Girl in the Dark, I

'It's been such a long time, I really don't know a thing any more. I'd like to help you, but I can't remember her face, that's just how it is. Mira, can you bring me another espresso? Thanks.'

Franck laid a photograph on the table. The girl was not smiling, a dark gleam covered her face; she defied the photographer with her gaze.

'Okay,' Jan Roland bent over the portrait, hands in his lap. 'That's her, Esther—no doubt about it. Who was it again who thought we were a couple?'

'There was a pertinent note in the police file.'

'A note.' He looked at the waitress as she put the coffee down. 'Thank you, Mira.' She nodded; in Franck's opinion, Roland was not one of her favourite customers and he could imagine why.

Roland—late thirties, ex-student, bike courier, a soft voice which he was unmistakably controlling—had a self-satisfied and condescending air about him which you did not notice immediately. At first glance he seemed friendly and charming; the more time you spent with him, though, the more his essential arrogance came out, which did not make him unpleasant exactly, just cold. When he ordered he just waved his hand kindly, and instead of looking at the waitress he concentrated on the man he was talking with. However, Franck was not sure if all that was really true. Roland was probably using the meeting to justify the present failures in his life, and no doubt the waitress knew his story all too well. In his line of work, Franck had met such characters far too often; they neither irritated nor baffled him any more.

'What does the photograph say to you?'

Jan Roland lowered his head as if listening to the paper. Franck folded his hands on the table next to his glass of water and indulged that patience he had developed over decades. The sausages he had had for lunch were making sad sounds in his stomach, or was it his intestine, and he felt more thirsty with every sip of water he took; he looked around at all the tables full of students reading or talking to each other.

The cafe was right in the middle of the university district. In front of the window pedestrians, drivers and cyclists seemed to be fighting a bitter war for freedom in the space available to them—or at least in Franck's eyes. Every few minutes the door would open and voices would drift in from faces on which Franck could not detect any trace of past malevolence.

I should come here more often, he thought, thumbing his nose at his growing senescence.

'Nice nose,' Roland said. 'In the photo she looks older than she really did.'

'You remember her now?'

'I remembered her all along, I just didn't have her face in front of me. Where was it taken? Her nose casts a shadow—I like that. Serious mouth, don't you think? Yeah, that's how she was, Esther, not easy to get close to. Thought she was better than everyone else, like most of the girls back then. And I supposedly had something going on with her? Who said that? I don't have any contact with any of those people any more. I was at our ten-year reunion, then never again. I didn't recognize most of them, all the guys had got fat, the women all married and comfortable in their little houses. Nine years of Gymnasium to end up a mother and a housewife.'

'You're not married,' Franck said. He had not understood some of Roland's words because of the feeble voice; all the same, he did not really think they were relevant to his investigations.

'I haven't had the chance yet. Could still happen, you never know. Esther. Sure, that was a real shock when we learnt that she'd hung herself. Where? In the park, yeah, right. For me, that wasn't such a surprise.'

'Explain.'

'She wanted to be something special and didn't manage. Sounds harsh, but that's how it is. If you set yourself such high expectations, it's easy to come crashing down. I think she had problems with herself, now I can think of something. She was always getting into it with her father, always. You know him? I met him once or twice, always seemed a bit dressed up, I forget what he did for a living.'

'He was a salesman in a clothing store.'

'Salesman, right. In any event, Esther and him always fought, strange that I'm remembering that now.' He drank from the empty cup, placed it back down and moved it back and forth for a while with his thumb and index finger. 'I think we talked about it once in class, about Esther and the eternal trouble she had with her folks. If you asked me about what exactly, I wouldn't be able to tell you, doesn't interest me either. But Esther and I were never a couple; sexually or whatever, though, I can't remember.' He pointed to the black leather folder. 'But you have evidence that something was going on. Right?'

'Witnesses' statements.'

'If I'd had something going on with Esther, then there certainly wouldn't have been any witnesses around, what kind of shit is that? How can someone say something like that? Snobs!' He had raised his voice and scrambled to find his composure again. 'They were just jealous because I'd gone to the movies with her a few times.'

Behind the counter the coffee machine buzzed, the conversations at the tables had grown louder, at the table next to theirs a young man was feverishly talking on his phone with a friend and sharing almost trade-secret-like details about his internship at an electrical company. Despite the carnival of decibels around him, Franck did not move, seemingly concentrated only on his interlocutor, he remained leant back in his chair and tried to establish connections between Roland's almost whispered statements.

'You get that?' Roland asked. 'We went to the cinema a few times; maybe we messed around a little bit, why else is it dark in there? Nothing more. I think. I don't remember. I really don't.'

'Were you at Esther's funeral?'

'No idea. Why? I think so.'

'You don't remember if you were there or not?'

Roland stared into his empty cup. 'All of us were most likely there, the whole school. It's not written down in your files?'

'Of course.'

'Oh. So that was a test.'

'No,' Franck said and leant forward a bit, for he did not want anyone to hear their discussion. 'No students' names are mentioned in the files, only that there were about one hundred of them at her funeral.'

The courier pulled his mobile out of his jacket and threw a quick glance at it. No one seemed to have contacted him. He laid the phone down on the table and observed the photograph again. 'There were a number of them, Sandra, no, I mean Sara, Leni, Hanna, I don't really know exactly any more, they weren't anything long term, just two or three weeks and then that was it.'

'Esther was not one of them.'

'That's what I was saying. No.'

'Did you ever, once you'd graduated, think about her death again, about events, the reactions of your fellow students?'

'Think about it again? Why? I don't think so. I was happy to be out of there and at university.' He looked at the window and then immediately away again. At the beginning of their talk he had told Franck about having interrupted his studies with, to Franck's ears, a somewhat arrogant undertone, as if the teachers and professors had not been up to the level of his aspirations.

'Back then you didn't speak about Esther's motives.'

'I don't know any more.'

'Did anyone else in your school kill themselves?'

'What kind of question is that?'

'What do you mean?'

'I don't understand what you're getting at. Someone else? Why?'

'Do you remember anyone else?'

'No.'

'Esther Winther was the only one.' It seemed to Franck as if the ex-student was looking at him like he had three legs.

'The only one what?'

'The only suicide.'

'I don't get . . . '

'If Esther was the only student to have killed herself at your school, you no doubt spoke about it and exchanged ideas as to the reasons why.' Franck felt like he had to explain the meaning of the level of magnesium in his mineral water to his glass.

'Oh, yeah, of course.'

'Good. Why did Esther go with you to the cinema?'

'What?' After a moment Roland nodded slowly and seemed to have understood.

Maybe, Franck thought, he had been in his profession too long, and that explained why in the meantime he found self-complacency to be worse than phoniness or scheming. He let the man think of something.

Roland continued to nod. 'I think she knew who she let in, I didn't talk shit with her, I was honest with her.'

'Very good.' Franck reflexively turned into the interrogator he once had been; even his smile wore work clothes. 'Did she want more from you?'

'She? From me? What do you mean, more?'

'A steady relationship.'

'I don't know. Maybe. No. I didn't want one.'

'But you had sex with her.'

'Of course.'

Franck noticed the contradiction to Roland's earlier statement and smiled. 'Is that why you had trouble with Esther's parents?'

'Why? No. Are you interrogating me now?'

'As I told you on the telephone, I am going through the circumstances surrounding Esther's death once more, any information can help.'

'What do I have to do with her death?'

'You knew Esther well, you spent intimate time with her, she trusted you with personal things.'

'Yeah and?'

'Nevertheless, even today you cannot imagine why she hung herself.'

'Sorry. Sorry. You're overwhelming me with all these kinds of questions and accusations. What I wanted to ask you was this: How'd you find my number? I'm not in the phone book.'

'I didn't look in the phone book, I was on the Internet, on Facebook, your profession's listed there.'

'Yeah, shit. Then you just called all the different courier services.'

'There aren't all that many.'

'I get it. I'm not hiding. You said that you'd pay for the coffee?'

'Of course.'

'Other drinks too? I'd like to have some red currant juice and water.'

'Please do,' Franck said.

After the waitress had placed the glass down, once again, without a word, Franck awaited the long swallow during which Roland was clearly trying to reconstruct his story. With an even voice and a studied and well-practised friendliness distributed across his tanned face, he began to speak again.

'Thanks for offering. Why did Esther hang herself? That's the question. Now that you mention it, we all were surprised, I think. She wasn't the type. But, really, who knows what kind of person's behind the mask? And students always wear masks. For self-protection. Against teachers, parents. Students with no masks at all are lost. Don't you think? They just get a lot of trouble, get shot down by others, and when it's real bad, bullied to the end. Doesn't have to be that way. You can protect yourself. I did, just like most of the others. Esther, too, naturally.

'With her, though, no one knew what she was thinking, what was wrong with her. I went with her to the movies, no one else trusted themselves enough. People were scared shitless by her. Other students, I mean. Not a single kid trusted himself enough. Well, maybe just one other kid did. Jannis was his name. A Greek kid. Same as me—Jan, Jannis.

'There was competition. Well, not really. She didn't want anything from him, he was just pushy. Didn't let himself be intimidated, got to give him that, I can remember him now, that guy. Real terrible student. But the girls lined up for him. Not Esther, she saw right through him. No idea what ever happened to him. His father had a bar, he probably took it over, what else? Yeah. So. The movies.

'And then she goes into the park and hangs herself. No one would've bet on something like that. But, it happens. Girls jumping off bridges, girls that let themselves get run over by trains, girls that take pills. I can tell you this much: Esther didn't take any pills, she wasn't the type.

'What exactly do you want to find out? It's been so long. Why she killed herself? We know the answer to that one. She had trouble with her parents, her old man had pushed her so far that she didn't want to do anything any more, nothing at all. I said to her: Let's go see a movie. She said: I don't like them, don't want to. I don't know any more. She was in a bad way, I can tell you.

'That guy didn't let her do anything, did you know that? She wanted to go to a party: No! She wanted to sleep over at a girlfriend's house: No! When we had a party and she had a little to drink, he came with the car and picked her up. And if she *had* drunk something, there was even more trouble. He hit her, everyone at school knew that. He beat her even though she was only fifteen, or sixteen, or seventeen. Her old man was one of those types.

'And what did she do? She didn't defend herself. Why not? No one knows. That's how it was. She couldn't take it any longer. We didn't talk about it. We already had, but, in retrospect, what could we have changed?

'And her mother? Kept her mouth shut, the old man was the boss. Are you listening to me? You seem to be somewhat absent.'

'I'm not absent,' Franck said against the chaos of voices swirling about him. 'Esther was confused.'

'No idea. She didn't let anything show.'

'You knew that she was confused.'

'Me? Not straightaway. Afterwards everyone talked about it as if they'd known something. And her mother? Killed herself too. What kind of family is that? Is the old guy still alive?' He took a sip, carefully, without showing any noticeable emotion. He could have just as easily been talking about a trip to the country full of incomprehensible people and plants.

'*Herr* Winther is still alive.'

'Who?'

'Esther's father.'

'Of course. Winther was their last name. *Herr* Winther, the tyrant.'

'You think that Esther hung herself because of him?'

'How should I know? Because of him, because of her mother, because of school.'

'Because of school?'

'What?'

'Esther didn't have any problems at school, did she?'

'I don't know any more.'

'Her marks were good.'

'Then apparently not.'

'What do you mean by that?'

'What?'

'Back then the police asked you where you were on the afternoon Esther killed herself.'

As before, Roland stared into his drink. He twisted his mouth and looked as if he were considering something; then he suddenly raised his head. 'I can't remember. No idea where I was. How should I notice something like that? Talk with the old guy. He knows. If anyone had any idea, it was him. And something else, too.'

He paused, looked past Franck to the window, nodded again as if confirming something that only he knew. As Franck did not react, he hesitated a moment before he began to whisper.

'And something else,' Jan Roland repeated. 'Our parents said that the old guy didn't just beat his daughter. Get it? Whether that was just a rumour—no idea. In any case, something like that made the rounds, we didn't discuss it any further. Esther was dead, so what? But when her mother hung herself too we thought: Shit, who knows what the real reason was. Get it? If you want to know my opinion, whether you believe it or not. Esther never mentioned a thing about any stuff like that, I'd remember it. On the other hand, who knows what goes on in a family, you know?' He took another sip from his glass, held it for a moment, nodded.

Franck's glass was empty; he ruled out a beer. In his files it was written that various students had described Esther Winther as depressed and increasingly quiet and closed. 'Would you describe Esther as a loner?'

'Absolutely. That's why we got along well. I was also a loner, always had been. Today's no different. I just remembered that we went to go watch *What's Eating Gilbert Grape*. Those kind of movies. *Interview with a Vampire*. No one else understood. Forgot everything. Yeah, she went her own way, right up through the end. Shit. If she killed herself because of the old guy, then I'll kill him myself.'

'Why?'

'What?'

'Why would you want to kill him?'

'What? Well, because . . . Haven't you been listening to me? If he . . . And she hung herself because of him . . . What does that question mean?' His voice had got away from him again, and he abruptly stopped speaking. Franck decided to order a beer. It occurred to him that he was no longer on duty; in fact, he had a look at himself to make sure he was not wearing a tie.

'You were not particularly close to the girl,' Franck said. 'Why, two decades later, would you suddenly want to get revenge?'

'What? Why? That's your question? I can tell you why. Because I'd kill every single rapist if I could. Is that clear enough?'

CHAPTER EIGHT

# An Invisible Companion

On his way to Marienplatz along Ludwigstraße with its Romanesque and classicist facades, Jakob Franck suddenly found himself surrounded by people and had no idea where they had all come from. The one-kilometre long, six-lane road was usually just full of cars while the sidewalks were crowded with university students hurrying to classrooms or to the city library and tourists busy taking photos of the once-crown's stately buildings. In Franck's experience, the stretch between the Feldherrnhalle and the Victory Gate was not really all that much of a great boulevard in the traditional sense of the term, except when there were some typical parades or other big cultural events.

After his talk with the courier, he had needed some fresh air but what he got instead was the cutting smell of perfume and cologne, damp clothes and exhaust. In the growing darkness, it had begun to drizzle; and though the rain did not get any stronger, the people around him streamed off the sweaty tension of overly motivated joggers.

Franck could not find any corner or place to escape. Jostled and eyed grumpily he pushed on through the crowd, chasing his thoughts. He would have preferred to be sitting quietly by himself in a bar; as a matter of fact, the overcrowded, loud cafe where he had been earlier in the afternoon now struck him as the better place to be alone. He asked himself why he had left and where exactly he wanted to go.

After paying the bill and saying goodbye to Jan Roland in front of the door, he was overcome by such a strong desire for movement and solitude that before he knew what was happening he had rushed off and become ensnared in the throng.

He pressed his shoulder bag to his chest like he was afraid of being robbed and hunched his shoulders as if to protect himself from a series of punches. In short, he was a bit of a mess.

It was not only that with every step the courier's demeanour and statements perplexed him more and more but that, above all, he wondered about his ability to read people and his perception in general. Furthermore, he slowly seemed to have lost control of his greatest skill: deciphering the genome of any lie whatsoever.

By the time he had almost reached Odeonplatz he seriously wondered whether he might have been fundamentally wrong about Ludwig Winther; whether Esther's former classmate might possibly be telling the truth; whether, back then, he, Inspector Franck, and all of his colleagues had failed; whether they had let themselves be distracted and driven away by her grieving parents instead of intensifying their questioning at the school and around the family; whether Doris Winther had not committed suicide out of despair over her daughter's incomprehensible death but because she could no longer handle the black silence and had broken down under the weight of shame.

Assuming, Franck thought, he woke up in the middle of summer at five in the morning and it was still dark outside—how could he be sure there had not been a total eclipse of the sun?

He finally escaped the crowd. He turned onto Galerie-straße and ducked through an archway into the abandoned Hofgarten. The gravel crunched beneath his soles; he stopped and listened; not a sound, only the hiss of traffic from beyond the archways.

Just as he was about to move on in the direction of the temple or into the deeper darkness beyond the light of the shop windows behind him, the bells of St Cajetan began to ring. Franck jumped; he could not remember the last time anything had startled him. He almost began to tremble; he was overcome by a shudder the likes of which he had not experienced since being a child; his heart beat wildly; his thoughts whirled like talking snowflakes; a burning drummer beat through his stomach; the air he breathed was more fragrant than fresh bread.

As if the most natural thing in the world he folded his hands over the strap of his shoulder bag, lowered his head and moved his lips as in prayer. The bells of the Theatine Church rang unceasingly over the rooftops and trees. For a few moments, Franck did not move. Then the silence returned.

When Franck finally took a look around, bewildered—as if waking out of an impenetrable dream—in the dim light of the archways he saw a boy, ten years old or thereabouts, dressed in a white parka with a knit cap pulled down low over his face; the boy waved. Franck too raised his arm. The very next moment, the little white face with the bouncing pom-pom on its head darted back through the archways and on to the street.

With an irrepressible desire for solitude, Franck set off for the suburban rail.


He did not turn on the light in the hallway of his flat on the Industriestraße; instead he lit the tall, white candle in the glass candle holder in front of the balcony door to his office, rolled down the blinds, hung his shoulder bag on the chair and only then, in front of the half-dark wardrobe, took off his leather jacket and shoes. He took a bottle of beer out of the refrigerator, opened it, went back into his office and closed the door; the constant flickering of the candle bathed the room in soft light and welcomed him like a mantle of silence.

For a number of minutes, Franck continued to stand in the doorway sipping his beer and observing the noise in his head—the jabbering in the university cafe, the clicking of heels, the roar of motors on the Ludwigstraße, the drone of the train and its slamming doors, the bells of the local church in Aubing feeble compared to those of St Catejan—slowly quiet down until all he could perceive was a buzzing, the echo of his own presence.

Then he sat down at his desk, spread out the documents and pieces of paper in front of him, snapped on the art-deco lamp with its milky, pressed glass and chrome-plated brass base—a gift from his wife on his fortieth—propped his head on his hands and tried to form an idea about the case.

As with any murder investigation, Franck began by studying the obvious; he evaluated what was irrefutably demonstrable or at least based on sound findings. According to her parents, Esther Winther left their home on Bernauer Straße that Monday morning, fourteenth of February, at around a quarter past seven on the roughly two-kilometre way to her school on Schlierseestraße. There had been nothing out of the ordinary, Doris and Ludwig Winther had explained when they spoke with Chief Investigator André Block the next day once her husband had returned from his training seminar in Salzburg. According to a number of students, even that morning at school had been more or less unremarkable—with the exception of Jan Roland getting on everyone's nerves at break with his theatre monologues, especially the group of girls around Sandra Horn and Esther Winter; the girls were used to ignoring their classmate's attempts to show off; Jan always said that one day he would be a famous actor and they all would have to look up at him from the cheap seats.

After lessons, around one thirty or so, Esther told her friend Sandra that she had to take care of something in town and would meet a friend; she did not say who she was referring to and Sandra did not ask; she was familiar with Esther's habit of 'making a secret' where there really was not one. Towards the end of the funeral, André Block and his colleagues had asked some of the younger mourners, but they did not know who Esther had met that afternoon either.

Although the medical examiner did not rule out the possibility that a second person could have helped Esther fix the rope with knots, the investigators did not reconstruct any of her classmates' timelines. From what Franck found out from Inspector Block, no further investigations were made, for the parents accepted their daughter's tragic decision and—if Franck understood the notes properly—showed almost no interest in the exact circumstances while the investigators did not want to make the situation worse through speculation.

Investigators were able to retrieve microfibers from all fingers, the base of the thumbs, wrists and inside of the hands thanks to adhesive tape, but only to conclude that they matched the traces found on the rope. Sweat and tiny particles of skin were run through the INPOL system for comparison with any saved DNA—with no results. Injuries to her feet and elbows attested to the body's having swung against the tree trunk at the moment of hanging and, according to both the criminal investigators as well as the doctors, not as a sign of natural defence against a potential second person, a perpetrator. Haemorrhages in the eyes, traces of saliva, bleeding from her ears and other further marks allowed for no doubt that the young girl had killed herself and not been killed first and hung afterwards in order to cover it up.

Unexplained traces on the rope as well as the professional art of the fivefold-tied noose—'a hangman's knots' in the words of the forensic doctor completing analysis of the abrasions on the throat and nape of the neck—could have pointed to someone with experience in ropework. Where, Franck asked himself, could Esther have learnt how to tie a rope so that she could then hang herself with it?

And another question bothered him as he read through the papers: Was there a particular reason why Esther had chosen that way to end her life? He had known young people to jump off of high-rises or—as Jan Roland had mentioned—throw themselves in front of trains, to take pills or drugs or to fast until their organs gave out.

Maybe, Franck thought, I should forget the question or concentrate on the more pressing problem first: Could Roland, the bike courier, be right? Was it possible that the seemingly perfect male-clothing salesman Ludwig Winther had abused his daughter and that no one around them had noticed anything, not even Esther's best friend Sandra? Not even her mother?

Was it possible that on the afternoon of the fourteenth of February, Esther had not gone to a meeting but instead had stayed away from all her friends in order to go and buy rope and turn a long-secret plan into reality?

Was it possible that the mood swings her classmates had reported had had to do with her father's transgressions and her mother's inability to help?

Was it possible that Doris and Ludwig Winther had kept silent after their daughter's death and lied openly to their friends, relatives, neighbours and the police?

Everything was possible when it came to people; he knew that much after forty-two years of police work.

Had Doris Winther no longer been able to breathe under the iron mask after a year and therefore made an irreversible decision, above all, to get back at her husband? Is that why she had left behind those terse lines: *I'm going. I never want to see you again?*

Everything, Franck thought, everything was possible.

He had to take care of the spoon.


Of course he had not had any sealable plastic bags with him, so he had wrapped up the spoon in a paper tissue and stuck it as carefully as possible into his bag; Jan Roland had gone to the toilet, the waitress was busy, and there were piles of plates and coffee cups on the table next to him; Franck took one of the dirty spoons and laid it in front of Roland's cup from where he had palmed the other one—a purely precautionary procedure should the courier, for one reason or other, suddenly miss his spoon; the waitress did not notice a thing.

For Franck, even a far-fetched clue was a clue to be followed up. Without making any official fuss, he would ask his friend Block to compare the fingerprints and whatever other genetic traces remained off the spoon to those taken from the plastic bag that was found near Esther as well as to the other evidence from the rope and the body.

On top of it all, Franck still did not know what to make of Jan Roland's monologue. In his opinion, the guy was just a frustrated show-off; on the other hand, Roland had no reason to spread those kinds of lies and Franck did not think he was crafty or sick enough to be planning revenge after so many years.

Maybe Ludwig Winther had spoken poorly about Jan back when Esther was still alive, maybe the student had become a bit too pushy with all his theatrical affectations and so Esther, not least because of her father's pressure, had turned away from him. No one had looked into the seventeen-year-old girl's relationship network. Not a single word in the files as to preferences, habits, arguments, friendships. From out of the notes, comments and transcripts of the students' rather superficial statements, Franck was able to piece together the biography of a girl whose marks were always good, who occasionally suffered mood swings—a fact which, however, did not make her any different from any other girls her age—and who had only recently seemed morose and unapproachable, but the reasons why remained in the dark. Her friends were not at all concerned, the fact that Esther had a loner streak in her had made her more interesting than unusual to her classmates and since she was a reliable friend with a propensity for playing pranks on her teachers, over the years she had even enjoyed a lot of sympathy.

Esther had been selected to be class representative numerous times but had always declined; in the school photos which had been given to investigators working

with André Block—one of which was in Franck's files—
Esther always stood off to the far left in the back row,
towering above everyone else. She seemed to like it; her
lips formed a mischievous smile and even though the girl
next to her was touching her with her shoulder, Esther—
Franck imagined—remained aloof and, so he surmised,
the very next moment took off out of the frame.

In the light of the old lamp he continued to look at
the photograph, which was no less of a mystery than
Jan's statements and the police's notes. Esther Winther,
Franck thought, belonged to no one; for seventeen years
she had cast a shadow and not a single person had
noticed how the shadow had slowly taken possession of
her and, in the end, driven her to commit a murder for
which she found no one more worthy than herself. Whoever she had intended to accuse through her act to that
day remained free—unpunished, unrecognized, guilty.

No, Franck thought, the truth had another, more hidden face.

On that cloudy, forbidding, lightless February afternoon Esther Winter had not been alone in the park on
Balanstraße; someone had been accompanying her for
hours, from her school down by Giesinger Station and
into the inner city; on the train; in the underground.
Unnoticed, surrounded by hundreds of others, only a
fraction of whom could have been blind, visually
impaired or deaf, she had walked through the streets and
stores, had perhaps even been asked by a stranger for
directions and answered politely; whoever she might
have met, whatever she might have seen, heard or
thought, nothing had had any effect on her deadly desire.

Someone, Franck thought, had been close to her the whole time, had not left her side, had encouraged her all along and even accompanied her back towards her home, up the hill, back to the underground and the tram stop from where it was no longer too far; there where she felt at home, where she knew every metre, every shortcut, every dark corner she could steal an important kiss, every cafe, every silent space when everywhere else was just too loud.

There is no way she could have been alone—Franck stood up from his desk and walked around his room, startling the flame in its glass; the neighbourhood was not outside the populated world, the park was not in a hidden corner of the Aubinger Lohe, lights burnt in all the windows, cars lit up the edges, cyclists were on evening errands, people were busy walking their dogs, and not only around seven o'clock. Animals needed to walk between six and six thirty too, they had to crap or mark their territory; hundreds of people in the two adjoining neighbourhoods delegated their loneliness to their four-legged companions who would bark in alarm day and night even if they had only caught the scent of a porcupine in Newfoundland.

Frieda didn't bark, Linda Schelling had said to one of the two police officers who first arrived at the scene. The dachshund was at a loss for words, Franck thought, and its little owner should have postponed gossiping with her best friend until later on, then she would have been at the right place at the right time and done life a service. I was talking with my friend, Linda Schelling was quoted as saying in the files, and then I wandered through Pfälzer Straße before turning onto Bad Dürkheimer here and, as always, Frieda walked ahead of me into the park and then I saw a figure hanging from a tree and as I got closer I saw that it wasn't a puppet but a person and not only that but Esther, from one of the houses around here, I thought, and couldn't believe my eyes and Frieda just stood there and didn't make a sound, she's never like that.

That's right, Franck thought, and felt like smoking a cigarette and having a schnapps, life's normally not like that at all; life is usually very different before the police show up.

But he did not want to open the door or leave his room, his eyes fell onto the classroom photo, onto the open, headstrong face to the far left in the back row. He looked at the pieces of paper, the notes, the files and file-cover spread across the table and asked himself whether he had kept everything because in some way he had known that the dead women from Ramersdorf would one day come back to him—just like Vera Balan who had thrown herself in front of the train and whose name graced the street Esther had had to cross in order to die, like Paulus Landwehr who had stabbed himself to death after splitting open his wife's head, like all the other guests who took up their places next to him as if a given right, drank his schnapps, ate his biscuits and stared at him as if they had never been born and longed for his breath.

There was no one else around, Linda Schelling had said to the police and then repeated her statement later on to André Block, I was alone in the park, she said, believe me, there was no one else around, just Frieda and I.

'And Esther,' Franck said to the copies of the files. 'Esther was there, just in front of you, you saw her hanging there twenty centimetres above the ground in her cowboy boots and jeans; and how proud you were when you showed the police your grey mobile that you'd only bought a week before; no one in your circle of friends had a mobile phone back then, the epidemic was just beginning; and then you added: "What luck I already had a mobile so I could call right away and report the accident."' Franck had circled the word with a blue marker. Accident. What luck.

'What goddamn luck,' Franck said and with a single arm movement brushed everything off the table, the pieces of paper scattered chaotically across the wooden floor. Franck looked around as if he could not understand what he had just done. But it did him good, he saw the hectic flickering of the candle flame grow weaker until it once again softly and evenly spread its light throughout the room which was once more as quiet as it had been when he had come in and closed the door. He had no idea how much time had passed since then; he thought it was entirely possible that he had spent the entire night with the dead women and would soon have to be on his way to new, as of yet unheard, witnesses.

Franck was convinced that the truth to be found—he snapped off the desk lamp and walked over to the candle in front of the balcony door—at the centre, in the middle of the ruined order just like how at a violent crime scene where nothing made sense or hung together any more, there was still a hidden fossil that bound the past to the present and pointed to the future, towards the solution of the case.

Finding that fossil—that had been his responsibility his entire life on the squad. And even if so much time had passed since the death of Esther and Doris Winther, more than eighty seasons, and the scars of the crime had become dust and dirt and rotten remains, living earth, new grass and bright leaves, he would find the fossil and decipher it.

Franck swore this to the two silent women and blew out the candle; he moved over to the window and closed his eyes. Darkness streamed in.

When he opened them again, how would he be able to recognize a solar eclipse?

Then he knew: by the absolute silence of the birds.

# CHAPTER NINE

# Tell Me It Isn't True, II

At first he had almost pushed her away to show that her behaviour was inappropriate; how arrogant, he thought immediately and took the woman's touch to be like a missed greeting instead, a clumsy plea for company. After a while, he wondered how it could have gone so far but did not realize that an hour had already passed.

An hour in which he had simply leant against the wall in the hallway, next to the oval-shaped mirror, and heard the woman's soft whimpering at his neck; in the air, the scent of freshly baked apple cake. As if completely normal his hands rested on the stranger's back, that stranger who was a whole head shorter and who wore a flower-patterned smock; and the sentence he had uttered had faded into the past as if meaningless or even a lie.

'I must tell you that your daughter is dead.'

It was not the first time Franck had used those words.

He regularly delivered terrible news using that very same sequence, the same thoughtful tone, without stammering and in an almost permissive way; he refused to cry; then the blaze of panic-stricken glances; the imploding voices; and often the scream of a relative who had just been torn out of the protection of the life he or she had made and plunged into the glaring reality of death where from then on they would have to live and who in the blink of an eyelid had understood that there was no turning back.

Franck would draw on those experiences the next time and sometimes—weeks or months later—would even receive a thank-you letter or a small package filled with sweets, coffee and cognac together with a card that said he had acted with dignity and 'in no way like a police officer'. And then, in the middle of his day-to-day routine, for a few seconds he would commemorate the person who had willingly or unwillingly embraced death, that person whose file number he had already forgotten.

In Doris Winther's home, at first he had felt like an amateur who did not know what to do with his hands, thoughts or sentences. Strangely, he did not find the woman intrusive, he had been surprised by his natural reaction and the easy way he had laid his arms around her, pressed his hands onto her smock and, as if he wanted to create a relaxed atmosphere, taken a step back to lean against the wall.

It seemed to him that during the first few minutes they both just gave in to the startling closeness, relieved that neither had said a word. Franck had noticed the silence; no radio was running, no TV, not a single sound made its way in from outside. Earlier, as Franck had been getting out of the car, a dog had begun to bark and soon another, and the barking, he remembered, continued when he rang the bell and the woman in the smock opened the door.

Then he had become aware of the woman's voice; a chirping beneath his chin—he could feel her lips on his throat—that slowly grew louder and turned into a wail whose intensity, sustained by a warm, melodic tone, amazed him. He feverishly wondered what he was supposed to do; he did nothing; he stayed still, kept his hands calm, concentrated on the tiny voice so that he would not miss a word, a syllable, a letter.

Never before had he stood that way immediately after delivering the news of someone's death. Never before had a relative's understandable speechlessness turned him into a mute witness he was not allowed to be. They had been alone, he had not yet learnt where her husband was; other than Esther and her parents, no one else lived in the house on Bernauer Straße, he had learnt that from the computer back at the department; the couple had no other children; the woman had baked an apple cake which, once it had cooled overnight, would taste particularly good the following day; maybe Esther was supposed to take a piece with her to school.

The reason why Franck had asked himself who it was that Doris Winther could have been waiting for when he suddenly rang the bell was a mystery to him; Esther had a key, she kept it in her bag, Franck knew that from his colleagues too, and Ludwig Winther? Why would he ring the bell instead of simply opening the door? Useless questions ghosted through Franck's head and he had been very close to asking one of them just to be rid of it.

'Tell me it isn't true.'

He had not been listening.

He had understood every word but had not been listening properly; he was so far away in his thoughts that he had to clear his throat before he could speak. Once he began to respond, Doris Winther shook her head and let out a hissing sound embedded within her feverish whimpering. Franck was taken aback and remained silent. He wondered if he should say the words anyway: Would you like me to call a relative? Or: Tell me about your daughter. Instead, she nestled her head even closer to his throat, it seemed as if her wail would burrow into his blood and spread throughout his body. He told himself that keeping silent was the wrong thing to do, that it was no way to act and, in fact, he had never acted that way before.

What was happening to the woman? Was she having a nervous breakdown, was she falling unconscious, and that was why she clung to him so strongly? Should he already have contacted a doctor? What kind of reaction was she expecting from him? She had asked him to simply tell the truth, but naturally she had meant a different one than he had.

Or was he reading it all wrong? It was impossible to let the woman go now, that had become clear, she had demanded the closeness and he had reacted too late; nothing like that had ever happened to him; he was shocked to realize that he had let himself be overpowered, that he had not been in control of his senses and that he continued not to be.

Occasionally she would sob softly. He had gone on holding her. No, he thought, what he was doing could not be called anything other than an embrace; there was no professional distance any longer, they had established an intimacy beyond warrant or any possible explanation.

When he was finally able to look at his watch without having to move his head, two hours had already passed. It seemed inconceivable but he had to look one more time. Something's wrong, he thought, he was missing something, something that would be impossible to get back; something would no longer be the same; something that had to do with him alone and that he would not be able to tell anyone at all.

His life as a police officer was taking a turn that he was helpless to do anything about.

His life as a man and a husband had lost its familiar meaning. He began to suspect—and this bothered him so much that he had to control his breath so as not to transfer his shock to the woman—why it was that over the last few years he had taken on a role that all of his colleagues, both men and women, despite their experience, education and psychological courses, shied away from.

No one had forced him to it, he had not had a single discussion with his chief on the subject nor the responsibility he was vicariously taking on for the whole department.


Once, after being placed in charge of the investigation of a man's murder, late one night he drove over to the fiancée's home to deliver the news. She had had two girl-friends over to discuss wedding plans; they were drinking wine and her mood could not have been better; Franck could hear her laugh from outside the door. Then the young woman was standing in front of him—twenty-eight years old, long blonde hair, a bright face with glowing blue eyes, cheeks reddened by wine and anticipation—and he said, 'My name is Jakob Franck, I'm a police officer. I must tell you some terrible news.' She had looked at him—and as if the two women in the living room had heard, their conversation stopped abruptly and immediately thereafter the music too—and he added, 'May I come in and we'll sit down a moment?' The young woman—she was, as far as Franck knew, a dental assistant—could not stop staring at him. She stood motionlessly in front of him, her mouth half-open, the blue now completely gone from her eyes; she looked as if she were about to go limp. The woman's two friends appeared behind her, they were just as young as she was, one of them also blonde, the other a brunette, they took her hand and did not dare take another step and with lost looks waited on a word from the inspector.

'Your fiancé,' Franck said, 'was robbed in his jewellery store and shot down by one of the perpetrators. He died while being treated by the emergency doctor.'

No one reacted. Footsteps could be heard from next door, a shuffling sound, then a clicking. Franck said, 'On behalf of my colleagues as well, I offer you my most heartfelt condolences. Should we all have a seat at the table?'

They went to the table which had glasses, wine and water bottles, piles of magazines, brochures, catalogues and photographs; Franck sat down in one of the chairs, the three women across from him on the sofa, the fiancée—her name was Anja Ring—in the middle, her hands pressed between her knees, her eyes on the wardrobe with all their framed photos. The only thing that she had said until that moment was, 'Please, come in.' She had barely had enough strength for that; one of her friends had taken hold of her under her arms and led her back into the room.

Then all of a sudden she jumped up; with both hands she pulled the colourfully embroidered tablecloth towards herself sending the glasses, bottles and papers tumbling across the floor; with a simultaneously instinctive as well as practised movement from uncountable training-hours, Franck turned to the side so that no liquids landed on his clothes, and slowly stood up. Anja whipped the tablecloth through the air and ran screaming back and forth across the room, from the TV to the door, from the window to the wall; her voice shrill and frightening, the women on the couch had no idea what to do. Franck sidestepped the woman but did not let her out of his sight.

Then she suddenly paused and went silent; a hoarse wheeze escaped her throat, her body shuddered, the piece of cloth fluttered in her ceaselessly twitching right hand; once again, as at the door, she stared at the inspector from colourless eyes overflowing with tears. One of the women stood up indecisively from the sofa while the other continued to sit, her face similarly covered in tears. With a rough, hard movement Anja threw the tablecloth over her head and collapsed on the floor; hunched up by the wall, she pulled her legs towards her body, fell to the side and stopped moving.

Franck knelt down beside her, took her hand and said, 'I will stay with you as long as you like.'

Around midnight, after Anja's parents and her fiancé's father had come, he left the flat. After the funeral at the Western Cemetery, he sat next to Anja Ring at the inn and she thanked him multiple times for having been there that night, for his words and for his patience.

*He* was the one, Franck suddenly thought that night between the fourteenth and fifteenth of February and was startled when he looked at the clock for the third time—*he* was the one who had been looking for closeness, solace, silence, dedication and patience; it was not any sense of selflessness or awareness as to how necessary love for one's neighbour was at the darkest hour— an understanding, in any event, that was not set down anywhere in a policeman's duty—which determined his behaviour, or maybe, but only to a degree. For, above all, he recognized *himself* in those others he was duty-bound to visit; when they opened their doors to him, he not only stepped into their universe of desolation but also returned back home to his own. In the rooms and hallways of those who were no longer considered relatives but the left-behind, he recognized himself far better than he did in his own life, his togetherness, his marriage, his household.

That night, in Doris Winther's embrace—and there his suspicion turned to certainty—he did not want to be anywhere else; he was in the right place. Even though the day no longer had a name, for death always takes the name of those days away, time still existed and he would use it to do what he was supposed to do; he would not run away, he would not make any excuses, he would not hide behind his duty and official demeanour, lie or make any promises.

Yes, he thought, that's who I'll be from now on, myself alone.

Three years after meeting Doris Winther and their seven-hour embrace, something he never told anyone about, his marriage with Marion ended unequivocally, and he never again entered into a committed relationship.

'Tell me it isn't true.'

And he said, '*You turn people back to dust, saying:* "*Return to dust, you mortals." A thousand years in your sight are like a day that has just gone by, or like a watch in the night.*'

She stopped whimpering and touched his neck with her lips; he was not supposed to have noticed.

At Esther's funeral, she asked the priest to repeat the Psalm.


'Distance reigned at the funeral,' said Inge Rigah. 'We never really spoke with each other much, we were simply too different. Today I'd say that we were really just strangers to each other. Does that sound terrible?'

She took a sip of her white wine and looked around the crowded restaurant on Stuttgarter Platz in Charlottenburg. Doris Winther's older sister suggested it after Franck had called her and asked to meet.

He had managed to get a seat on a midday flight without any problems, had booked a room in a reasonable hotel near Savignyplatz and had flown to Berlin one day early. He had not been in the city in a long time but immediately got angry, just like he had in the past, because he could not visit all the sites on foot due to the size. Just after exploring Potsdamer Platz and the surrounding area, he had had to tumble into a taxi in order to continue his tour.

For a while, he blamed his state on the circumstances, the great distances, the huge, unavoidable number of tourists, the traffic and the lousy air. Throughout the course of the afternoon, however, it became clear to him that something else had exhausted him: his age; the internal effort it took to become curious; his being alone. There was no one he could have shared his observations with. He walked around and looked at things; he saw apartment buildings, monuments, turn-of-the-century architecture, canyon-like streets, inner courtyards, churches and parliamentary buildings, the present hewn in stone. He kept thinking about how he did not belong to any of it any more, wasted the rest of the time he had left and fed himself on stale memories which he had been chewing on for far too long already; his drive to be hungry was gone.

He had become, he thought while sitting in a pizzeria on Savignyplatz gobbling down a dinner of overcooked rigatoni, an old, grey-haired man in a world that was too big and too blinding, a man who had sought death in order to be closer to others and from time to time even embrace them.

'My sister told me about you,' said Inge Rigah. 'You were with her when she learnt about what had happened.'

'What did she tell you?'

'That you were there, apparently for quite a long time, nothing else. Why?'

To help digest his food and the day itself, after a litre of cheap red wine, Franck had had another four grappas and had subsequently spent the following morning trying to balance out his dehydration. In the bar where they now were sitting, however, he was drinking a Pilsner and enjoying it. Apparently, he thought, a few of the old appetites hadn't died after all.

He asked, 'Did you speak about Esther's potential reasons back then?'

'Of course, I asked them both how it was they hadn't noticed anything, there had to have been some clues, some warning signs. He just kept repeating: Not a thing, not a thing.'

'With "he" you mean Ludwig Winther.'

'A peculiar man, I hardly know him and don't want to say anything bad about him. That was her choice, and I never said a word. But from the start I didn't like him. I met him for the first time three, maybe four, days before their wedding, Doris had asked me to come and help her with the preparations. It surprised me. Like I said, we had very little contact. When I was eighteen, I moved to Berlin and she stayed behind, she was sixteen and still at school.'

She drank from her glass, something was on her mind, she looked past Franck to the door where new guests came in, looked around disappointedly when they saw there were no more chairs, then left.

'I think I would've taken her with me if she'd wanted to come. No, I really think so. I liked her a lot, that little girl with the freckles, I wish she'd been a bit more assertive in life instead of being such a conformist.'

'She married too young and had a child.'

'In my opinion, yes. She wasn't even in her mid twenties when Esther was born and afterwards her life was over. That's how I see it. Is that unfair? Could be. But after all these years, with all the distance, what else am I supposed to say? She'd studied, Doris had. Art history, literature. She could've become a professor, she was well read and really passionate about her interests; she could've had a career, but what did she do instead? She married a trouser salesman. Yes, he worked for a famous retailer, that's true, but all the same he was a salesman and nothing more. Why did she do that? Why did she give everything up?'

'What did she tell you?'

'Nothing. She ignored those kinds of questions, she didn't like being criticized—my life is my own, she'd say, and your life is yours, and I don't question that. Direct quote. I tried to explain to her that I was not questioning her life but trying to understand why she had decided to do this and to do that.

'But you couldn't get anything out of her, never, right up till the end. The funeral, the one we talked about a little while ago—there were an unbelievable number of mourners, half of Esther's school was there. Everyone came up to gather around Doris, to be by her side, to keep her company on that difficult path. And what happened? She refused to accept any of their condolences.

'People wanted to give her their hands and express their sympathy, but she didn't want any part of it. Didn't want to step up to the grave, she just stood there, motionless; it was like she'd gone unconscious standing there, I was worried. She just shook her head whenever someone came up to her.

'Afterwards, in the restaurant, I tried again to talk with her, I didn't want to pressure her or come down on her at all or criticize her, I just wanted to understand her. Impossible.'

'How did Ludwig behave?'

'Not all that differently with the exception that, as opposed to Doris, he would give people his hand and threw the first spade-full of dirt into the grave. He made an effort, I have to give him that much; I was still distraught and waiting for explanations, for any sentence at all that would've made Esther's death somewhat understandable. But there was nothing. Not a word.'

Her glass was empty. Franck looked for the waitress and when he found her, hesitated to wave her over. He turned back to Inge Rigah. 'Looking back now, from the perspective of today,' he said, 'in your memory: What kind of person was your niece? Why do you think she took her own life at the age of seventeen?'

In front of her was a green case with her reading glasses; for a while she pushed it back and forth, turned it around, her head lowered. Franck became aware of a letter engraved in the silver ring she wore on her little finger and, if he was not mistaken, it was an E.

'She was a quiet person,' Inge looked into the inspector's eyes. 'She kept her own counsel. She visited me here in Berlin three or four times during her school holidays, even when the Wall was still there; at that time, she was about ten or so and couldn't understand what she was seeing, the people were so different from the ones that lived where she did, then there were all the old buildings, the wide streets, and the city was so big; dogs, punks, young people just hanging out. She wasn't afraid at all, she just held my hand and went everywhere with me, into every dark corner, every bar.

'Later on, I sometimes blamed myself for not having paid more attention to how old she was but she seemed to enjoy our day-trips immensely. She wrote me letters telling me how impressive she thought the city was and that she wanted to live here too, if possible, right after her taking her graduation exams. She never talked about it with anyone, I know that. Her parents didn't have the slightest idea what was going on with her, what she was thinking, what she wanted, she was very reserved and careful.'

'What do you mean by that?' Franck had an idea but needed confirmation.

'She didn't trust the people around her.'

'That included her parents.'

'Parents, teachers, friends, she didn't feel like any of them were being honest with her, she felt like they were all just pretending to be interested in her, that they liked her simply because she was nice and didn't hurt any one's feelings. Maybe she was right.'

'Did she have boyfriends, any relationships with young boys?'

'I don't know, she didn't talk about it.'

'When did you meet her last?'

'About a year before her death, she came to Berlin again, and we had a lot of fun together. The trains were stopping constantly, you had to get on to buses, nightly chaos all over the place. It was a few years after the fall of the Wall, the lines were being redone, the city was getting a completely new face and every day Esther just wanted to get out and look. She seemed to be happy.'

'She always came to visit you by herself,' said Franck, 'never with a girlfriend or a boyfriend.'

'Always by herself.'

'Was that because of you?'

'No, I told her that she could bring someone with her, naturally, I thought about a boyfriend, someone she could just casually hang out with. I was certain that she had problems at home with that kind of thing. That her square parents were afraid she could get pregnant, that they didn't want Esther to have a boyfriend.'

'That is not simply conjecture on your part.'

'I had the impression that Esther felt controlled and that her father gave her rules, which annoyed her. She was a young, good-looking girl, and we're not living in the fifties any more. But I don't know—my sister had changed, inside, outside; she wore these old-fashioned clothes, smocks, for goodness' sake! She espoused strange ideas about raising children and politics and life in the city, it was growing more dangerous, chiefly because of all the foreigners. Those kinds of things. Even at our mother's funeral she started up with that crap. Was that his influence? Could be.'

'You mostly speak about your brother-in-law in the third person,' Franck said.

'He is a third person. Do we want to have something else to drink?'

'Of course.' Franck gave the waitress a sign, and she brought a fresh Grauburgunder and a Pilsner. 'How had your sister's ideas changed?' he asked.

'They had become more conservative, repressed. She wasn't like that before; she was lively, funny, a people person. No idea what happened. Esther never talked about it, just alluded to it, ultimately what her parents thought didn't seem to interest her too much.'

'At the same time, she let herself be bullied by them.'

'Bullied? Yes, she kept to herself, I would say. If I'm going to be honest, I had the impression that she kept things from me as well; she seemed open and cheerful but in her deepest self other forces were at work. Perhaps she was lying to herself, perhaps she was struggling with herself for not being more resolute, for allowing herself to be too likeable, I don't know. You're asking me why she might have killed herself and I'm sitting here, twenty years later, racking my brain for an answer, can you believe that?'

'Did she suffer from depression?'

'I asked myself that for a long time. The answer is: I don't know. I don't think so, but who really knows? Whenever she was in Berlin she didn't seem depressed or defiant, she was a teenager with all a teenager's normal problems and thoughts, she was looking for something, what else are you supposed to do when you're fifteen or sixteen? She was always on the search, she was confused and, at the same time, abounding in self-confidence, at least on the outside so that others wouldn't catch on to how overwhelmed she really was. We all know something about that, some people stay that way until they're quite old.'

She cast him a glance, which he refused to interpret; she did not know a thing about him and that was how it was going to stay.

Franck said, 'Could you please try to remember the exact details of the funeral again, the discussions you had with your sister and your brother-in-law, the atmosphere, your impressions. Did you speak with any of her class-mates?'

'No.' She took a drink, put the glass back, then suddenly raised her head. 'Or wait!' she said, paused, took off her colourful cardigan, hung it over the back of the chair and rested her head on her hands. 'I totally forgot. I did actually speak to one of her schoolmates, a lanky type in a black suit, hair gel, white shirt, thin tie, like a rocker from the sixties. He came up and started to talk to me, seemed pretty self-confident. How could I have forgotten him! Josef, Jakob, Jens . . . I don't remember his name any more.'

'Jan,' Franck said. 'Jan Roland.'

'Yes, could be. Jan. Entirely possible. Do you know him?'

'I've met him. He maintains that he went to the movies with Esther somewhat often.'

'That's right! He told me that too.' As if taken aback by her memory, she went silent and needed to drink from her wine twice before she could sort her thoughts back out. 'He told me something else. Unbelievable how I never thought about it again.' She fell silent once more, but this time a bit too long for Franck's patience.

'This student,' he said, 'told you about how he was afraid that Esther might've been abused by her father.'

'No!' Inge Rigah looked at him in surprise. 'What are you talking about? No. Not her father. A neighbour had made a pass at her, he thought, an older man from the neighbourhood had manipulated her and forced her into having sex. Something like that. It's outrageous that I repressed something like that!'

The sixty-four-year old painter could not remember the man's name. Franck asked her about Paul Jordan; she maintained that she had never heard the name before.

'Did you ever talk to your sister or your brother-in-law about it?'

'No.'

Franck waited for an explanation.

Inge Rigah avoided his eyes. 'I found the accusation to be absurd.'

'Why?'

'The kid came off as a pompous ass to me, he was grinning the whole time, I can see him again now in my mind's eye. I had to think of a young mobster, sounds unfair, I know. I just couldn't believe it.'

'Did you have the impression that other students also knew something about it?'

'I only spoke with the one.'

'And then?'

'What do you mean?'

'What did you do after speaking with him?'

'I don't know any more.'

'Where did they conversation take place?'

'After the ceremony, by the exit to the cemetery, I think. Yes, I'd left my sister and her husband behind because I couldn't stand their behaviour any longer, and there was a group of students standing around. I lit a cigarette and suddenly that black-clothed kid came up to me. He was alone, his friends continued to stand off with the group. And then he asked me whether I knew that Esther had had something going on with an older man.'

'That was how he phrased it?'

'Sorry?'

'Esther had had something going on with an older man.'

'That's how he expressed himself, I think.'

'And then?'

'Then he said that the man had harassed her and forced her into having sex.'

'That's a little bit different from what he'd said just a bit earlier.'

'You think so? I really can't remember the exact words any more.'

'Try.'

'So, like I said: The man had forced her into having sex.'

'And,' Franck, who in the meantime had taken some notes on his notepad, said, 'at the same time, Esther had had a relationship with him.'

Puzzled, the woman put down her glass from which she had wanted to take a drink.

'Those are two different assertions.'

'How so? She could have indeed had something with him and he still could have forced her into having sex.'

Franck tried to temper his annoyance. 'Let's stick with this for a moment. Did you ask the boy, let's call him Jan, why Esther hadn't put up any resistance against the abuse and gone to the police?'

'I did!' She snapped her fingers. 'How long ago is that now? It's really uncanny how unexpectedly you show up and the details from back then occur to me again. You're right, I asked him and he said that she hadn't wanted to.'

'How did he know about the course of events?' Franck asked. 'Did she tell him about it?'

'That's what it sounded like.'

'You don't know for a fact.'

'No.' After taking another sip of her drink, she furrowed her brow and tapped the table-top with her index finger. 'I have to ask you something: Why did you believe that Esther's father was the guilty one? Who'd think, I mean, someone?'

'Yes.'

'Who?'

'Please concentrate,' Franck said without raising his voice or seeming impatient. 'Give yourself a little time, don't pay attention to the noise or the voices here in the bar. Imagine that you are at the funeral at the Eastern Cemetery in Munich, the coffin is being lowered into the ground, everyone has offered your brother-in-law their condolences and are gradually beginning to move away. You are standing by the grave, observing your sister, force yourself to keep calm; at a certain point, you can't take the situation any longer and make your way towards the exit. It's February and cool, in the distance crows are cawing. You're walking down the gravel path thinking about Esther and her visits to you in Berlin; you have no explanation for what's happened; you desperately need a cigarette. You come out of the cemetery where a number of people are talking, their heads lowered; only the group of school kids is somewhat louder, they're talking about Esther or homework or one of their teachers who gave a weak talk in the chapel. You pull out a cigarette, light it, inhale, your thoughts continue to spin and then this slender, black-clad young man is standing in front of you; you start, but something about him makes you take notice and grow curious. And he begins to speak.'

'Yes,' she said with closed eyes, head in her hands. 'He says: I'm a friend of Esther's, sometimes we go to the movies. I thought you should know: There's a guy, fifty or so, an old man she meets and has sex with, and he forces her to do things. Maybe it's his fault she hung herself.

'And I can't believe what I'm hearing, and say to him: How do you know that? And he replies: I know it and now you do too. And I ask him: Did Esther talk about this with her parents? And he says: No idea. And I ask him: Why didn't she go to the police if the man was harassing her or even abusing her? And he says: No idea, it probably embarrassed her. And I say to the young man: Are you not imagining this all? And he says: I don't give a shit what you think, I just wanted you to know.

'Then he went back to his friends and I saw him bum a cigarette, turn back towards me and look at me with a cold stare. At that moment, I didn't believe a single word.

'By the time my sister came out of the cemetery, I'd decided not to say anything about the subject. I can still see his smirk as he began to talk to me, that crooked mouth of his. Maybe that's why I thought: He looks like a mobster, not only because of the black suit and the greasy hair.

'Then we went to the restaurant; I observed my sister and Ludwig to see if maybe I'd notice if they knew anything. But when Ludwig began to cry at the table, right in front of everyone, and couldn't stop, I felt sorry for him, and my sister too, and I thought: What am I doing mixing myself with her life, it's got nothing to do with me; then everyone was quiet for a few minutes and just handed over tissues, it was almost comical. As for me, I only cried much later, when I was back at home on Mommsenstraße and had lit the seventeen candles I'd bought especially for Esther.'

She opened her eyes and reached for Franck's hand. 'Do you think that Esther did not willingly kill herself? Do you think that someone forced her to do it? Why would someone do something like that? You're a police officer, you have to know why.'

Unlike Inge Rigah, it was difficult for Franck to concentrate in the middle of all the noise in the bar. It was not as if he thought the other guests were being particularly loud and the clattering of the silverware, the clinking glasses, the bartender busy behind the bar seemed completely normal. Nevertheless, he felt a pressure in his ears and imagined a whistling that seemed to grow stronger and stronger the closer he listened; perhaps the noise level had to do with the fact that the two large windows of the big room did not have any curtains to soften the sounds; or that the echoes of his hangover had come back and were reforming themselves; all the same, he was in the mood for another beer.

If what the woman remembered was true, one dubious trace might lead to Winther's neighbour—Paul Jordan, the one Ludwig Winther had spoken about so insistently—and another, no less sketchy trace, to Esther's father who the by-now grown boy with the gelled hair—

unlike when he had spoken to Inge Rigah out in front of the cemetery—had indirectly accused of abuse back at the cafe.

What kind of game was Jan Roland playing with his classmate's death? Franck wondered.

'I wouldn't rule out the fact that Esther was not alone at the time of her death,' he said, fully aware of how amateur-like such a statement sounded to his criminally trained ears; there was no evidence, there were no witnesses, no conclusive arguments. However, at that moment, he was convinced he had discovered a shard of the fossil he desperately needed in the case concerning Esther Winther. Something in the distorted picture of all the inconsistent statements corresponded to the truth, Franck thought, he had to look and to listen even more intensely.

Indeed, now he truly had a case, it was irrevocable, and he was head prosecutor, investigator and witness in one.

He nearly cried out 'no'.

'Then she was possibly murdered,' said Inge Rigah in shock. After that, for a while she did not say anything else, nor did Franck; they ordered another round of drinks and the painter watched the detective write illegible words down on his paper.

Once he had filled a number of pages, Franck leant back and pushed back his chair, crossed his arms and then his legs.

'Why so glum?' Inge Rigah asked.

Franck looked at her blankly. 'You're still keeping something from me.' He was not sure if it was true or not, it was more of an occupational, conventional hope.

'Don't be ridiculous. I cancelled a course of mine because of you, because you were so pushy. And then you go and say something like that. What should I be keeping from you? I went deep into my memories, as you could see, I made a real effort, and a lot of things came back to me.'

Her glass was empty, and she seemed surprised. Franck motioned to the waitress and ordered another round.

'Would you like to eat something, *Frau* Rigah?'

'Maybe in a moment. You're welcome to call me Ingrid.'

'I will, if you have nothing against continuing to call me *Herr* Franck.'

She looked at him as if he had told a joke she had not immediately understood but soon would. A smile appeared on her face. However, his stoic demeanour quickly frightened off any joyful expectations. 'Ah, yes . . . I mean . . . *Herr* Franck, of course . . . no, nothing against that.'

'Thank you.'

Wordlessly, as before, the waitress placed their glasses down and went on to the next table; Franck supposed that the two of them knew each other but chose to avoid personal exchanges; he liked being witness to an everyday secret and acquaintanceship he was unable to gauge—as so often when he would sit in a bar and observe people with their habits, tricks and flirts and imagine what they were like in reality and all the things they had already experienced or dreamt.

He had only been retired for two months but already two years prior to that he had lived like a hermit who only left his burrow every morning for one reason and that was to forage through the woods and to take care of things from whose deeper meaning he had long been excluded and which, therefore, were unspeakably difficult for him to overcome.

He had long led his life in as routine a fashion as he handled the cases that came across his desk: he no longer went to crime scenes; he waited for his colleagues' reports and then discussed strategies with them before they all went to the cafeteria to fill up their trays.

When around six o'clock he would call out his usual '*Servus*, have a nice evening, Dieter!' his voice seemed to him as metallic as a primitive tape recorder. But barely out on the street, into the overbearing August light and the Hansastraße overflowing with its hundreds of cars, rushing evening shoppers, gambling addicts, pimps, whores and onlookers, he morphed back into the nameless and faceless old man who looked back at him every morning from the bathroom mirror. With the exception of him, everyone else belonged there.

After saying goodbye to the department, nights he would sit in his office, which had never become a child's room, and play poker in the virtual world against pseudonymous opponents, drink beer without getting drunk and shake his fists a little when he won just like he would hit the desktop when he lost; in all honesty, he had to admit that he was not playing properly but only seeking distraction, perfecting his feeling of being absent. In his dreams, he believed he was being impersonated by a man he had never seen. And in that respect, the first day of his retirement would be a blessing because from then on no one would be able to bother him, he would simply be a non-descript passer-by and bar guest, insignificantly alone in the middle of a society made up of strangers.

'If you would like to know, *Herr* Franck,' Inge Rigah said, emphasizing the title, 'Jutta and I have known each other since the eighties when we shared a flat together. Then we went our separate ways, she wanted to be a singer, I wanted to be a painter, what can I say? She became a waitress and I give painting classes in the evenings. I still paint, I already told you that, and Jutta still sings, she even still gives the occasional show, she's good.'

'You avoid each other a bit,' Franck said.

At that moment, the waitress passed by the table and Inge Rigah smiled at her. 'Perhaps, maybe we're a little embarrassed; absurd.' She took a sip of her wine, and her voice seemed to brighten. 'I come here two, three times a week, we see each other regularly but we don't talk much. Back in the day, we used to talk all night long, downing wine and smoking like chimneys, politics and all, that was normal, every day the divided city was a challenge. So what?'

She cast Franck a timid look. '*Tempi passati*, it's the present now and the only thing that matters is that we're still here. You as well, *Herr* Franck.'

He lifted his glass. 'Let's drink to that.'

'I'll drink to anything, if I must.' They toasted each other for the first time since they had been sitting together. 'And? Do you still think I'm keeping something from you?'

'It's possible.'

'You're stubborn.'

'You don't understand me,' Franck said and put down his glass. The alcohol had begun to affect him a bit, but he was not bothered. 'I don't think that you're consciously holding anything back from me, I just think that you could tell me more about Esther, details, incidentals.'

'Incidentals? I've told you everything I know. And I don't know a lot, she'd come to visit, we'd wander through the city, she'd ask a thousand questions, then she'd go back home. She didn't drive, she'd fly, flying was such an adventure for her.'

'You hadn't mentioned that until now.'

'Is that incidental enough?'

'Yes.'

'How so?'

'It says something about your niece.'

'What?'

'That she liked to travel and probably wanted to travel more often and to distant countries too.'

'You're right, *Herr* Franck.' And because she could not do anything else or because his observation had annoyed her, Inge Rigah repeated his name, 'Pay attention, *Herr* Franck. She absolutely wanted to go to America at some point, to South America too, we talked about it, it's true. I think she really would've liked to fly somewhere else during her school holidays, not just to Berlin but a foreign country, far away. But her parents couldn't afford it, you can understand. A trouser salesman doesn't earn all that much. To America. Friends of hers had already been there a number of times, she'd mentioned that, it occurs to me now. Ah, *in vino veritas*. Does the invitation still stand?'

'To the last glass,' Franck said.

A shadow darted across her face; she shook her head forcefully. Franck watched her. 'Oh well,' she said. 'Had to just think of a friend of ours, of Jutta's and mine, he's no longer with us. Where were we?'

'Did Esther's parents forbid her from travelling abroad?'

'Perhaps. But what does forbid mean? If the money wasn't there, it wasn't there.'

'She could've got part-time jobs and made her own money.'

'She did, she waited tables in a cafe around the university. On the weekends and during the Christmas holidays. She'd come to Berlin around Easter or in the summer, not at any other times.'

'Can you remember the name of the cafe?'

'No.'

'Café Ludwig?'

'It's possible. Is that important?'

'I don't know yet.' Franck had met Jan Roland at Café Ludwig; indeed, he had suggested it.

Then the waitress came by their table again. Inge Rigah said to her, 'This is *Herr* Franck from Munich, a detective, we're talking about Esther. *Herr* Franck believes that her suicide might not have been a suicide at all, but a murder.'

'That's what I told you back then,' Jutta said before Franck could qualify the statement. 'Such a spirited girl doesn't kill herself; I always thought there was more to it.'


Tilting her head back, Doris Winther looked at him. Seven hours had passed, seven hours in which they had held each other almost without moving.

As if seeing her for the first time, Franck observed the woman in the blue kitchen smock, and she did not look at him any less confusedly.

Once again, minutes passed in silence.

Then Doris Winther ran her tongue across her lips. 'Shall we go into the kitchen?' she asked quietly.

Franck nodded in order not to disturb the silence. She nodded as well, turned and walked away and he followed her into the middle of the smell of the apple cake.

# CHAPTER TEN

# The Wave from Behind the Wall, II

I still have never heard a silence like that. Today I think that's why no one found me behind the sofa, 'cause the silence was so comfortable, it overwhelmed me: What was I supposed to have done? Tell me, how would you have reacted in that kind of situation? How? You wouldn't have, how much you want to bet?

Would the same thing have happened if I'd been at school? Who knows? Our teacher was ill, I forget her name; she wore funny glasses, I remember that much, had spikes on the side; just decoration, but to us kids they were spikes. That's why we called her *Frau* Hedgehog, that's how it was.

Suppose she hadn't been sick and we would've had the first hour with her just like we always did and I would've left the house at seven thirty just like I always did, and everything would've been like it always had: I would've eaten a slice of bread, the radio would've been on and my mother would've been listening because something huge was going on in big Berlin, as she put it back then, and how fantastic it would be if she could be there. My father would just laugh about those kinds of things. In fact, he probably laughed that morning too and accused her of being unrealistic—that was one of his favourite phrases; my mother was unrealistic, he thought—and I didn't understand what he meant, I was too young, too silent, should've been able to ask.

It didn't matter to me at all what realistic was, what was more important was my father leaving her alone and not insulting her and accusing her of things she didn't have any idea about.

Sometimes he'd come home at night and say she'd let him down, that she hadn't supported him enough, which was why he'd lost yet another client to a competitor who could offer better personal service than he could. It was always everyone else's fault, I'd understood that much by the time I was four and, above all, my mother's, she was guilty of everything; he'd yell at her and she always stayed quiet: always.

He would shout and she would simply sit there and stare at his face; that was eerie and cool at the same time. Only when he'd get up and go to the refrigerator and grab a beer would she jump up and tear the bottle out of his hand; then she'd sit back down as if nothing had happened and look at him like someone who was important. I don't know when I gave up thinking my father was someone important, in kindergarten, I'd guess, at the latest.

Why didn't I do anything? Why did I cover my ears and hide behind the sofa like a coward?

Let's suppose that *Frau* Hedgehog hadn't been sick, suppose that *Frau* Goose hadn't had time only at a quarter to nine but at eight and that we all would've been

136

there, the whole class, Martin, Christian, Jan, dim-witted Dennis, Julia, Nina, Jasmin, Anna, all thirty-one of us; and suppose that *Frau* Goose had said to us that *Frau* Hedgehog was sick and that she would therefore be our teacher until noon, and that she had driven over especially for us from Lake Starnberg; then all of us would've stood up once more, just for her, and said: Good morning, *Frau* Goose! and everything would've been normal and nothing would've happened. Right?

I don't know any more if *Frau* Goose was really named *Frau* Goose; I just called her that so I can imagine her better but it didn't work; I've no idea what she looked like.

But she only had time at a quarter to nine, or her car wouldn't start, or her telephone there on Lake Starnberg was broken, when we came into the classroom, she excused herself for being late. The headmistress had called our parents at seven o'clock to tell them that we had to come for the second lesson. That had already set my father off. He was standing in the kitchen and yelled out into the hallway where my mother was on the phone, I was still in the bathroom. In fact, I was already done but didn't trust myself to go out. Only once it suddenly became quiet. As quiet as it was later that evening, twelve hours later.

Everything started off that morning; as soon as my father came to know that I'd have to stay home and my mother said she would stay with me, he accused her of doing so with the intention of hurting his business and ruining him.

For some time already he had begun to think that my mother wished him ill—that's how I understood it— she wanted bad things to happen, therefore she was the bad person; he hurled a cup at her and she threw a dish that smashed against the wall. I sat at the kitchen table eating my bread and jam and drinking hot chocolate until my heart was beating so heavily I couldn't get down another bite. As far as my parents were concerned, I was probably invisible; my father lifted his arms and stuck out his hands, I'll never forget that, because I saw it twice, once in the morning and once at night; in the morning between his wide, pale hands there was only air, in the evening my mother's head.

I've asked myself over and over again what would've happened if my mother had gone with him to the store and me to school and *Frau* Hedgehog with her strange glasses had shown up at work on time—would that evening only have been dark and nothing else?

It was dark when they called out my name, my mother and the woman on the TV; not a light was switched on in the room, just the flickering of the screen; and the dim light from the hallway only cast shadows.

Over and over again I've asked myself what must've happened before I heard the first scream, there behind the sofa where I'd crawled because it was the only place I hadn't already looked for my race car. I was so happy it was there; I pressed the car to myself and was happy— then the scream.

At the very first moment, I knew that it was my mother screaming but in the second I thought, that can't be. She can't scream, I thought, and her nickname which only other adults could use came to mind: Low-Voiced Liese.

Low-Voiced Liese just didn't scream, but there she was and the scream became louder, and I crouched down even further.

Then the scream was almost above me; she had walked into the living room, my father behind her. How do I know? I peeked around the corner, just once, for one whole second, I swear. And there he was, his arms raised, and between his wide hands was my mother's head; and she was screaming.

My father still had his jacket on, his green, silk scarf hung off one shoulder, his work scarf, as he called it; I saw it, and I saw how he ripped it off and wrapped it around my mother's throat, as quick as a professional, a goddamn contract killer.

That's what I think today; back then, I didn't think a thing; my thoughts probably splintering apart in my mind like the dish my mother threw against the kitchen wall.

One more scream, no.

No more scream. There weren't two screams, the whole time there was only one; from the hall—or wherever it was—my mother screamed once, I don't think she managed to get air in between, no, I don't think she managed, then the scream simply split as if someone had hacked it off from the voice.

And because I couldn't stand the voices from the TV, I slid on my knees to the other side of the sofa, my

Porsche clutched tight to my chest, softly, so the murderer wouldn't hear me.

At that moment, I knew that a murder had taken place; what I didn't know was what it was like when someone died, when someone was murdered.

She lay on the floor, her legs wriggling; she thrashed about like a baby; my father was kneeling behind her and pulling the scarf tight; he pulled and pulled, my mother's legs sought air and her arms fluttered up and down; I had peeked around the corner of the sofa. My father was too busy to notice; he held the knotted scarf around her neck, my mother's face grew red and began to swell, almost like a roll in the oven; her tongue hung out of her mouth, spit sprinkled out like water; she gasped, but not for too long.

Everything happened so quickly. My father didn't let go, he continued to hold the scarf around her neck, I know that much even though I wasn't looking any more but had hidden myself behind the sofa again. On the TV people continued to run around shouting: Crazy!

In the meanwhile, I had laid down flat across the floor, pushing my face into the rug and shutting my eyes so tight it hurt; I didn't want my crying to startle my father; I dug my face so deep into the wool that I only noticed the stench a little while later, a nauseating smell that was worse than the one in the school toilets.

Afterwards, the police explained to me what had happened immediately after my mother was killed.

My father had vomited next to her corpse. Unintentionally, as he stressed once he was in custody, where, together with my uncle, I'd gone to see him against the wishes of my aunt; I never would have wanted that to happen, he repeated whenever we saw each other; I don't think he meant the murder, but the vomit.

Till today, no one knows that I was a witness to the murder; officially, I was in bed asleep as the tragedy unfolded. I read something to that effect later in the newspaper; I collected everything I could about my father's crime, the trial too.

As the tragedy unfolded.

Only the good Lord knows that I was there and saw it all; but the good Lord keeps his promises to the dead, that much we know.

CHAPTER ELEVEN

# Everything at Long Last and Right Away

He looked down into the main hall and saw too many people all at once; fortunately, however, he was alone at his table and no longer surrounded by people talking too loudly to one another or blabbering away on their mobile phones or stabbing blindly at their food with their silverware—he was alone with the exception of the woman in a dark coat and skirt sitting five tables away drinking a latte and writing in a book.

There was not much business on the first floor of the terminal at that time of day; most of the tables in the row of airport restaurants were empty; downstairs, in front of the check-in counters, long lines had begun to form without any one seeming to be too upset.

After Franck had left the packed airplane—next to him in the thirty-second row there had been an obese man who, so it seemed to Franck, was more afraid of flying than a child who had to go to the dentist—and picked up his bag from the baggage carousel, he did not feel the least desire to go back home, and certainly not in the commuter train which on Friday afternoon would doubtless be full. On top of it all, it was raining; he still felt the icy Berliner wind in his bones and although he had only drunk beer the whole evening, since waking up his body had been acting as if it were offended by twitching in strange, unfamiliar ways.

Maybe, Franck thought, it would have been more intelligent to eat something or at least drink a bottle of water than have two double espressos; furthermore, the man next to him on the flight's tense, barely repressed fidgeting and sweating seemed to have robbed him of his last reserves.

The idea of spending time in an airport and going to have something to eat, an idea which occurred to Franck for the very first time in his life, manoeuvred him on to the escalator and up to the first floor where, contrary to every routine of his and, quite frankly, thoughtlessly, he ordered a wheat beer, a sausage and artichoke pizza with extra Grana Padano and a tomato salad with tuna. By the time the waiter brought his food, his glass was already half-finished; bent forward with his arms outstretched, which was not in the least his style, he began to cut individual slices of pizza and push them into his mouth with his hand. At the same time, he continued to observe what was going on down below in the departures hall.

A little later he wondered exactly when he had managed to finish off both the pizza and the salad; he leant back, folded his hands across his belly and cast another glance at the knotted-up, red napkin on his plate and the leftover onions in the salad bowl: it all seemed rather incomprehensible. What else could Franck do but order a second beer? His stomach began to make peculiar sounds, and he started to look around for a toilet.

Apparently, the woman in the dark coat and skirt had been watching him for some time.

From a distance of five tables, Franck thought he could recognize a hopeless, irreversible confusion in her eyes; he immediately forgot the disturbance racking his insides, his desire to escape and his unease. He took his coat from the seat next to him, picked up his bag, paused a moment to make sure that the woman was still sitting there—turned towards him, immobile—and walked over.

'May I sit down?'

She did not respond. Franck placed his bag down in front of the railing, folded and then laid his coat on top of it, hesitated. The waiter had seen Franck switch places from the front of the restaurant to the inside and nodded; the inspector briefly raised his hand. The movement freed the woman from out of her trance-like stare; she turned her head, observed her empty coffee cup, raised her eyebrows; a flat smile crossed her pale lips.

'Please do,' she said. 'And please do not think I am intrusive.' When she spoke her smile seemed to float across her mouth.

Before taking a seat, Franck cast one more glance down into the faceless comings and goings of the hall— still relieved to be upstairs in an almost brazen stillness and in the inescapable presence of a woman whose eyes reflected a particular coldness.

When he furtively studied her hands, the wrinkles, little veins, spots and fine cracks, the unmade-up skin around her throat, her face benevolently marked by the years with the lines around her temples, the not-perfectly-enough-covered traces on her eyelids and nose, the in-some-places-undyed or frayed, light brown hair, her clean but along-the-arms-and-collar-worn coat which shapelessly hung off her shoulders; when her voice, ragged from cigarettes, alcohol and other storms which seemed to come from the polar circle of her life, spoke to him, he asked himself how old she might be. At best, he guessed around late fifties; if it turned out that she was ten years older or younger, it would not have surprised him at all.

'You mustn't think that I was observing you,' she said, tugging at her black coat, which made her seem nervous. As Franck soon realized, however, it had more to do with some kind of tic, as did the way she frequently opened her eyes wide and stared into the distance, aghast, or how with the index and middle finger of her right hand she would perform a little dance upon the table-top for a few seconds. She did not seem to notice, everything simply happened, like her smile.

'I didn't think you were. My name is Jakob Franck.'

'Adriana.' She looked at him; for a moment, he thought she was about to cry. But her glance froze and had nothing more to do with him.

Franck looked on past her in order to alleviate her tension; after a while, she sighed and sank her head. Franck turned around and signalled the waiter. In the meanwhile, three other guests had come in, an older married couple and a fully bearded man in a suit, around forty, who was busy working on a laptop next to which were two smartphones.

'May I offer you something to drink, Adriana?' Franck asked when the waiter arrived.

'You don't have to do that.'

'I'd like to.'

'Then I'll have another cappuccino.'

'Would you like a water with that?'

'You really are quite thoughtful. Then a glass of tap water, please.'

Franck decided upon another wheat beer, nothing else came to mind; he had only called the waiter over because he had wanted to order the woman something, to make her talkative, to give meeting her a personal note, to justify his having come over—he did not know why.

Her eyes, her slightly curved posture, the aura he thought he perceived of her having been expelled from somewhere, the unspoken desire for unobtrusive close-ness reminded him of Ludwig Winther, the man he had smoked and drunk schnapps with although just an hour before their meeting he never would have believed it was possible. And as little as he could be sure about the real motives of the 'trouser salesman' (as Inge Rigah called her brother-in-law), the signals that came from Adriana were quite clear indeed.

Right in the middle of the confusion of a Friday the woman had lost her way, and now—like a forgotten suit-case on a motionless and broken baggage carousel long after midnight—she was waiting for someone to turn the light back on, she was waiting for a mechanic to repair her or to at least explain how it all could have come to that.

'Would you like to tell me a story?' Franck asked.

A minute passed before she trusted herself to look at him. 'Why? Don't you have anything better to do?'

'Is this your diary?' He pointed to the book with the black leather cover and little bookmark hanging out the side.

The waiter brought their drinks and Adriana watched him go as if she were interested in him, but Franck thought that her glance had frozen in the air again. Her coffee must have got cold by the time she finally took her spoon and stirred it even though she had not added any sugar. Her behaviour did not stop Franck from drinking on his own; nor was he looking at her constantly, he simply kept her in the corner of his eye.

'My whole life is in there.' By the time her eyes reached the black book, she had already begun to speak again. 'And when I close it, it seems as if it were already over, or, in any case, interrupted. Do you think I'm crazy?'

'Tell me more,' said Franck.

'You have to give me an answer.'

'Of course I don't think you're crazy.'

'You didn't answer my question earlier either.'

Franck thought for a moment, then said, 'I don't have any plans other than listening to you.'

'Are you something like a priest?'

'No.'

'A psychiatrist?'

'No.'

'A hairdresser?' Her smile came like a crack in the skin of her seemingly frozen-over face.

'I was a police officer,' said Franck.

'Oh God.' Not a trace of a smile remained on her lips. She turned her head and raised her shoulders as if wanting to turn to the side.

'Responsible for fatalities.'

'Oh dear.' With an abrupt movement, she bent herself closer towards him. For the first time since he had sat down at her table, she looked into his eyes for longer than a few seconds.

She would never have imagined anything like that as she watched him eat, the way he was slouched into his chair, the way he kept pushing his napkin from one hand to another; he seemed quite agitated; he also seemed to be keeping a dubious secret behind his middle-class facade; a man who, judging by his bag, had just come back from a short trip and instead of getting home to wife and child first wanted a beer and a pizza; an insignificant man, just like she was an insignificant woman; two nameless guests sitting in an airport restaurant in the afternoon, for no particular reason really but on a whim, in a state—she was convinced—similar to that of an iceberg, she vaguely hoped that he would notice her and, without any needless delay, come over, sit down and answer all the questions she wanted to ask and for one reason only: so that she would not have to think about her sister.

It was unlikely, that was clear to her; but in the presence of a man who did not himself know where to go, she would be able to survive the day; she would not drown, as she had all the previous years; maybe, she thought—and, once he was finally standing in front of her, she eagerly invited him to take a seat—through this encounter she would find the strength, after all the wandering, invocations, evocations, starless nights and icy tears, to let go.

Let go, said the voice in her head, and she did not stop looking at the man whose name she had forgotten; take all the medicine out of the kitchen cabinet, open the heavy, French red wine Sofia gave you, fill the bulbous, green Roman wine glass all the way to the top, load your hand up with the tablets, stick everything into your mouth at once and swallow, then drink, and again, until the glass is empty; stand up, take the framed photograph into your hand, kiss it and hold it tight; then lie down on the floor, close your eyes, forgiven and forgotten; out.

'Oh dear,' Adriana repeated. 'If you only knew.'

'Someone has died,' said Franck. 'And you are in mourning.'

'Yes.' How strange, she thought, the word just slipped out.

'Would you like to talk about it?'

'With you?' Her glance belonged to the distance behind Franck once more; her eyes widened, her body hardened into stillness.

'Who died?'

The silence that followed lasted minutes.

'She was murdered,' said Adriana. 'We were only five hundred metres away, but we didn't notice. And kept on sleeping. And only woke up when the telephone rang. The woman at the other end of the line said, "Please come quickly to Reception." We weren't dressed, neither my partner nor I.' She paused. 'Do you think I'm crazy?' she asked a second time.

'No,' said Franck. 'When did it happen?'

'Oh.' Her eyes strayed off again. 'Today. Around this time. We shouldn't have been allowed to travel, not at this time of year, not on account of my sister, not that, everything, not that. Do you understand?'

'Who died, Adriana?'

'She died.'

'Your sister.'

'Sofia.'

'Tell me more.'

'I don't think I really want to.' She looked at him but before her eyes could freeze, he shoved his right hand under her left and took hold of her. A shudder ran through her body, Franck could not believe how cold her fingers were; she did not let go of him, instead, she took a breath through her half-open mouth, nervously, hesitantly, close to panicking. Franck lightly increased the pressure and she looked at him. 'You're holding my hand,' she said. 'Why are you doing that?'

Franck did not say anything. Her fingers had not warmed up even one degree; he laid his left hand on top of hers as gently as possible, as if incidentally, as if by accident.

'Goodness, the things you're doing.' Surprised, she stared at her cup. 'Do you think the coffee still tastes any good?' After a moment, she took a sip, put the cup down and shook her head. 'Bitter. That's okay. I don't remember your name any more.'

'Jakob Franck.'

'Right. Adriana Waldt, with a *d-t*. Most people forget the *t* when writing it down. It was like that back in school, you can imagine. At a certain point, Sofia would only write our surname with *t*. A real pain for the teacher. Our mother thought it was funny, I didn't. We rarely agreed with each other, my mother and I, she and Sofia always understood each other. I think. Today I'm no longer so sure. In fact, I'm not really sure about anything any more. Not about anything.'

He began to like her voice. There was something familiar in it, the echoes of another, forgotten voice; he could feel the beer, but to the degree that it sharpened his senses and placed him into a timeless spirit; two beers later, though, he knew that the force of gravity would pull him back. 'Tell me about the hotel where you were.'

'The hotel.' She lowered her eyes. 'You're still holding my hand, and I hardly notice any more. What does that mean?'

'Nothing,' said Franck.

Her next sentence was lively. 'It doesn't mean anything, you're right.' She came to a halt. 'Hansen Beach Hotel. From the second floor, you could see the sea. On the first floor, you only see the dunes. But that's nice too. *Herr* Hansen. And *Frau* Hansen. And little Jens Hansen. But he's not that small any more, he's already fifteen or sixteen. But back then he was really small, the first time we ever went there, I mean. Sofia would drive there every year. Sofia's my sister.'

'Yes,' Franck said.

'You know that, I already told you. I forget what's only just happened, but I recognize things that happened a hundred years ago.' From one moment to the next, she was overwhelmed by a boundless wash of blissful memories; she saw people and places, the dunes and the sea, the sky, the seagulls snapping ice cream from little Jens' hand; she could even smell the sweet scent of the crepes stand on the promenade, the rosebushes and the sand; it was as if she were there and Sofia was kissing her lover all over again.

Angry with sadness, she pulled her hand away; she wanted to flee but was caught up in his presence; the man across from her, she had understood, would not let her go, and it was her own fault. And a policeman on top of it, a poorly shaven apparition but one with a clean, white shirt that despite his outrageous munching away he had managed to avoid staining; a beer-drinking retiree but one with manners. Her left hand felt different than her right and she wondered: What's going on with me?

'Which sea were you at?' he asked as if nothing had happened, she thought. How was he supposed to suspect what had just happened, she wondered, and said, 'At the North Sea, naturally.'

'I've never been there.'

'Why are you lying?'

'I'm not lying.' Franck said and drank his beer, which was slowly growing flat; his eyes rested on her.

'No one has ever not been to the North Sea,' said Adriana Waldt with a serious face.

'Well, then I'm the first.'

Shaking her head, with her thumb and index finger she reached for her cup handle but otherwise did nothing.

'What happened then?' Franck asked and folded his hands on the table. She looked over and closed her eyes, then opened them again and past him.

'We'd gone out the night before. La Strada. That's a pizzeria on Paulstraße, not far from us, from the hotel. We always go there. Eat a bit, drink some Nero d'Avola, talk the whole evening. The hostess has known us for a long time.'

As if his face were a movie camera she was not allowed to look into, her glance flitted to the side. But nothing was staged. 'It was snowing when we left. Beginning of November, what a stupid idea. I'd told her that we should postpone the trip and only fly to the island for New Year's. We had already done that once before, and were happy. Sofia, Hagen, Kai and me. Hagen was Sofia's partner and Kai was my boyfriend. The men didn't want to fly either.'

Franck sensed what she wanted to tell him; he recognized the form of self-torture from hundreds of interrogations and speaking with relatives and the bereaved;

yet again he was the listener, not a colleague, fellow traveller or a random guest. Excluding the possibility that, he thought, he would have gone to one of the other restaurants in the terminal—where he would have felt completely out of place—to quieten his hunger; his table in sight of the woman had been reserved, he now realized humorously but did not let it show.

She turned towards him. 'May I ask you something, *Herr* Franck?'

He nodded.

'Are you listening to me?'

'Every word,' he said. 'What did you do on the evening before your sister died?'

'She didn't simply die . . . '

'Yes . . . '

'Yes. May I ask you something else?'

This time he showed no reaction at all.

'How old are you?'

'Sixty-one.'

'Oh.' She forced herself not to say anything else.

'You thought I was older,' Franck said.

'No. I didn't want to hurt your feelings. Don't you have to go?'

'Where would I have to go?'

'Home. To your family.'

'I live alone.'

'Me too. For almost two years now. And you?'

'For almost twenty.'

'Why so long?' For a moment of surprise her slight body, hidden under the far-too-large blazer, perked up and a fleeting, rosy light appeared across her face of snow. 'You must stop living that kind of life immediately. Are you listening to me? No one's allowed to live alone for twenty years. Is that why you eat so quickly and thoughtlessly, because no one's there to pay attention and share the table with you? Promise me you'll make an effort to change your life. I'm begging you, *Herr* Franck.'

He had no idea how to reply. He already feared the woman was on medication and needed a partner for her erratic stories full of dramatic hyperbole; evidently his look was so intense that all traces of colour faded from her cheeks and her body disappeared once more into the shadow of her coat, which to Franck in the meantime seemed voluminous and tattered.

'Excuse me,' Adriana Waldt said. 'Now I've offended you, I was just afraid for you all of a sudden. But I don't even know you, I know nothing about you, only that you were once a police officer and are now retired. Will you forgive me?'

'You did not offend me. Why didn't your friends want to fly to the island that day?'

'They just didn't want to. They had a feeling. Sofia didn't listen to them, like always. She had decided to spend her birthday on the island again, that was what she wanted to do. She'd celebrated her fiftieth there, she'd invited ten people for it, flight and the stay all free. You couldn't discuss those kinds of things with her. Once she'd made up her mind, any objections were futile. Futile, pointless, absurd.'

The index and middle fingers of her right hand danced back and forth across the top of the table as if someone other than Adriana were playing with a marionette. 'Can a person you know so well disguise themselves that, in the end, you don't really know them any more? No. That's impossible. The reality is that we all disguise ourselves, all of us, you and me and every one, and we shut our eyes and imagine a person we might've known before, a long, long time ago, do you understand, *Herr* Franck? When the person was still a child. When the person sat next to you in bed or on the couch or played in the garden. We always, our whole lives long, want to see the same person there. No one else. They've got to remain how they were. But because that's insane, because no one stays the same as they were, we see them through our own concepts as if looking through a window into the past, a past that hasn't existed for a long time.

'There's a voice within us that says: Lies, all lies. Right, *Herr* Franck? Right. We push the voice away, it's quite simple, and then the person walks into the room and we look at them and take them by the arm and talk with them the whole night long, for half a lifetime, we talk with them like puppets we made ourselves just to be less alone in the silence.

'*Herr* Franck, my sister was three years older than I am, we were like twins, and from the very beginning I was the first person she ever showed her poems to. She trusted me from the very beginning. No one in the family knew where her talent came from, she had it and used it, and whenever she wrote, she reeled through the flat and even the city. She grew intoxicated by the words she wrote and the words themselves, and when she'd read out her poems to us, we just couldn't see that they came from her mouth or that they were even hers. From Sofia, who was usually so quiet and didn't want to be noticed by anyone. Even when she was drunk she'd scribble verses on newspapers and beer coasters and napkins, then she'd stand up on a table and read what she'd just written out loud. People would be amazed and would clap. And Sofia would start to dance, right in the middle of the bar, right there on the table, and she would dance to a music that only she could hear, for there wasn't ever any other music there.

'That night at La Strada she didn't dance. She sat quietly at the table with Hagen, Kai and I. Hagen was talking about his new website and Kai was making fun of him, as always, and we were drinking our Nero d'Avola. And then some Ramazotti which the hostess gave us for free. Her name is Gianna. Her husband's the chef. He's also responsible for the music. He set up an extra speaker and ran a cable from the restaurant into the kitchen. If it was up to him, the guests would have to listen to Gabriella Ferri every night. She was from Rome, just like he is. A haunted soul. Fell off her balcony. Or threw herself off. We hummed along with some of the songs. Sofia too. We never learnt Italian. Did you, *Herr* Franck?'

'No.'

'No. We never even learnt Spanish. Though our father was from Madrid and lived with us for a while. Two, three years. Then he disappeared. Took off, as our mother put it. She was alone, and we grew up with her. She would go for walks a lot, along the river, through the English Garden and far away into the north of the city. Sometimes we'd sit in the kitchen and hold hands. Waiting for Mom. She always came back. Never said where she'd been, what she'd done, who she'd seen. She would open the door, hang her coat on the rack, take off her shoes, slide into her house slippers, as she called them, and hug the two of us. She always smelt on fresh air. And then she'd make us pancakes, and the whole flat smelt sweet.

'And that evening at La Strada, Sofia suddenly said: Do you still remember how Mom would always make pancakes for us when she'd been away? And immediately I had the smell in my nostrils and could taste the powdered sugar in my mouth, it was wonderful. Sofia hugged me at the table to the music of Gabriella Ferri and the men went outside to smoke. We were the only two left, all the other guests had gone already. We were always the last ones there at Gianna's.

'Nothing else happened, *Herr* Franck.

'The next morning Kai and I slept in. Hagen too, over with Sofia. We slept in because we'd agreed to see each other at ten in a cafe nearby. It's more relaxed than in the hotel, and you can look out at the sea.

'*Herr* Franck?

'*Herr* Franck?'

Her hands, palms facing upwards, lay flat on the table, one next to the other; Franck laid his hands on hers and the cold fingers closed around them, her nails driving into his skin. '*Herr* Franck? Say something.'

'Who killed your sister, Adriana?'

'It was the sea. The sea killed her. She let herself be killed by the sea. And we were there and didn't notice. And we were there and watched. We watched. And I hugged her at the table in La Strada, and Kai waved to me from outside but I couldn't wave back because I didn't want to let her go. Do you understand that, *Herr* Franck? Do you?'

'Yes,' he said.

'She was done with her life.' With an expression of deep reluctance, she moved the coffee cup to the edge of the table and pushed back her chair, and Franck saw that she was wearing loosely cut, black cloth pants that were full of bright spots and a pair of black boots which, Franck thought, looked as dirty as Ludwig Winther's loafers. Now he also recognized the vague undertone in Adriana Waldt's voice again, the husky echo of a woman's voice, a woman who had gone silent two decades before: Doris Winther.

'She was done with her life,' he repeated; agitated by his remark, she recoiled when she noticed her two fingers standing on the table, those two bony stalks balancing her thin, spotted hand. My goodness, what all I've told this strange man! she thought, and he was in no hurry.

'We shouldn't have flown,' she said. 'The men were right, they'd sensed everything, and I didn't understand a thing. I'm trying, look at me, *Herr* Franck, I'm trying very hard to understand. I wear my sister's clothes, I put on her shoes, I don't fit, even her clothes push me away, even her shoes. My hair just can't take her old headscarf, I can feel it as soon as I try to tie it. That's why I've taken it off, though I really should wear it because it's black and it suits me. The sea murdered my sister.'

Then she went silent; her eyes off in the arctic distance, her hands, as if exhausted after strenuous activity, lay on their sides between the two of them. Franck hesitated to say anything; when he began, she cut him off.

'And now,' she said, standing up and taking her black handbag from the seat next to her, 'I must leave you, for I would like to be outside.'

'I'll accompany you,' he said.

She pulled the bag with the gold rings. 'By no means.' Today's the day, she thought, and wanted to tell him that for two years she had not spoken with anyone that way, and that she had missed it and had always hoped to, so that she could go—oh, to finally be able to go. And he, who had also stood up and waved to the waiter, had done her the favour of listening and letting her speak. She thought she could already feel the heavy red wine in her mouth, everything at long last and now, and she would have already thanked him had he not grabbed her arm.

'What are you doing?' she asked while he, sensing that he could not allow her to leave alone, let go and controlled his voice.

'I am going to stay with you until I'm sure that nothing will happen.'

'Never!' she cried, reached back and, with incredible strength, hit him in the face with her bag.


They sat next to each other with their backs to the other guests. After the waiter—whose disgust, Franck thought, had more to do with the small turnover than the woman's assault—had withdrawn into the depths of the restaurant, he repeated his version of events to one of his colleagues while waving his hands in the air.

With her bag pressed to her stomach, Adriana soundlessly rocked back and forth; this man, she thought, had ruined everything, and she had let it happen; she was a coward, and her sister would despise her for it.

'Should we call your partner?' The dull throbbing in his face gradually began to fade; even though it had caught him completely off-guard, she clearly had not had any hard objects in her bag and had only raised her arm once; on the second try, it fell back in fatigue. Franck had not moved an inch, nor had she; for a while a heavy silence spread out around them until the waiter appeared with a series of helpless phrases. Franck quieted him down with a few terse words and led Adriana back to the table.

'Who?' she asked; startled, she raised her head; she had not thought of him in so long, she had almost forgotten ever being together with him.

'Kai,' said Franck.

'No, no. Kai's gone.'

'You separated.'

'He had to leave me,' she said and abruptly turned her head to Franck. 'Did I hurt you very badly? I don't know why I did that.'

'You didn't want me to accompany you.'

'I didn't want you to, and I still don't want you to.'

'Why did Kai have to leave you, Adriana?'

'Because I wasn't there any longer. For him. I wanted to be there for myself. With Sofia. No one else. He couldn't understand that.'

'You didn't let him be there with you in your grief.'

'That's right.'

'When did you separate?'

'One year ago.'

'He left you,' said Franck.

'He said that he had the right to a life but that I would only live for death. I tried to explain to him why I couldn't leave Sofia and he always responded that I needed to go and see a doctor, I was sick, like Sofia—only that you could see I was sick, and no one could see it with her. Fifty-six years. That's how long I lived with her. Half a century and more. Is that possible, *Herr* Franck? That much time and that much silence? Although we talked so much, every week, sometimes even every day. On the telephone. Although . . . and her? What about her? Fifty-six years. I have no idea how long. When she began to keep quiet about the truth. And that's what she did, *Herr* Franck. I really didn't know a thing, my Kai was right about that. No one knew a thing, not once at La Strada that evening.'

Eyes wide she stared at the shiny floor; her voice reminded Franck yet again of that timeless night in the attractive single-family home when a woman he did not know began to lose her life.

'And then,' said Franck, 'your sister went into the water.'

'And then she went into the water. And I asked Hagen what had happened during the night. Whether they had fought. I wanted to know what was wrong. There had to have been something wrong. Right? No. He said: As always, we held onto each other in bed; I put my arms around her, and we fell asleep. And then they fell asleep, and when he woke up, she was gone. I don't believe that.' Her voice could barely be understood any more. 'She simply left us, as if we hadn't even existed.'

She stopped speaking. But just when Franck began to answer, her flat voice returned. 'Can you imagine, *Herr* Franck, that at that very same time many other people went away for ever too? Ten thousand. That's a fact. So many go leaving so many others behind at the end of the universe. Here I am, yet somehow am no longer. I'm just a shadow with clothes that my dead sister casts; and happily. That's who I am.'

'Did Sofia leave behind a note?' Franck asked.

'Only a single line on a piece of paper from the Hansen Beach Hotel. She wrote: In the casket I want to be wearing my black Dorothy Perkins blazer and my black trousers from Anna Field. That's what she wrote. That's it.'

'And you honoured her wish.'

'Yes, we did. And she had a second Dorothy Perkins blazer and a second pair of Anna Field trousers, she was head secretary and needed to be able to change her clothes and have enough to go out, she had to be around people a lot, although she preferred to spend time alone, like me. She made more of an impression than I do, she was more solid. That doesn't bother me. And so I spend time with her every day and I talk with her and ask her questions though I know I will never get an answer. I'm really sorry for hitting you. Please forgive me.'

'It's all right,' said Franck. 'Is your mother still alive?'

'No.'

'Did your father attend Sofia's funeral?'

'No. Why?'

'Are you still in contact with Sofia's boyfriend Hagen?'

'No. I'm not in contact with anyone. Aside from Sofia.'

'She died two years ago today.'

'Yes.'

'Did you sit here in the airport last year too?'

'Yes.'

'And you're writing in your diary.'

Her hands gripped the bag on her lap more tightly. 'I write all of my questions and thoughts down into the book, and I write letters to Sofia too and tell her about my life. What I see when I go to work and what I do when I get home in the evenings. I often cook soup.'

'Would you cook me a soup too, sometime?' Franck asked out of the blue, she looked at him, a veil of dusky pink across her cheeks.

'Unfortunately, that won't be possible.' She paused for some time without moving her eyes from his face which, whenever she looked at it, reminded her of an anchor; you would've liked him, she thought all of a sudden, and as if he could read her thoughts he nodded.

'Promise me something, Adriana,' he said, and she answered: No. But, closer to her than anyone had been in two years, his unshakeable presence made her feel shy.

'What?' she asked quietly.

'At some point over the next few weeks, go with me to visit your sister's grave, I'd like to see it and be there with you. I'd like to hold your hand, just like you used to hold Sofia's hand. We'll just stand there and think of her. I didn't know your sister, I don't even know you, I know very little about you. You are inclined towards hitting unknown men in the face with your bag when you feel like you're being harassed. And I can see that you're in mourning and that you come to the airport not to fly anywhere, but to drink coffee and write letters to your sister.

'Two years are nothing, Adriana, you have every right to come here to sit and write, to wear your sister's clothes, everything you do in order to think of Sofia, no one has the right to take that away from you. That's your way, these are your steps; and even if you don't receive any answers to your questions, you have to continue asking them. It's the only way.

'But you should also understand one thing: You are not the shadow your dead sister casts. She would never want that. If your sister didn't let you be a part of her troubles, it's because she couldn't do otherwise. She didn't want to be a burden to you, she wanted to carry her burden alone, just like she'd done her whole life long, voluntarily and without complaint. You don't need to answer me, your eyes already have.

'You're still wearing Sofia's clothes, every day of the year you still think that your sister betrayed you and lied to you, you're still unable to reconcile yourself to the life that from now on you have to live. But you'll learn, you'll make it. Apparently your sister—we don't know why, and we never will—could not reconcile herself to her life, and she didn't ask anyone to help her with that pain, she carried it for herself alone.

'Sofia wasn't quiet because she didn't trust you but because she couldn't find the words, and that caused her infinite pain, for half of her life, I'm sure of that.

'Adriana, you cannot let the sun set on your anger for one day more, not a single day. Promise me you'll take that to heart. And promise me that you'll call me and go with me to the cemetery. And, last but not least, I'd like to invite you to dinner. Or only if you promise not to hit me when I offer to accompany you home. Repeat the phrase I just said: I cannot let the sun . . . '

'I cannot let the sun . . . I cannot let the sun set on my anger one day more.'

'One more time, Adriana.'

'I cannot let the sun set on my anger one day more.'

'Today's a good day,' said Franck and, unable to contradict him, she reached for his hand; it was the first time since that evening at La Strada that another person's skin was something other than the thin disguise of a lie.

In the milky light of the old lamp Franck read the poem over and over again; that evening he had looked around rather randomly for something to read, for he wanted to spend it behind closed doors and in the comfort of his trusty books and files.

Promising to call him soon, Adriana Waldt had left the airport with the S8 in the direction of the centre city. Franck took the train east and got off in Laim. On the way from the restaurant downstairs, he had originally thought of accompanying Adriana all the way to her front door but she had sworn to call him and he had made the effort to believe her; furthermore, she had resolutely refused to tell him her address, and he did not want to push her.

As expected, the train was overcrowded, but he was able to find a window seat; huddled up in his coat, he looked forward to getting home to his empty room.

About one thousand nine hundred years before Christ, a man in Egypt wrote a poem he called 'The Debate Between a Man and His Soul', its final lines read:

*Death is in my sight today*
*As when a sick man becomes well,*

*Like going out-of-doors after detention.*
*Death is in my sight today*
*Like the smell of myrrh,*
*Like sitting under an awning on a windy day.*
*Death is in my sight today*
*Like the perfume of lotuses,*
*Like sitting on the shore of the Land of Drunkenness.*
*Death is in my sight today*
*Like a trodden way,*
*As when a man returns home from an expedition.*
*Death is in my sight today*
*Like the clearing of the sky,*
*Like a man who discovers what he ignored.*
*Death is in my sight today.*
*As when a man desires to see home*
*When he has spent many years in captivity.*

The poem is considered to be part of the oldest suicide letter in existence, written by a man who, Franck thought, was struggling to find redemption and who had to express one last time all the things that had weighed him down his entire life, but that he did not want to burden anyone else with.

His name is unknown.

CHAPTER TWELVE

## To Go and Live

That weekend Franck did not speak with anyone and slept longer than usual, which surprised him. His trip to Berlin, all the talks, impressions and contradictory information had worn him out and reawakened an old, half-forgotten quality inside of him; he called it 'thought-sensitivity'.

He had discovered it—or invented it—during the extremely complex and constantly flagging investigations surrounding a double murder; a combination of thin facts, flickering half-facts, bifurcating statements, confusing crime-scene traces, contradictory motives and a trauma-tized eight-year-old witness with an excessive imagination had driven the detectives to their limits. One morning Franck decided not to go to work; he closed the door to his study, pulled the blue, woollen blanket off the couch, spread it out across the parquet, lay down, stretched out his arms and legs and began to project his thoughts onto the white of the ceiling while paying attention to what he found in each piece of the puzzle, like he was watching a film for the first time, curious to see whether what was happening would change him from being a distant viewer into a reflective human being.

He was not allowed to think about the images beforehand; he had to be able to perceive the terrible, the incomprehensible, the incoherent, the chaotic and the labyrinthine nature of the crime as something natural, as something that touched him as simply as a hand or a glimpse of the sea when he was a child.

To recognize the truth of the case, he could not be a criminologist of any kind; he had to try and forget everything he had learnt and trust the reactions of his body, the neurotransmitters of his cells.

For two hours that morning he lay there motionless; he stared at the ceiling and registered hundreds of pieces of information without trying to understand them. Then, all of a sudden, he fell into an open-eyed, sleep-like state; he was not met by any dreams but by a house and its inhabitants; what he saw shot through him, for he had become one of them, overwhelmed by rage and violence.

Once he had got up and stepped under a cold shower, he realized he had not solved the case, but felt that he had at least understood it; back at headquarters, he ordered the files and the evidence once more; he asked the disturbed little boy new questions and went through the rooms in the fourth-floor flat where the crime had taken place one more time; he spoke with all the neighbours again and arranged new appointments with every single relative, friend, acquaintance and colleague of the family's—seventy-three people in all, who, together with a colleague, he proceeded to examine over the course of several hours.

He later described what had come to him as he had lain there on the floor as a moment of happiness through simple inner perception. And although his colleague André Block suggested that he might not necessarily want to report his experience in his lectures to the Police Academy—the students might think, as he did, that something with the Inspector, Salary Grade A12, was not quite right—Franck returned to his method a number of times, and always with useful results.

Indeed, after five months of investigations, they were able to solve the double murder in the high-rise on Petuelring thanks to witness testimony, readjusted windows of time and one of the eight-year-old boy's incidental remarks; the main suspect, a close friend of the murdered couple, denied it but was nevertheless convicted thanks to unambiguous DNA traces left at the crime scene; he was sentenced to life in prison, the judge finding the nature of his guilt particularly serious.

After getting back from Berlin, for the first time in a long time Franck spread out the blue blanket across the floor and began his ceremony; one hour later he stood up in disgust. A number of people had been complicit in the young girl's death twenty-one years ago, something they themselves had to have been aware of even back then; they were all deceiving and lying to one another simultaneously and did not let the detectives, who apparently were just following routine, trick them out of their reserve with their questions. Someone from that circle had let Esther down at the most crucial moment. And, angered by his thoughts, Franck thought he knew who that was.

'You can by no means simply come here and insult me,' she said loudly as she closed the door to the conference room. 'This is outrageous. I'm going to file a complaint against your superiors through my chief editor. How did you put it? I sent my friend to her death? Are *you* completely innocent? You're lucky that I'm even speaking to you, man.'

'I don't have any superiors,' said Franck. 'And I did not say that you sent your friend to her death, I said that I believe it's possible you belong to a handful of people that did not prevent your friend's death. Do you understand, *Frau* Horn?'

'No, I don't.'

The thirty-eight-year-old editor had stuck her hands into the back pockets of her black jeans and was pacing back and forth in front of the window. Sandra Horn's thin, tastefully made-up face was dominated by designer glasses with a red-brown frame and when she shook her head, as she often did, her glasses slid down her nose and she had to push them back up with her finger. Hoop earrings dangled from her ears and she had folded up the collar of her white blouse which she wore untucked from her jeans. As opposed to the way she dressed and the subtle scent of her perfume, Franck found her behaviour inappropriate. 'And what is that supposed to mean, you don't have any superiors? You're a police officer, after all. Or a detective. What's this all about?'

Franck sat down in one of the ten chairs, pulled out his pen and notepad from his bag, opened it up and looked at the journalist. 'Would you please sit down for a few minutes?' She showed no reaction whatsoever. 'I'm retired, I told you that downstairs at reception, if you'd like to remember. Nevertheless, I am involved with your friend's death once again because there still are a number of inconsistencies, contradictions and unanswered questions.'

'Like what? After all these years? How did you ever come up with that idea? What do you have to do with Esther's suicide?'

'I was the police officer who informed Esther's mother that she had died.'

'That was you?' With her finger on her glasses as if she had to hold on to them, she sat down and rested her head on both hands. 'I see. *Frau* Winther told me about you. Supposedly you spent half the night with her, quite unusual. And how did you suddenly arrive at the idea that something was off with the suicide? Did someone say something to that effect?'

'It's possible.'

'And who might that be?'

'Back then you went to Esther's parents and told them you'd had the feeling for a long time that Esther had wanted to do something to herself. Can you remember?'

'Why do you keep asking me if I remember? I definitely remember that you aren't a police officer any more. That's quite clear. In any event, I don't remember what I might've said to her parents any longer. Is it important?'

'Yes.'

'And why's that?'

'Did you have evidence to support your claim?'

'I don't know, I certainly must have. Who are you trying to find all of this for?'

'Do you remember your classmate Jan Roland?' Franck asked. He had found the address of Sandra's parents in his files; her mother seemed upset by his request and said that she had never understood why Esther had taken her own life; in her opinion, the schoolgirl had been a rather quiet, reserved person but also adventuresome and vivacious; after her friend's death, Sandra had never wanted to talk about it again; the name Jan Roland meant nothing to her.

'Jan?' Sandra Horn fiddled with her glasses, then took them off forcefully and threw them onto the table. 'One of those assholes you find in every class. I hate these glasses, my contact lenses are ruined and it's taking ages for the optician to get me a new pair. What's with this Jan?'

'He has some peculiar ideas.'

'Well, he was peculiar himself. Shifty, sleazy. Didn't he want to be an actor? I bet he became a bin man. Is he the one who hired you?'

'No. He thinks that Esther might've been abused by her father.'

In the matter of only a few seconds, Sandra Horn seemed to be transformed from a naturally arrogant and proud woman into a being robbed of all of its certainties whose eyes displayed nothing but panic and disbelief; even the sweep of her lips had disappeared, and her mis-shapen mouth made no sound. She fell into such a glaring silence that two female colleagues passing by the glass door stopped to stare in shock. Franck was pretty sure that verbal reserve did not belong to Sandra Horn's every-day repertoire.

He took a few notes and waited; the journalists out-side had walked on, whispering. Only now did Franck notice a small, square-shaped watch on Sandra's right wrist which was as gold as her earrings and ticked silently. Hands flat upon the table, she shook her head numerous times and made no attempt to say or to do anything. When her eyes fell onto Franck's notepad with its spidery handwriting, she began to stare at it as if she could make it talk and learn a truth that would annihi-late the power of her imagination; then they wandered aimlessly and fearfully throughout the room until they again met Franck's face and stayed put; their pleading penetrated through to her voice.

'That can't be,' she said through an almost closed mouth. 'That's a terribly mean lie.'

'Are you sure?'

The question made her silent again. Embarrassed, she put her glasses back on and then, as if taken by a slowly growing fury, tore them back off with both hands. 'Anyone who'd think something like that is a bastard. And Jan Roland was always a bastard. And you believe him? And you're here because of him? And trying to talk me into something? And want to make me insecure?

What kind of police officer are you? One of those devious ones. Our conversation is over.'

Her words were more powerful than her conviction; she remained seated, compulsively cast a glance at her watch then shook her head again.

'He also had something else to say,' said Franck.

'Of course he did, he always had something to say.'

'Supposedly Esther was friends with a man from the neighbourhood.'

Sandra Horn twisted her mouth into a grimace that to Franck seemed tremendously contrived; maybe the messenger and failed actor's memories were not such a mess after all and he was not just flattering himself by exaggerating; on the contrary, maybe he really did know more about the girl he went to the movies with than the others.

'And what does "friends with" mean exactly?'

'Most likely that she had a relationship with him.'

'And "most likely"?' She had unmistakably taken up the role of being superior again, of being the authority, which were the tools of her trade and personality; increasingly annoyed and at the same time insecure, which caused her to be both furious and transparent, his stoic manner made her feel like she was being pushed into a corner, just like the worst moments of being at school.

'Do you think that could be possible, *Frau* Horn?'

'Do I think what is possible? What exactly? That Esther fucked older men? That we were all whores? That we also drove her to her death? What do you really want from me? Who got you on to all of this? Who puts such vulgarity out into the world? You're defiling the memory of my best friend, understand? More respect, Inspector, or else there'll be something about you in tomorrow's paper that you won't like one bit, I guarantee you.'

Before he had set out for the offices of the tabloid where Sandra Horn ran the society column, he had read a few stories and interviews with her on the Internet; the wittily written articles introduced him to public figures he had never, or only vaguely, heard of and their statements about matters of being were, in his opinion, characterized by a shockingly flat-screen-TV-like quality; during his time in the criminal investigation unit, he would leaf through the tabloids every day and attentively read all the police reports; fundamentally, he had nothing against that form of journalism, it was simply that brazen self-confidence and asinine threats irritated him.

'What you write about me,' he said, 'is irrelevant, just so long as you don't print an old photograph.'

Intending to be anything but funny, Franck had only wanted to establish a short timeout in the middle of the inner-assault the journalist was allowing to drive her to making pointless attacks; a good joke coming out of his mouth, his ex-wife used to say now and again to friends, is about as unimaginable as one day seeing a green-eyed Hans Albers in front of the cameras.

After a while, Sandra Horn, without looking again at her watch, scratched her hand and leant back with a suppressed sigh. 'You're doing me in,' she said. 'You're confronting me with things I didn't expect. Let's try again. That guy, Jan, came to you and maintains that Esther was sleeping with someone from the neighbourhood and, moreover, that she was abused by her father. Have I understood all that correctly?'

'You have.'

'What do you think about all that? Apparently you've spoken with the asshole. Didn't he seem completely suspect to you? What's he even doing these days?'

Staff members hurried through the hallway at regular intervals; some of them waved to Sandra Horn, but she did not wave back. Franck had already filled up four pages of his notepad with observations and estimations and as he turned over the next page, the journalist put her head back onto her hands and patiently and with a sad smile watched him continue to write. Eventually, he laid the pen across the page and concentrated on the direction he would have to take to finally discover at least a dim light in the sleet-filled dusk of that fourteenth of February.

He said, 'At the moment, Jan Roland is working for a courier service. As far as your friend is concerned, so he implied, Esther's father might've been guilty of doing something. After the funeral at the East Cemetery, in any event, he went up to Esther's aunt and told her that he knew about a relationship your friend was having with an older man from the neighbourhood . . . '

'How can you . . . '

'I must interrupt you,' he said quietly. 'That's one side of things. The other side has to do with you.'

As before, she scratched her left hand, this time, however, more forcefully; Franck acted as if he had not noticed. 'The day after Esther's death,' he said, 'you visited her parents and said that for a long time you had thought Esther might do something to herself.'

'I did not!'

'What did you say then?'

'I have no idea any more, man.'

'You do not deny the visit.'

'Is this some kind of interrogation now? What exactly do you want? What would you like to hear? If you have some kind of suspicion: Here I am, say it to my face. In Esther's name, what are you accusing me of?'

'Nothing,' he said and meant it. 'I am trying to bring a dead case back to life and, ever since, Esther's ghosts have been haunting me. You are also a part of this, *Frau* Horn.'

Clearly incapable of doing anything else, she shook her head. Her face, Franck thought with a touch of humour, had even taken on the pale appearance of a ghost; he did not find it in the least bit funny, however, when she began to scratch open the nail beds of her thumbs with both her left and right hands while sucking air and blowing it back out through pursed lips—just like someone who was having a panic attack.

'*Frau* Horn?'

She cast him a frightened glance.

'Stop that.'

'What?'

'That thing with your fingers.'

She defiantly rubbed her skin two more times, flapped her hands as if to scare off the nervous plucking, then let her arms hang down at her sides.

'Where would we like to begin?' he asked. 'Maybe it'd be best to start with your visit to the Winthers the day after Esther's death.'

'I don't know any more,' she said; it sounded both despondent and truthful. 'I was there, it's true, but there's no way I said something like that to them, that's impossible.'

'It doesn't matter what you said. What's more important is what you thought. You thought that Esther was carrying a secret around inside her and you didn't get the chance to talk with her about it.'

'She didn't have any secret. She just stopped talking. I don't know what happened, I really don't.'

'You must know.'

'Why?'

'If not you, who else?'

She put her hands on the table, then in her lap, then back on the table. 'Really, I don't know. Why don't you ask—'

'No,' said Franck.

'Sorry?'

'We're not talking about Jan Roland right now. I'd like you to tell me what had been going on with Esther from the beginning of that year. Why she changed. Who the neighbour was that she supposedly met quite regularly.'

'That I can tell you.' Relieved to give a straightforward answer, she stretched her back and propped her hands on her thighs. 'That was the dentist, Dr Jordan. But she didn't go to meet him. She was just there a lot because she got on well with *Frau* Jordan, and with their son, he was still pretty young, ten or maybe eleven. The Jordans lived across the street. There was nothing going on there, I'm sure about that.'

'Then why is Jan Roland saying there was? And don't say it's because he's an asshole. I tend to believe he didn't tell me any lies.'

'So what? First he says that Esther had something going on with the dentist; then he says that her father sexually abused her. Just how is he supposed to know all that? What does he get out of spreading those kinds of lies?'

Franck's silence confused the journalist; she would have liked to continue talking but noticed the inspector's absent stare and his morose expression and paused; as he continued to remain silent, she shrugged her shoulders and, offended, looked over at the glass wall.

'What was wrong with your friend?' Maybe, he thought, it would be a good idea to ask her to go and bring him a coffee; or to go to the cafeteria together; or maybe he could call Ludwig Winther, invite him over and let the two of them loose on each other with the misdirected ploys they had perfected over the years of playing threshold guardians to a suicidal girl—until the moment when, unable to bear their respective pride any longer, they would come to their senses and make a confession.

After a long silence punctuated by ringing telephones and incomprehensible pieces of news drifting over from a TV, Sandra Horn stood up and walked to the window where she remained standing with her back to the table, hands in the back pockets of her jeans.

'I dream about her, you know,' she said. 'We're swimming in the Isar then lying naked on the Flaucher, we ride our bikes through the city and go shopping; most of the time we don't buy anything, we just try on clothes and have fun. Whenever I dream about her, it's summer. Strange, don't you think? The sun is shining and we giggle about everything, total kids. But you know . . . '

She turned around and looked at Franck, 'In reality, we were never like that. I can't remember us ever laughing that much. You didn't do fun things with Esther. Don't misunderstand me, she wasn't the brooding kind; she laughed, but just not like that, not when someone told a joke or a dumbass like Jan Roland would dance around or act out some scene or other from a play he hadn't understood. She didn't like it when someone tried to amuse her.

'I don't know. Now that I'm telling you all this it's becoming clear to me just how weird the two of us must've seemed to others. I was always in a good mood and straightforward, ready to fight when there was trouble not only verbally, I'd hit you if I didn't have any other choice, and she—Esther was quiet and watchful, unyielding, pitiless with her stares.'

She took her hands out of her pockets, looked as if she were about to gasp for air; then she walked back to the table with heavy steps and propped herself up against the back of a chair; it became more difficult than ever for her to talk. 'I once dreamt that I meet her shortly before she . . . before she goes into the park. We're on the street, on Bad Dürkheimer or somewhere close by, and I ask her what she's up to, and she says: I'm going to go and live. I'm going to go and live. And what do I do? Me? I let her go. What does that mean? I've never told anyone about that, you're the first. It's been years since I had that dream but I've never been able to forget it. Why are you looking at me like that?

'All I know is that Esther shut me out. We continued to go out together, we were still friends but, when I watched her in secret, I could just tell that she was somewhere else. With something else. Someone else. Good. Jan Roland wasn't the only one saying that Esther had problems with her father, that he was pressuring her or worse. Yes, there was talk about the neighbour; the dentist was known to show up at clubs and invite young girls to drinks. And he did. He invited me too, Esther as well. He liked her, it's true. But there was nothing going on there, I stand by my previous statement, Esther knew exactly when she had to draw a line. That's how she was. And her mother? What else do you want to know? She was unable to cope with Esther's death.'

'And you're convinced of that?' Franck asked, writing it all down.

'I am.' She paused, looked towards the glass door, held her breath. 'People said some other things too, I know that. People said she hung herself because she'd believed the rumours and been ashamed.'

'Doris Winther believed the rumours more than she did her husband?'

She nodded.

'And you?' He waited until Sandra turned back to him, then he bent over the table and reached for her wrist. 'Tell me what else you've never told anyone. Now's the time. Let's go and live, Sandra.'

She shook her head again forcefully; she could not get her ideas together; everything she thought, whatever she tried to remember, pulsed inside of her, belonged more to her heart than her mind; she was on the edge of losing control. She pulled back her arm with a jerk and smacked the table with her palm.

'That's what I want to do,' she cried. 'I do! What do you think? Right away I thought it was true. And that that's what Esther had been unable to talk about. What else could it've been, man? Of course he mistreated and sexually abused her, and we all looked on, all of us, that asshole Jan just like me and everyone else. We should've understood that. But we didn't. Not a thing. We're guilty. You've got to bring the guy to court and lock him up. Why were we such cowards? Why, *Herr* Franck, why?'

He stood up and helped her to sit back down; her whole body was shaking.

# CHAPTER THIRTEEN

# The Girl in the Dark, II

Up to a certain point, police work in a case of death was, in Franck's experience, always a kind of mutilation of the dead as well; to him, however, that had least of all to do with the work of the forensic scientists whose often spectral-like and completely emotionless post-mortems and findings made up the basis for the official closure of an investigation.

What Franck meant was his very own professional and, if need be, ruthless dismemberment of the circumstances, the exhumation of half-rotten truths, the disclosure of all those understandable, if similarly dirty, tricks of survival.

Solving a murder or a clearing up a dubious death gave an investigator the right to turn the world of the violently deceased upside down, and with unrelenting exactitude tear its inhabitants away from everything they had once used to structure their lives until they were standing out in the cold and aware of their essential wretchedness. Only then, Franck was convinced, could the victim be upon his or her way to everlasting peace.

He did not want to exclude the fact that the ghosts chose to haunt him because the dead still wandered the earth and, thanks to his austere, bureaucratic and incomplete final reports, intended to make him responsible. Nevertheless, he continued to put out cookies and tea and sit at the table, managed to withstand the horror and so far had not had to escape into any kind of therapy.

However—and this became clear to him while talking with Sandra Horn—one thing he would not be able to handle under any circumstances would be to have *her* at his table: seventeen-year-old Esther Winther; the one whose family and circle of friends, as far as Franck could tell, had incomprehensibly not been torn apart but, on the contrary, had spared the investigators, as if the girl had to be forced into silence a second time; as if she had to pay for something she had done to others, not to herself; as if her life, her death, was the result of a succession of plausible incidents and reasons; as if one morning she had decided on her own to don the mantle of dejection to the mute astonishment of the world; as if to even her closest friends her growing distance was simply a passing cold; as if the watching was all-around applause; as if everything had been the same as always.

Nothing, Franck thought, had been the same as always; and though here and there the investigators had uncovered new clues, in the end, they contented themselves with the relatives' silent mourning.

During the long interruption of their talk in the conference room while Sandra Horn was busy discussing the latest news with her colleagues and Franck was alone, he began to work himself into a frenzy thinking about how all the people Esther had known had found her irritating, baffling silence to be like a hiccup and presumed that, in order to get rid of it, the girl had simply held her breath too long and suffocated.

The image offended Franck so much that it triggered an irrepressible anger he did not spare the journalist when she returned with two coffees; inwardly he accused her as much as he did his colleagues, Esther's parents, teachers, classmates and neighbours; he crossed his arms and did not deign to give Sandra Horn a single glance.

She pushed him a cup and took a gulp from her own. 'What's wrong now?' she asked. 'Can't you see I'm trying to be open with you? I really don't know what else to say.' She realized she had forgotten to close the door. She put down her cup and when she came back, sat diagonally across from Franck so that she would not have to look him directly in the face.

Eager to chase off the image of all those contemptible people, he looked at her and reached for his pen. 'By now the loss of your friend doesn't pain you in the least,' he said in a tone that was a bit harsher than he had intended.

'What makes you say that?' she asked, on the verge of tears just like a moment earlier with her colleagues when, in the middle of a back-and-forth about the size of a celebrity's photo, she had suddenly begun to sob; frantically pulling a tissue from her pocket, before blowing her nose she had covered her face, hoping to free herself from the trap the investigator had placed her in with his incantational questions, for as soon as she had left the stuffy air of the conference room, she thought she would get her head straight and finally be able to defend herself against all the subliminal accusations. Instead, she was shaken by a crying fit next to the local-news office which led one of her colleagues to push her a chair and get her a second glass of water. Then everyone stood around her while two women kneeled down and patted her shoulders; she felt like a schoolgirl out on the playground after seeing her boyfriend cuddling another girl; the only good thing, she had thought to herself shortly thereafter in the toilet, was that the detective had not seen her. Then she washed and powdered her face, turned on the coffee machine in the kitchen, reassured her colleagues that everything was all right after they offered to ask the uninvited guest to leave, and went back into the room with her face composed.

Now hardly five minutes later she was sitting there with her good intentions gone and a forgotten feeling of guilt that, as much as she wanted to, she could not pin on the man sitting diagonally across from her.

From what she remembered, after the funeral twenty years ago—and the strong, black coffee which usually helped her through the day tasted stale and bitter—she had gone to her room and lain down on her bed with the exact same feeling: an appalling sense of emptiness.

'Talk with me,' said Franck.

'I can't.'

'Tell me what you're thinking about.'

'Nothing. About back then. About what you're accusing me of. About nothing. I don't know a thing any more, I wanted to . . . I didn't want to accuse the man . . . But . . . Back then I thought, yeah, there's something to all this . . . Do you believe that?'

'I don't know,' said Franck and took a sip of his coffee, which was still hot and had come just at the right time.

'No one knows a thing. I don't understand . . . You spoke with Jan Roland and he believes that Esther's father is guilty. Why didn't he say that then? Have you had a look at the old police reports?'

'There are no statements from him there.'

'Wait. You said that he'd said something to Esther's aunt . . . '

'Yes.'

'What do you mean, "yes"? What's going through your head?'

'A young, seventeen-year-old girl hangs herself in the park. For some time, the circumstances surrounding her death lead only to confusion; our questioning of neighbours doesn't turn up any useable clues, her parents accept that their daughter committed suicide. Case closed. Many of her classmates attend the funeral. One year later, Esther's mother chooses to commit suicide in the same way as her daughter. The reason: apparently, the inability to get over the pain of the loss. Her father loses his job, starts drinking, his friends turn away from him, only through luck and self-discipline does he manage to keep from landing in the gutter. One day he shows up at my flat with the hypothesis that his daughter did not kill herself at all but was murdered, quite possibly by a neighbour who wanted to impede a minor, with whom he'd had a relationship, from going to the police. I question the witness Roland who tells me that Esther's father sexually abused her which led her to do what she did. Now I'm talking with you and you confirm this suspicion. Everything clear?'

She stared at him; for a moment her eyes reminded him of Adriana Waldt whose search for an anchor in the icy sea of her thoughts caused her to freeze to death over and over again. Sandra Horn's lips formed empty words; she noticed and tried a second time to no avail. 'I tried . . . I really . . . Did I confirm what—'

He cut her off. 'You confirmed the suspicion. Which means that we can go home now and enjoy our Sunday.'

Something compelled her to drop her head; her golden earrings brushed the upturned collar of her blouse. 'What?' the journalist asked doubtfully. 'Sorry? What do you mean we can go home now?'

'The crime has reached the statute of limitations, the victim is dead. Consequently, investigations are automatically discontinued.'

'Automatically . . . '

'Automatically.'

'But . . . ' There was a great sincerity to her words. 'You're no longer a police officer, you're not investigating Esther's death but looking into it again on your own, that makes a difference.'

He took another sip of his coffee. 'I am concerning myself with it because her father asked me to.'

'Her father!' She stood up, brushed her blouse straight, pointed to the notepad with her outstretched index finger. 'That's why you didn't tell me who'd sent you. You're on his side.' Then she lowered her head again, and changed her tone. 'I don't mean it like that, it's just that you make me . . . You're right.' She took two steps backwards, leant against the wall, tilted her head and crossed her arms. 'No, no, it's good that I can't talk my way out of this, no one who was there can. The point is, I cannot imagine that this Jan Roland really knows a thing. How could he? Do you have any kind of explanation?'

'You also considered abuse to be a possible reason back then. Even though at the same time there were rumours that a neighbour had started an affair with Esther. Or she with him.'

'What do you mean by that?'

'The man chatted you up too and made a pass, he had a soft spot for minors.'

'My reasons were . . . I thought that . . . I have to confess something, before, outside, with my colleagues . . . Never mind.'

Franck stood up as well and did what he had been meaning to for an hour: he took off his suit jacket, threw it onto the table, stretched and began to slowly pace back and forth, his hands crossed behind his back, slightly bent over, just like he used to when he was on the squad.

'I heard you crying,' he said and did not wait for any reaction. 'We have to consider three questions: If Esther's father was guilty—did Esther trust her mother? And if she did, why did Esther Winther stay quiet about it?

Three: If Esther did not trust her mother or you, Sandra, why didn't she go to the police or to a doctor? She was a self-confident, wilful young girl, she could put up a fight when she had to, she wasn't a coward. She might've been a bit reserved when she felt she might achieve her goal better that way, and she was without any doubt an extremely observant person as far as her fellow human beings' moods were concerned, she could also see through con artists more quickly than others. And she was, I believe, an absolutely reliable and trustworthy friend.'

'She was indeed,' Sandra Horn said. 'I told her everything, and she did too, we were always honest with each other and could laugh about others, above all, the drooling boys. We were a team, inseparable.'

'But one day you realized that you weren't a team any more.'

'Something had happened but she didn't want to say what. I didn't push her, that wasn't the way we did things, we didn't annoy each other with questions; we weren't glued to each other like other girls who'd march to the bathroom arm in arm or stand in the corner whispering. We weren't little bitches. Basically, we could rely on each other.' As if confirming what she had said, Franck nodded; she looked sad and confused.

'When,' Franck asked, 'did that phase begin? How long before her death?'

'It's been such a long time.'

'No.'

'Sorry?'

'It's taking place here, now, with us. Esther died on the fourteenth of February. What had your relationship been like since the beginning of that year? No doubt you spent New Year's Eve together. What do you remember from that night?'

After she had watched the inspector pace back and forth two more times then walk around the table and up to her without a word to stand just a hand's width away, she let her arms sink to her sides. 'I swear, I don't know any more, we were probably on the Reichenbach Bridge because that's where kids always set off a bunch of fireworks. Still do. We must've been there, where else would we have gone instead? But what her mood was? No idea.'

'And your memory of the day Esther died?'

She shook her head and closed her eyes. She did not know if she had ever thought about that day again; but ever since the inspector had come into the room and chased her into that labyrinth of old shadows, she could sense that deep inside there was a moment whose reality— if she truly became aware of it—would humiliate her and unmask what she had become in all the years since Esther's death: an apathetic, made-up careerist who denied their common destiny and whose only professional and private success was writing pseudo-journalistic, flattering articles as a well-paid, metrosexual single woman in a relatively well-known big city.

And now that moment had come. She knew it and did not flinch. 'We had a fight,' she said. 'A kind of argument.'

She stretched out her arm and pointed to the window; she spoke past Franck in its direction as if someone were standing there. 'Because of the complete nonsense Jordan had been telling me for weeks. And why? Because you told him.' With a quick glance at Franck, she continued. 'Because she told him. That was her strategy. And now I remember . . . I think it was the first or second of January, right after New Year's, when all of a sudden I thought: She's leading me on, she's screwing around with me. She'd never done something like that before, she wasn't the type. Why is she doing that? I wondered and then I was sitting with Jordan in a cafe off the Münchner Freiheit and he asked me if it was true and I said: What? And he asked if Esther was having trouble at home, and I said: What kind of trouble? And he said that she'd told him that her father had started to go too far, coming into the bathroom when she was taking a shower, that kind of thing. I didn't believe a word. He carried on just like Jan, the windbag. And so I went over to her house that same day, I now remember, and asked her what was going on and she said that she might've talked with Jordan about it. But after that, not another word. That's how it was.'

With a casual but powerful movement, she pushed a chair against the side of the table, walked past Franck, turned back around and waved her hand through the air.

'What's this supposed to mean, man? It's not like we didn't talk to each other any more, we still met every day after school to go shopping or to a cafe or to study if there really wasn't anything else to do. Somehow we were still a team. And yet, at the same time, somehow we weren't.

'And that day . . . that day we fought again. Because Jordan had started with all that crap again, and that idiot Jan Roland too, and I think Viola as well, they all had something to say but in reality didn't know a thing. And so I confronted Esther again and told her that, if everything that people were saying was true, she had to go to the police, man! Press charges against her old man and have him taken to jail. And I asked her what her mother would have to say about it. Yes, I know that I asked her about that because . . .

'We were in the cafe near Giesing Station, like always, eating pretzels and drinking coffee, we were the only girls who'd drink real coffee, not that milky shit like all the others, by the way. I asked her and what did she do? She looked at me, just like you are right now, she looked at me and told me not to get upset, nothing had happened. I thought, what's going on? Is my best friend messing with me? And she looked at me slyly, that was something new, and said that she'd show them who she really was and make them all aware of the crimes they'd been committing against her for years, that they'd now have to pay for everything and to stay away. Those were her words. Stay away. I didn't have anything to do with any of it. Isn't that totally cruel?'

Franck had not dared go and grab his notepad so as not to interrupt her; he returned her glance which was already darting away towards the glass wall, the door. 'What crimes did she mean?' he asked.

'I don't know. In any event, not any sexual ones. I asked her, in the cafe, a few people were listening to us but they weren't from our school, so I didn't care. I asked her if her father had sexually abused her and she almost laughed and said that he was far too much of a coward to do something like that. She'd been telling the story of being sexually abused just to get back at him, just like that, in general. To get to him. Why? Why would you do that? I screamed into her face. Because someone who makes their father out to be a child-fucker when he isn't, that's a god-awful thing to do. And she replied quite calmly: Because he doesn't allow me to live my life. A pause. And then: Stay out of it, it's got nothing to do with you.

'I was standing at the bar table, she was across from me, like you, and it was quiet. Everyone was listening to how neither of us said a word. Then I'd had enough and said: I'm supposed to stay out of this? And she said: Yes. And added: You're all keeping me from living my life, none of you know a thing about me, you included, she said to my face, but you'll come to see what kind of life I really lead, and then she said: And now it's time for me to go, I have an appointment in the city.

'She laid her money down on the table, a bill, I can still see it, it's lying there, a green bill, and she said good-bye and, instead of hugging and giving each other a kiss, like we always did, she disappeared from the cafe without turning around once. Not even that. And I didn't understand a thing. I just stood there stupidly, like the two of us here now. Then I ordered another coffee, and then I went home. I didn't hear anything else from her. Just the next morning at school when the police officers

196

came into our classroom. Would you mind hugging me, please, just for a second?'

He walked over to her and, without pulling her towards himself, laid his arms around her shoulders; her arms still dangled at her sides; then he let her go and she walked silently past him to the table, picked up her glasses and put them back on. 'And then she was dead, and I was alone with all my questions,' she said.

'You did not mention a word of any of this to the police officers at the school.'

'What was I supposed to have said? I didn't know a thing. She walked out of the cafe and no one knows who she went to see. No one knows why that person didn't keep her from hanging herself. What was I supposed to have said? Should I have kept her back somehow? How could I have known . . . I should've gone after her. Is that what I should've said? If I had gone after her and kept her back, then . . . then what? Would everything have been different? Really? Where did she go? Who was more important than me, man? Who was she really, my best friend? Who did I sit next to all those years? Look at me. Hey, it's me, Sandra, who are you?'

When he got home, Franck thought, and was over-come by a fear that was hard to conceal, maybe Esther Winther would already be sitting at his table, waiting patiently for his return.

# CHAPTER FOURTEEN

## Eternal Silence

She was not there. The table in the living room was empty, the silence in Franck's ears a blessing. He sat down, crossed his arms, laid them on the table and looked up at the framed picture of the forest, into the hazy light of an eternal present. No dead today, not even Esther Winther, whose cruel end had remained as un-investigated as the ones of his usual guests, defaced for all eternity.

Seven hours, Franck thought again, he had held Esther's mother in his arms for seven hours, and all that had come of it had been disappointment, not trust. In the name of their dead child at first the parents had under-standably walled themselves up within their clean, sin-gle-family home that smelt of roses and apple cake and spent a year together alone; outwardly, time seemed to be shaped by mourning and pain; inwardly, they were dominated by a hellish and reciprocal damnation. And then, one year later, Doris Winther ended her martyrdom by her own hand whereby her husband became ostra-cized by his friends and colleagues and turned into a drunk who was forced to leave both his home and his neighbourhood and to give up everything he had counted on to give him stability and a future.

Sitting at his table recapping the day, the whole week, Franck did not believe a word himself.

His conclusions were based on unverified statements and obsessive reaffirmations. As long as he could not find the person Esther had met the afternoon before her death and whose identity she had hidden from even her best friend—something 'completely unusual' as the journalist Sandra Horn had said— accusations of abuse against a neighbour or her father would not bring him a single step closer to the truth.

The longer Franck thought about it, the more groundless the allegations seemed, especially if he took the journalist's statement seriously that Esther had wanted to humiliate her father in such a devious way.

What was going on in the young girl's life to make her want to do such a thing?

He decided to go back to the beginning, to the primordial germ cell of Esther's extremely short-lived universe.


At Franck's urgent request, they met the following day at the East Cemetery; the mother and daughter's grave was still covered with evergreen branches due to the cold; in the middle was a red candle which, Ludwig Winther explained without being asked, he had neither placed there nor lit.

'Why are you telling me that?' Franck asked; his doubt, his incomprehension, his anger at having let himself be taken in so easily had grown overnight and if he had still been a police officer, he would have called the man in and recommended he get a lawyer.

Winther—stooped over in a worn, brown jacket and the same black suit coat and roll-neck sweater as the week before, his hands loosely folded, arms limp at his sides—stared at the flickering flame. 'What do you mean by that, please?' he replied.

Franck—lined, black leather coat, black jeans, sturdy shoes, feet warmed by solid winter socks, alert, tense— had his shoulder bag over his left shoulder as if to establish a barrier between himself and the widower; in his coat pocket, his right hand enclosed the notepad and pen. 'Who takes care of the grave?'

The third unanswered question after their curt, formal greeting. Franck, as always more or less, had shown up too early; he had had to wait until the twenty-something person funeral procession had left the chapel and moved towards the freshly dug grave besieged by wreaths and flower arrangements; based on the sign by the room with the coffins, he had gathered that five funerals would be taking place that day. When he was a child, he remembered, hurrying out into the biting wind, the coffins would be left open behind the glass pane with the body peacefully bedded down in white inside them— that is, as long as death had left the dead their faces and not, as in the case of Vera Balan, sent an express train to Budapest to snap it up.

Two darkly dressed women rushed past him and delicately scurried across the gravel to join the other mourners.

Then Winther asked one question too many. 'What did you find so important that we needed to meet here at this ungodly hour?'

'There are clues pointing to the sexual abuse of your daughter,' said Franck, without raising his voice. 'You too are said to have been hard on her and to have ignored her wishes. The most important thing to me is the fact that you lied to my colleagues and me, and used your daughter's fate to systematically hide the destructive affairs within your family so that we declared your daughter's death a tragic but understandable act of doubt which was the result of inner conflict or depression.'

'But I *did* tell you that . . . '

'You came to me and gave me a motive for a potential crime. You said a neighbour hoped to cover up a crime, a rape, by making your daughter's murder look like a suicide. But I'll tell you why you actually came to see me. You can't handle the guilt any more, neither your own nor your wife's. You can't take your lie of a life. Shame is what drove you to me, not the realization that your daughter fell into the hands of a murderer. If there is a murderer, then he's part of your family circle. That's what I wanted to tell you at your wife and your daughter's graveside. I'd like you to make a confession, *Herr* Winther, right here, right now.'

As if in shock, the sixty-five-year-old man began to rock his crooked upper body back and forth, his mouth stretching ever wider until his face was made up of a single, misshapen grimace. His body seemed about to tip over and from out of his throat came a hoarse wheeze that, as it grew louder, sounded like the death rattle of someone about to suffocate. Franck prepared himself to grab hold of him, support his head and then, as carefully as possible, lay him down on the narrow gravel path between two headstones.

'Please.' Winther took a step to the side, turned towards the inspector with a jerk, raised his arms and pressed the fingers of his folded hands into one another. 'What you're saying isn't true at all. Esther was everything to me. I didn't do a thing to her. I couldn't have killed her, that would've been a form of suicide.'

As soon as he realized what he said, he threw his hands in front of his face and screamed; the longer and louder he screamed, the more tightly he pressed his hands into his face; his voice sounded like the howling of an animal off in the woods, a single, mournful wail behind the bony lattice of his fingers that ended as abruptly as it had begun.

Winther let his arms fall, with a childlike begging in his eyes tried to say something but could not make a sound. Franck lost his patience.

'Don't lie,' the investigator said, 'the dead are listening to you and have been the entire time.'

His mouth still half open, Winther turned back to the tomb and stared into the candle; bent down further than before, his hunched back deformed the threadbare jacket and his legs began to tremble; his eyes became one with the flame and it was as if the flickering were to blame for the tremor of his body.

All at once he seemed to become ancient, a man undone for decades by the incomprehensibility of his family's grave.

When the chapel bell began to ring and, at the same moment, a crow took off cawing from the branches under which they were standing, Winther crossed himself.

'Inspector?' He did not look at Franck, and the latter made no sound. 'If I admit something to you, will you continue to look for my daughter's murderer?' He listened to the air, wiped the corner of his mouth with a crooked index finger, sighed and nodded. 'You don't trust me,' he said. 'I don't deserve that.'

'I've got to distrust you,' said Franck. 'You've left me no other choice.'

'That's not true; you turn everything around; who have you been talking with that makes you say such things? As if I were responsible for everything? Sorry?' Then something occurred to him; he straightened up and tried to stretch his back which was met by a stabbing pain that made him wince. He instantly fell back into his regular stooped posture and wiped his mouth again. 'The dentist,' he said in a tortured voice, 'he's convinced you of all this, he's been allowed to talk his way out of it and you've fallen for it. You can't do that!'

'I haven't spoken with Paul Jordan yet.'

'Excuse me?' Winther tried to appear furious but managed only a grey frown.

'All that came from a talk with your daughter's best friend,' said Franck. 'And with your sister-in-law.'

Winther shot him an incredulous look. 'That would surprise me.'

'How so?'

'This city is meaningless to Inge, she thinks it's the most boring place in the universe.'

'I met her in Berlin.'

'You travelled to Berlin for that? Why? Couldn't you have talked on the phone? Do I have to pay for the flight?'

'Of course not.'

'I don't understand . . . What did you expect to learn from talking with her? She doesn't know a thing, she was always far away, Doris hardly had any contact with her. I just don't understand.'

'Esther had visited her aunt.'

Winther made a growling sound, shrugged a shoulder and looked back at the candle sticking out between the spruce branches. 'I never approved of them, those visits. She came back a different person every time, I didn't like it, and I shouldn't have allowed it; we could've gone somewhere together, the three of us, during the holidays, as a family. Inge was never family and never had been, but Esther defended her. My wife too. Both of them. Aunt Inge. I could never stand her.'

He gave Franck a helpless look; then he folded his hands again, took a deep breath and fought back a cough. 'Now you're accusing me of things, and I don't know if that's right. You want me to confess, but you can only confess when you've done something wrong. We're standing here at the cemetery on a Monday morning and the cold wind's cutting right to the bone, can't you feel it? I'm not standing in front of a judge. Or am I? No.'

As if driven by some incomprehensible interior force, he kept looking back at the inspector and seemed terribly confused by the latter's apparently unshakable demeanour; vulnerable and bitter, at one point he even bumped into the marble edge of the grave with the tip of his shoe.

'No,' he said with a wheeze. 'I did what was right, and that's it; my father was a shoemaker, his shop was small and smelt of leather and oil and glue and wood and when I'd sit on the stool and watch him sew or work with the machine, I'd breathe the smell in deep because it was so comforting and at that point I was a part of my father's world. Can you understand that?

'My mother took care of the house, my father earned the money, and people came to him in droves, he couldn't complain. And he never did, in spite of all the work he had, even on weekends. On Sundays, we'd sometimes go for a walk, in summer we'd go to Nymphenburg Park, sit at the side of the lake, eat the sandwiches my mother had made; and although the air smelt of grass and earth and summer flowers, I could always only smell the leather from my father's shop, it was lovely.

'He died when I was eleven.

'He was ill but I didn't know that, my mother had kept it a secret. He went to hospital at the Brothers of Mercy and we went to visit and he didn't say a thing. Not a thing. He just lay in the white bed next to three other men and I didn't trust myself to touch him. Touching was uncommon among us; I would have gladly said or done something.

'Now I'm sixty-five years old and at the same time eleven again. I don't want to be.'

After glancing at Franck, he grew quiet, then kicked the grave and crossed himself vigorously. 'You see,' he said then stopped. Apparently he had noticed the mourners along the brick wall for the first time as they were taking their leave from the priest who was on his way back to the chapel with the two altar boys for the next ceremony.

'You see!' As if his behaviour were Franck's fault, Winther turned to him with a stony face. 'Although long ago I said goodbye to God, I'm crossing myself. How logical is that? It's a reflex you can never get rid of, like the smell of my father's shop. What suffering, everything, the shop useless, my mother with no income at all, me at the Gymnasium because my father wanted me to amount to something. I was supposed to have studied hard and gone on to an academic career; he would've liked to see me become a teacher, taken care of for my whole life, the family too.

'He would've liked to see that instead of me stooped over in a dark shop six days a week, seven in winter. So, at sixteen, I started an apprenticeship—salesman, retail; we had to have some kind of money coming in, my mother sat at the register in the supermarket six days a week. We didn't go hungry but we didn't go to Nymphenburg Park in the summer any more either, it was too far away and the tram was too expensive.

'So at twenty I became a salesman, met Doris and we became a family, then Esther came into the world and I wanted us to have a house, a garden, our very own home in a good neighbourhood.

'And then you come along and accuse me of failing and say that I treated Esther poorly or that I even abused her and didn't let her have anything and that I am guilty of everything just because I wanted to establish a comfortable life for everyone. Have you lost your mind? You live alone, you said so yourself, you don't have any children, you don't know what it's like but you judge others who are making an effort and breaking their backs to take care of their families. That's not right, it's unfair and simply untrue, believe me.

'I don't have anything to feel guilty about.

'I'm cold.' He crossed his arms, let them fall, crossed them again, stuck his hands into his jacket pockets and, tilting his head a bit to the side, listened; then he began to rock his upper body back and forth again.

'I'm not accusing you of anything,' said Franck. 'I'm trying to understand your daughter's life and you were a significant part of that life.'

'I know that,' Winther whispered.

'When Esther would fly to Berlin to visit her aunt, you'd accuse her of being extravagant.'

'No . . . '

'Not out loud, no, but silently, you didn't even say anything to your wife, you kept it to yourself, but nevertheless it was there, more powerful than if you'd trusted yourself to honestly say what you thought.'

'No . . . '

'Honesty, that didn't work,' said Franck and like the self-absorbed, shivering salesman looked over at the wavering flame. 'You never learnt how to be honest; you thought that your father was content there in his shop, happy about all the work he got to do on his own. It made him ill, his work, but he never said a word about it, just like your mother, they let you believe that everything was all right, that your future was secure, that you would complete your graduation exams and establish the foundations for a solid future at university. No doubt you even went to church every Sunday while your father was finally able to sleep in . . . '

'No . . . '

'You were a Catholic and went to Mass, I'm positive.'

'Yes . . . '

'And you'd go by yourself while your mother made lunch and your father relaxed a little . . . '

'You're wrong, Inspector. He didn't allow himself to relax and sleeping in was forbidden, something always needed to be done and Monday morning at seven thirty there were already customers standing in front of the door waiting to pick up their shoes, that's how it was, always, there was no time for messing around. Do you understand?'

'Yes.' Franck waited for Winther's weary glance, which inevitably followed. 'And so, just as your parents were silent about your father's health and all that makes living together in an open fashion possible, you too were incapable of telling your daughter to her face how you felt about her going to Berlin to experience new things; when she bought clothes and went shopping with her friends; when she asked you for money to go out and have fun. You couldn't manage to express what was bothering you; you prohibited everything instead, you said no without any explanation, you did not listen to your daughter even once because you suspected that some of her wishes might've been justified; because you couldn't allow her to have them . . . '

'No . . . '

'Because you thought that the future began later on, just like you did when you were younger and your parents explained to you why your father worked so hard: so that you could have a better life. And you were convinced that, if you went to church every Sunday and prayed to God, life would be fair and you would make it through school and go to university and have a future that would make up for everything you and your parents had sacrificed. And that's what you demanded from your daughter: she should follow the very same system and unconditionally subjugate herself to a future that *you* were convinced of, but which quite possibly had absolutely nothing to do with her own ideas.'

'Please stop . . . '

'How was Esther supposed to know what you were worried about, *Herr* Winther? You stayed silent. Or is it that, maybe, Esther understood you? Could Esther have freed you from your prison of the shoemaker's shop? She wasn't like you, you know that, she was an adventurer, every day was a journey for her and she accepted the challenge, she wasn't afraid. But you made her afraid; you and your wife both. And Esther began to distrust you, and her distrust transformed into the worst form it can take: self-hatred. All of a sudden she hated herself, she no longer had any confidence in her talents, in her freedom, in her feelings of happiness. She went silent and you thought she was simply offended and that everything would settle down later. But nothing settled down; just like your father's health although you diligently went to church every Sunday to pray and obeyed everything at home and were a good child and always did your home-work meticulously and on time. Nothing settled down, nothing got any better. And when you had a child she was supposed to be just like you had been and that is what you must confess at your daughter and wife's grave. If, that is, you still want to have a life.'

Minutes passed; the chapel bell began to toll once more; black-clothed people gathered under the arcades, a rose or lily in their hands; crows hopped across the gravel paths; the siren of a patrol car came to them from the distance; the sky grey, leaves driven by wind. Then the men came out of the hall carrying the coffin followed by the priest and the red-and-white-clothed altar boys, one of them swinging a censer on a chain, and behind them the procession of pain, right on time.

Standing in front of his family's grave, Ludwig Winther crossed himself a third time and said to the headstone with its two names, to the red candle, the protective branches, 'I confess, but don't understand myself. I confess, but don't understand myself.' Then he turned around and looked the inspector in the face. 'I confess, but don't understand myself.'

# CHAPTER FIFTEEN

# The Man at the Window, II

They walked next to each other without saying a word, Winther had not expected otherwise but he was also unsettled by the inspector's sudden and total silence. After they left the narrow lane along the cemetery wall beneath the railway tracks and set off for the East Station, he was overwhelmed by insecurity, which bothered him at that moment in particular.

All the same, Franck had been the one asking him to come to the cemetery and in a coolly insistent way; and when he thought about it, with a rather convincing lie that had turned him into a liar too. At seven in the morning he called his boss and told him—carefully and in a hoarse voice broken by tedious bouts of coughing—that he had been nabbed by a terrible cold and was lying in bed with a fever and awful headaches; his boss reacted understandingly—which relieved him as much as it astonished him—told him to get well soon and to take care of himself, adding, 'At your age, you don't want to mess around with the flu.' An observation that had caused Winther to look at his tongue in the bathroom mirror and touch his forehead.

'We have to talk about something, it's urgent,' Franck had said to him on the phone, before adding, 'I have important news.'

How else was he supposed to have reacted other than to accept, in spite of his responsibility to the beverage shop? And now he was walking next to the man and had learnt nothing—other than that to this man he was guilty of something he was supposed to admit, loud and clear, at the graveside of his loved ones. As if, Winther thought, he had been the one to dig his own family's grave, as if his daughter and his wife had taken their lives owing to his mere existence.

'No,' he cried out and stopped, his upper body still swaying. Cars rushed past the two of them. They were standing at the crossing of the four-lane arterial road in the direction of the highway, the noise of the trucks droned through Winther's head and he felt like he had to raise his voice until he was almost yelling. 'They accused *me*, both of them, and I didn't know how to defend myself, how was I supposed to? You can't just wash something like that away like you've been gardening, it sticks to you, and everyone knows about it, the neighbours, everyone. I was standing before a court though I hadn't committed a crime. And then you come and want me to confess to something. How can you not understand that I was murdered too? Me. And my Esther. And then my wife killed herself. You've got to be able to understand something like that as a police officer.'

Out of breath and with flailing arms, Winther almost tumbled out on to the road. Franck managed to grab hold of his shoulders, held on to him tight, then pushed him across the sidewalk against the picket fence around the former lumberyard. Winther coughed and doubled over, stamped his feet, balled his hands into fists but did not know where to direct his anger.

From half a metre away, Franck observed the fidgety man stagger and throw punches into the air; he only quieted down when a young, darkly dressed woman with a headscarf pulled low across her forehead passed by him pushing a stroller and, as if perplexed, he stared after her.

Then Winther stretched out his arm, pointed to the woman, who had remained standing at the red light, and opened his mouth; but instead of saying anything, he only moved his lower jaw up and down and, when he noticed, he held up his hand in front of his mouth, frightened, and looked at Franck with a profoundly uncomprehending look.

'Come on,' Franck touched his shoulder. 'We'll take public transport over to the bar.'

That's true, Winther thought, he had asked if they could go have a coffee or a small beer; he was cold and afraid that someone might recognize him and ask why he was not at work—it was rather unlikely, but the beverage shop was not too far away. The inspector had agreed and without thinking Winther had suggested the Enzianstüberl.

'In the corner building with the nineteenth-century hotel,' he said in the tram at Orleansplatz where they got on, 'that's where Jordan's office is. And the hotel, that's where he always went with his young lovers. Back then, the hotel hadn't been renovated, it was still musty and pretty seedy. In any event, that's where the *Herr* Doctor sits and rakes in his money and no one holds him accountable for anything, not even you.'

Franck wrote down the name of the hotel in his notepad.

Walking into the pub, Winther was startled. The old, tattooed man in the black shirt who until then had always sat in the corner was standing at the bar in Winther's usual place, in front of the beer taps. They were the only guests. The radio was quieter than in the evening. Micha, the bartender, was sitting on his stool behind the counter reading the paper; he looked up, seemed surprised for a moment to see Winter come in so early, nodded to him then continued reading. The old man, who had introduced himself as Enver, did not let Winther out of his sight.

They sat down at the narrow end of the bar close to the door. Without a word, Micha laid the open newspaper down on the dry edge of the sink, slid off his stool and waited for his new guests to order.

'Do you have any coffee?' Winther asked.

'Of course.'

'And something small to eat?'

'Every morning I buy fifty pretzels, there're still a few left, and some sausages, as always.'

'Then I'll have a couple of Vienna sausages with a pretzel and a coffee, please.'

'And for you, sir?'

Franck had not eaten breakfast, he had only had two glasses of mineral water but still did not feel like having a warm drink or something to eat, and certainly not any sausages, which would just remind him of the rough lunch he had had with his colleague Block in the cafe on the Hansastraße. 'A non-alcoholic beer,' he said.

'At the moment I just have unleaded wheat beer, I'm still waiting for delivery.'

'Wheat beer is good.' Franck turned towards the man with the grey hair and the furrowed face who had a nearly empty whisky glass in front of him. 'Hello. Do we know each other?'

'Why?'

'You've been looking at us nonstop.'

'You're a cop, right?'

'That's right,' said Franck.

'The people you let in here!' Enver exclaimed to Micha with a look. The bartender ignored him, pulled a non-alcoholic wheat beer out of the refrigerator next to the kitchen door and opened it.

'I know Ludwig,' Enver said. '*Servus*, Ludwig.'

Winther could not remember having introduced himself. Then he remembered that the man had mentioned a brother who was also named Ludwig. In retrospect, he regretted everything he had said to the intimidating man with the strange name of Enver that night before his sixty-fifth birthday, he found the fact that he had been staring at him since the moment they had entered to be a provocation; he did not return his greeting, just nodded his head imperceptibly. Winther had not unbuttoned his jacket, and it was going to stay that way.

Once the bartender had brought the beer and the coffee, Winther turned conspicuously from the counter to the inspector. The inspector changed his posture too, Enver took a drink and looked towards the tiny kitchen where Micha had disappeared.

Winther lifted his cup to his mouth with a shaky hand; Franck drank the foam off his beer and, in a brief moment of confusion, imagined he could taste alcohol, which he liked.

'Talk,' said Franck. 'Don't worry about the past, you can trust me.'

'I don't know.' He cast a quick glance at Enver. 'You saw through me, I'll admit it, and I don't understand. I just don't understand.'

'What don't you understand? What you did? What did you do?'

'What did I do?' Bent over the edge of the counter, Winther grabbed his coffee cup with both hands, in his thoughts he escaped back to his flat, he wished he could drive over to the beverage shop and pick up the evening shift, say he was suddenly healthy again and that he wanted to make up for the lost hours with overtime; he was not hungry any more either, and the coffee tasted like it had been standing around too long. He reached into his jacket pocket and pulled out a tissue to dab at the corners of his mouth; he would have preferred his handkerchief, but for that he would have had to unbutton his jacket, which was something he wanted to avoid.

'I did something by virtue of the fact of doing nothing.' He stuffed the tissue back into his pocket and kept his hand there. 'That's what no one understands. Just like no one understood why my daughter said that I abused her. That I sexually abused her—it's incomprehensible. When you hear those kinds of accusations, you just don't understand the world any more, and no one believes you. Isn't that right?'

'Be honest now,' said Franck. 'Your daughter is dead, you can no longer help her. You can only help yourself.'

'Yes.' Winther leant forward, then back again, hesitated, tried to find the right words, held on to the edge of the bar with his left hand as if at any moment he might fall. 'I'm not lying, I came to you on account of a suspicion, and that suspicion still stands, and I know for a fact that I did not drive my daughter into the grave but this man, the one who was with her in the hotel, he did.'

'Is that really true?'

After a moment, his back slouched, Winther shook his head. It was more difficult for the former salesman to sit, to just be present, Franck thought, than to speak. 'Well, I don't really know about all of that, I took it to be true and didn't find any evidence to the contrary.'

The bartender brought a plate with sausages, a pretzel and a sachet of mustard and put it down next to the coffee cup. 'Do you need any silverware, Ludwig?'

'No. I'm not hungry any more.'

'You can eat it later.'

'Thank you.'

'Enjoy your meal.' Micha sat back down on his stool and picked up the paper. The smell of the sausages brought back a useless memory to Franck.

'I'm really not hungry any more,' Winther said to the inspector and pushed the plate away towards the long side of the counter.

'You didn't abuse your daughter . . . ' said Franck.

'Never. I think . . . I really think . . . I think that she wanted to blackmail me, could that be? Could a man really think his own daughter capable of something like that? I feel sick, you can't say something like that out loud, no, that won't do.'

'You can. You have to finally say these things out loud: stop listening to your inner-critic, it only makes you morose and bitter and suspicious.'

'What do you mean by suspicious?'

'You've started to blame others in order to get rid of your own feelings of guilt; you know that. You can't walk away any more, it's too late. The dead are everywhere and they aren't interested in how fragile your soul is, they're rubbing their deaths in your face, they're laughing at you, they come every day, they live in your dreams, they sit down with you at the table . . . but they'll become your guardian angels, they'll protect you from your fear of redemption.'

'Excuse me? But . . . But they can't do that, they don't have any right, the dead . . . I just wanted to make sure that our money didn't go down the drain, that was my responsibility. Who else could've done that? I managed to get the house, the garden, everything. That was understood. There wasn't any money left over for long trips and the like, they had to have understood that.'

'Perhaps,' said Franck, 'you didn't explain the situation well enough to Esther.'

'What was I supposed to explain?' In a hushed voice he repeated the question. 'What was I supposed to explain? I don't have to explain anything, no, not me. I did everything and took care of everything, but I didn't talk about it. You don't talk about those kinds of things, you just do them, and others understand and act accordingly—that's how families work, or no? What was I supposed to explain? When? We didn't lack a thing. I earned the money and the bank treated us well, the plot of land was a real deal and I managed to get a very good interest rate, everything was just right. And earlier, when Esther was still a baby, we travelled to Italy, to Pisa and Rome, and we always stayed in nice hotels in Tuscany and we ate well and didn't hold anything back whatsoever; I never paid attention to money when we were travelling, I knew what I owed my family. And then she went and started spreading those rumours and everyone pointed their fingers at me. *Herr* Franck, why did my daughter do such an awful thing?'

'You knew what she'd been saying about you and yet you didn't talk with her.'

'No.'

Franck fell silent. Winther tore apart the tissue in his pocket with his right hand, his left hand lay on his lap, palm upward, pale and seemingly lifeless. Now and again Franck cast a glance at the guest in the black shirt who appeared to be caught up in his own thoughts and did not seem to be eavesdropping.

With the exception of Winther's occasional outbursts, they spoke quietly and the music from the radio drowned out their voices.

'No,' Winther repeated. 'I wanted to speak with her but didn't know how. I also didn't believe it could be true. I simply did not want to believe it. I still can't and, until I die, won't.'

'Who told you about it?'

'Indeed, who? My wife. One day she came back from a friend's and said she had to talk with me. It was a Sunday, and I was watching a football match on TV. My wife switched it off, turned to me—I can still see her standing there, there she is, right there—and said what it was I'd supposedly done with her daughter. I was still caught up in the match and didn't understand what she meant. Answer me, she screamed, and I cringed because no one had yelled at me since I was a child. Doris wasn't a person who yelled, she didn't really speak much at all, like me; we'd never been talkers. And I told her that I didn't understand what she was saying, and she screamed at me again demanding to know whether it was true that I had raped her daughter. For God's sake! I said, and she looked at me like she would never believe a word, like I would lie, like something like that could be true. But it wasn't true. Nevertheless, I was tainted and would never be clean again.'

Franck would have liked to take a swig of his beer but did not want to turn away. 'Did your wife speak to Esther about it?' he asked and the reply came more quickly than he had expected.

'She simply believed her, she believed everything from the beginning right up through to the end.'

'That can't be.'

'Why not? That's how it was.'

'What had happened between your wife and you? Why didn't she believe you?'

'I don't know. I never found out.'

'Be honest,' said Franck. 'What was the reason? What was it that led to that gulf between Doris and you?'

Winther now buried his left hand into his other jacket pocket, and slouched so low over the barstool that he had to look up at the inspector. 'All of a sudden it was simply there, the . . . rift. Everything. And Esther withdrew into herself, stayed in her room and spoke, if at all, only with her mother—tough times, puberty, nothing strange about that. However, I've got to admit I was happy to leave in the mornings, everything was easy at work, we were a great team, everyone supported everyone else when there were problems, when there was a difficult customer or a customer's wife—we were almost like a family, there was a sense of cohesion and a silent understanding—that's why we always went to training courses in twos or even in threes so that no one ever had to sit around on their own. It was lovely, really a great time.'

For a while, he stared at Franck without saying a word. 'But,' he said, and trying to sit up straight but failing, slumped back down. 'I tried once. I knocked on her door, I wanted to talk to her about everything, but she didn't open. I asked her through the door why she was saying things about me. There was a long silence. I could hear the TV, we'd bought it especially for her, with a satellite dish even, just so she could watch her favourite series, *Moonlighting*—perhaps she wanted to be a detective, I don't know. I waited outside her door, twenty minutes at least, then in a loud voice she said that she didn't know what I was talking about and wanted me to leave her alone, she was entitled to a private life too. What was I supposed to do?'

Franck let the ensuing silence die out to the sounds of a pop hit from the eighties. 'After that, you never spoke to her about it again,' he said. 'Or your wife.'

'No. No. We didn't talk, no. Not a word, not a sound. Five months later Esther was dead, and her friend from school showed up and said that Esther had been depressed—another lie, another crime against the truth—and my wife believed the girl immediately, just like she had believed her friend who'd spread those rumours out into the world in order to harm me, to destroy me.'

'Is that your impression? That someone wanted to destroy you?' Franck had almost asked the bartender to turn the music down; however, the music was a pleasant cover.

'No,' said Winther again. 'That's just my imagination, you're right. I have to be honest. I'm just trying to make myself important when I say things like that, duck out of the way, you've seen through it all along.'

'Even after Esther's death you didn't talk with your wife about the accusations of rape.'

Winther shook his head.

Franck thought of so many things at once that he almost knocked over his glass with his elbows.

'The real reason,' he began carefully, 'your wife decided to take her life in the same way as your daughter probably does not have to do with sadness over the tragic loss, but the shame she felt about what you'd supposedly done. Doris could no longer handle the uncertainty.'

'But why didn't she ever speak with me?' Winther cried, lost his balance, tried clawing the counter but slipped off his stool, which fell over, and clutched on to the inspector. Franck jumped up and held him.

Arms and legs quaking, for a while Winther could not calm down and needed to be supported by Franck while the bartender and the tattooed guest stared at him irritably. Then Franck carefully took him by the shoulder, pushed him back and leant him up against the bar like a somewhat stiff puppet.

Gradually, Winther gained control of himself. 'Please excuse me, please . . . ' He meant the bartender as well and wanted to turn around to the whisky drinker but the movement was either too much for him or caused him even more pain. He gasped and bent over to the side;

every breath cost him great effort. 'No talk, just silence and sleeplessness.'

Franck remembered Winther's sister-in-law telling him in Berlin how, at the funeral, Doris had refused all condolences and her husband had had to shake everyone's hands instead; she was deeply ashamed—Franck was convinced—and yet had no basis for her behaviour or her feelings. She felt that everything was possible and despised her husband's reassurances, and because she wanted at all costs to keep the police from finding out about it, she decided—for her husband too, whom she gave no choice—that Esther had indeed suffered from depression and that they were guilty of her death because they had not recognized the signs and got her help in time.

Who, Franck wondered, would contradict a conscience-stricken mother suffering from sadness and pain, who had lost her seventeen-year-old child in such a pitiless way? Who was that woman? He would not get any satisfying answer from her widower, at least that had become clear to Franck in the meantime.

The woman in the airport's black book came to mind.

'You mentioned,' Franck began, 'that your wife kept a diary. I'd like to read it.'

'I don't know.' Winther's stooping body swayed.

'Do you know what's in it?'

'No. I discovered the green notebook by chance, leafed through it briefly and put it back in the drawer; it's still there.'

'Lend it to me.'

After a pause, which encouraged the inspector to finally take a sip of his unleaded wheat beer, Winther said, 'I think I'd like to eat my sausages now.'

'Don't bother my guests,' said Micha after Franck and Winther had left.

'Are you spying for them?' Enver grinned, but his voice was hard.

Micha was drying glasses and putting them on the shelf. 'Me? I don't think so. Seems like that's something you'd be up to.'

'What makes you come up with crap like that?'

'You watch Ludwig every time he's in here. What do you want from him? Someone hire you?'

'The guy's paranoid, haven't you noticed?'

'Here no one's paranoid.'

Enver twirled his empty whisky glass in his hand, considered it, made a face. 'I was in prison for a while myself, I thought that everyone I met wanted to kill me to get revenge for my brother. But it was his own fault.'

The bartender went into the kitchen; Enver continued to talk as if Micha were still standing in front of him. 'He wanted to squeal on me—me, his own brother. After the last robbery, everything had gone smoothly until all of a sudden Ludwig got a conscience; after forty years of working together, it was probably the kid his new old lady had just had's fault. He threatened me, I had to defend myself. Dead. It should never have gone that far.

Grew up without a father, the kid. Give me another Jameson.'

When Micha returned from the kitchen, he reached for the glass and filled it up without a word.

'Ludwig,' Enver said. 'I take a good look at every Ludwig I meet, that's just how it is.'

Hours later, in the colourless light of the dwindling afternoon, Franck looked up from the street and saw Ludwig Winther standing at the window of his attic flat, a dark, distorted shape pressing its hands to the window—like someone who wanted to get out into the world.

# CHAPTER SIXTEEN

## Butterflies on the Beach

On the stairs up to the attic, Winther said that he could not invite anyone inside as it was unsuited for guests. Franck conveyed that he had nothing against waiting by the door until Winther fetched his wife's diary.

Once he had unlocked the door and opened it a crack, he hesitated. 'Earlier you invited me to the bar,' he said as if speaking to himself, 'and now I'm being rude. I don't mean to be. Please, come in, but don't look around.'

'I'll wait right here.'

'No. Please. Just go straight through and have a seat.' He took a step to the side, let Franck in and shut the door.

A small passageway led from the hall to the kitchen and another door, which was ajar, to the bedroom. Winther hung his jacket over one of the three coat hooks which already had two cardigans and a grey parka, took off his street shoes, placed them under the wardrobe next to a second, no-less-dusty pair, put on a pair of brown felt slippers and, soundlessly and almost silently, disappeared into the bedroom, closing the door behind him.

Franck took a look around. The sparse, threadbare and impersonally decorated room seemed like one in a hotel whose owner had not even invested in a halfway-modern colour TV. Nevertheless, Franck realized that—as opposed to such run-down rooms—the flat did not smell of acidic disinfectant. On the contrary: it smelt of nothing at all.

After a glance at the door, Franck sniffed around a little, more to pass the time than out of curiosity, and was surprised by the fresh air; to be on the safe side, Winther had opened one of the two windows, probably just like he always did, when he left his house. As opposed to the home in Ramersdorf where the family had lived before, the small, sparse attic flat must have seemed like a refuge, a temporary living space on demand for the underemployed beverage-shop employee.

The silence, Franck thought, had driven that family into an inner and insurmountable homelessness. The time to make a wish had never arrived for any of them; not even, he thought, looking towards the door again—no sound came from the other room—for Winther's sister-in-law in Berlin. Inge Rigah had escaped the approaching shadow in her family's world rather early, but in the place she had freely chosen to go she had instead become a prisoner of her dream, which she refused to realize or allowed only to remain as a sketch. In Esther she saw herself as a free spirit that no one could cage; and so, after her niece's death, all that was left was the wrinkled anger she had carried around from the very first time she ever met Ludwig Winther.

On the street, an old married couple walked by hand in hand wearing hats and Loden coats, taking their time, deep in conversation. Franck watched them until they disappeared behind a parked SUV; even with their hats, they did not reach its roof.

'You're not sitting down.' As soundlessly as he had disappeared into the side room, Winther unexpectedly came back.

Franck turned towards him and saw the green notebook; Winther too looked at it in his hands as if someone had just given it to him. They were silent, then Winther raised his head. 'I can offer you water,' he said. 'Unfortunately, I don't have any beer.'

Franck, who after the draining stops at the cemetery and the bar had indeed begun to feel the desire for some coffee and something edible, at the same time knew that he would be unable to leave just yet. 'Is there something else you'd like to tell me?'

'Yes,' Winther answered and seemed surprised by the promptness of his response; with a despondent gesture, he considered where to put the diary but then kept it in his hand. 'I'd still have a lot to say but you don't believe me any more—that's fine, I've been a liar . . . '

'No.'

'Sorry?'

'You are not a liar,' said Franck, taking a step towards Winther; all of a sudden, he was bothered by the cool wind coming in through the window. 'You lied because for half of your life you have been silent about your thoughts, your insecurity, your need . . . '

'Silent about everything, yes . . . ' Winther stretched out his arms; had he not been holding the green notebook, Franck might have thought he was asking for handcuffs. 'Please read it. I swear, I only just leafed through it now, I just wanted to have a look and see her handwriting and then I wondered when she wrote all of it—when I wasn't around, that's obvious, because I never saw her writing. You see, I've lied to you yet again.'

He clutched the notebook; Franck noticed the long, misshapen nails of his two thumbs. 'I did read the last page, I didn't just glance at it—I had to. I read it and am horrified. There are just two sentences, and I know them. I couldn't get any air. I sat down on the edge of the bed, *Herr* Franck, and almost suffocated, I couldn't move. I really didn't want to read anything, you have to believe me, please, I don't have the right, but I did anyway. Two sentences, and I knew what they were already—who can count on something like that? She planned everything precisely, my wife. Please.'

Franck took the notebook—on the cover: Exercise Book, A6, 32 pages—from his hand, hesitated, browsed through it briefly then went straight to the last page. Doris Winther had written everything in black ink; on some of the partially wrinkled and yellowed pages there were only three or four sentences, in a small hand but quite readable, no dates but with the days of the week; below the two notes that Doris Winther had written at the bottom of the otherwise empty page, Franck discovered two tiny numbers connected by a hyphen.

He looked over at Winther to gauge his reaction to the numbers; he seemed more rattled by Franck's careful reading than anything else.

'Yes?' Winther asked and, without taking his eyes off the inspector, reached into his coat pocket and pulled out the blue handkerchief to dab at the corners of his mouth.

Franck had read the woman's final notations himself once before—on a chequered, neatly folded piece of paper.

20–5.

The twentieth of May.

On twenty-first May, Doris Winther hung herself in the garden of her house; her suicide note was nine words long.

*I'm going. I never want to see you again.*

These nine words ended the diary.

Never, Franck thought, shutting the notebook with a solemn gesture meant to hide how upset the lines had made him, had he seen a suicide note the writer had secretly practised beforehand.

The desperate only came up with such letters once—if they managed to find the strength and courage at all. With her final accusation, Doris Winther, Franck was almost certain, had wanted to express something completely different than what her husband, sister and the police had believed all those years—for that matter, Franck too since that day twenty years ago when, after Esther's death, he had had to enter the house in Ramersdorf a second time.

'What's wrong?' Winther asked. 'You look horrified.' Shoulders askew, he was even more hunched over than a few minutes before.

'We're both horrified.' Franck pointed to the green notebook. 'She finished writing with the same words that she ended her life.'

'I don't understand.'

Only once Franck was absolutely sure about his thesis would he, possibly, talk with Winther about what the message in the diary and her farewell letter really meant. 'You give me the book,' he said, moving up close to the oppressed-looking man. 'And just as you are finally letting go of it, you must also let go of your wife and your daughter.'

'That's impossible.'

'No.'

'It is. It is.' Winther held his hand in front of his mouth, turned it and observed the inner side as if he might find the impression of his quivering lips.

Franck looked at him. 'How did you get your scar?'

'A dog bit me,' Winther said in a thin voice.

'When was that?'

'A long time ago, on the beach near Pisa; back then, with Doris and Esther; a big dog.'

'Did it attack you?'

'Not me. My daughter. Maybe he just wanted to play, he bared his teeth, like this.' For a second Winther made a face; looking at the diary again, Franck almost missed it. 'I went over to try and scare him away; he was just running around on the beach, no one was calling him; a real beast with no fur; bit me right away; just once but deep; then he walked off, the mutt. I would've kicked it, I swear. Blood everywhere. My wife wrapped a hand-kerchief around the wound. Esther cried and cried, she was more frightened than I was; she often said that she was responsible for me being bitten. It wasn't her fault; she wasn't guilty of anything, nothing, nor was my wife. Yes, the scar's still there but Esther would have forgotten, Doris too, I'm certain of that.'

'Repeat after me,' Franck said. 'Cross your hands over the diary and listen to me.'

'What am I supposed to listen to?'

'*I'm letting you go, Doris . . .* '

'Excuse me?'

'Just repeat after me.'

'No.'

'*I'm letting you go . . .* '

'I . . . Please . . . *I'm letting you go . . .* '

'*Doris.*'

'*Doris.*'

'And,' said Franck, '*I'm letting you go too, Esther . . .* '

'No. I . . . *I'm letting you go too, Esther . . .* '

'*In gratitude and love.*'

Winther made no sound, his hands trembled on the notebook Franck was holding on his flat hand; and, just like at the bar, he began to sway back and forth.

'I'll repeat the sentence one more time,' said Franck. 'And you repeat it, word for word, and twice, once after the other.'

Winther bit his lips, a pain that reminded him of the night after Doris' funeral surged through him as he crawled across the floor of his house in his shoes and black suit but could not get the lump of a scream out, as throughout the night he writhed and whimpered like a dog that had been shot, ran into walls and wardrobes but, though bleeding to death, was not allowed to die.

'Are you ready?' Franck asked.

'I . . . '

'*I am letting you go, Doris, my wife, and I am letting you go too, Esther, my daughter, in gratitude and love.* Now you, Mr Winther.'

He did not speak; he wanted to but, in the chaos of the darkness surrounding him, was unable to find his voice. Two minutes went by, the room was filled with cold air.

Franck took him by the arm, led him to the couch and told him to sit down. Exhausted, relieved, out of breath, Winther sagged into the cushion, leant back and closed his eyes for a moment.

'Try it later,' said Franck. 'You cannot forget.'

Winther defensively shook his head.

Franck looked around again. 'There's not a single photo of your family here. Why not?'

Winther pointed to the hall. 'Over there,' he said softly.

'I promise I'll continue to look into the circumstances surrounding Esther's death.' Franck got ready to go. 'And I would like you to do what I asked you to do today.'

Winther wheezed and bent forward. 'Help me, please.'

Clutching the inspector's arm, he stood up, sighed heavily and shuffled over to the bedroom door; he opened it, snapped on the light—the blinds were down—and allowed his guest to have a quick look around.

Across from the narrow bed, on which was strewn a brown bathrobe, hung a roughly twenty-centimetre colour photo of Doris Winther in a yellow dress with butterflies and a more or less eight-year-old Esther in a white T-shirt and straw hat; both of them held ice-cream cones, in the background you could see the sea. Otherwise the walls were as bare as those in the living room. Next to the door was an old country armoire, probably the only piece of furniture Winther had brought from Ramersdorf, Franck thought.

They shook hands silently. At the same moment as Franck pulled the front door shut behind him, Winther left the bedroom for the living room, walked to the window and held his hands flat against the pane; he did not know why but as the cold crawled from his fingers into his body and he saw the inspector come out on to the street, he was overcome by the irrepressible desire to wish for something. He almost cried with joy at the unexpected thought.

But did not. He simply stood there, hands pressed to the glass, unable to think of anything.

As twilight came down, he stood there still, forehead against the window, thinking about nothing more than going to work the next day and the phrase he had found and was not to forget.

In his office, which should have been a child's room, the white candle was burning in the glass. Franck had placed the plate with the butter cookies on the desk, as if a given, as if he had always welcomed the dead there. He sat on the couch, blue blanket covering his knees, next to him the green notebook dimly lit by the antique standing lamp with the chrome arm.

A half hour in silence.

On his way home, he had stopped by an Italian cafe to have a double espresso and a ham *tramezzino* and after that even a chocolate croissant. But that day, he thought while travelling westward through the city on the tram and then the S-Bahn, he had most likely—doubtless he was not yet himself again—discovered something that would give him a glimpse into the shadowy realm of the Winther family, into the courtyard of the two women's violent deaths.

The fossil.

Or a part of the fossil.

Or maybe just a new silence.

In any event, he thought, he should continue reading the green notebook; he should trust himself at long last. No one had the right to the dead's confessions. Whatever Doris Winther had written belonged to the past—just as did his role as the inspector informing relatives of the death of their loved ones. Others had been responsible for the case and had judged the death of the schoolgirl to be a suicide, and her parents had agreed—no objections, no doubts. Just more evidence for the statistic that every forty-five minutes someone took their own lives. Next piece of evidence: Doris Winther, the same day that she turned forty-two, hung herself. Reason: a broken heart.

Which probably wasn't the case, Franck thought just like he had back in the small flat in Berg am Laim and sat up straight, his thoughts somersaulting over one another again. The nine words changed everything, or at least cleared Ludwig Winther of all responsibility.

Franck stood up with a jump and began to pace back and forth; hands crossed behind his back and nodding his head with every round, he threw a glance at the green book on the couch.

*I'm going. I never want to see you again*, he said to himself: The words had not been addressed to her husband, they had been directed at herself.

She was accusing herself, Franck thought by the closed door and headed towards the wall across the room, to the shelves with their hundreds of novels, reference books, collections of poetry and photographs. Doris Winther had understood that her daughter had lied to her too, not only her schoolmates, some of whom, in turn, had retold the lies to their parents.

One year after Esther's death, an abyss opened up at her mother's feet. Doris had trusted her daughter all her life; had found explanations again and again whenever Esther was desperate over her father's apparent tight-fistedness, stubbornness, meanness; had probably secretly slipped her money, had often not accepted her daughter's rudeness but never said anything, had really believed her, had even believed Esther's best friend when she came the following day talking about bleak depression; from the very first, had believed all her talk about going too far or even sexual abuse, had likely found signs where there were none, Franck thought with ever-quickening steps. She had punished her husband with silence; and had stayed silent out of pure conviction; out of pure self-righteousness which all of a sudden she had become aware of maybe when Sandra Horn came by suggesting that her friend Esther had only wanted to make her father angry, scare him out of his petty-bourgeois mentality. Something like that had to have happened, Franck thought, and again Doris Winther had immediately believed it was true.

With a sigh, he came to a stop, pressed his hands into his thighs, looked over at the green notebook and stayed still until he had calmed down. Then he walked over to the desk, grabbed a biscuit, ate it and took a second one. He was ready for the woman's past, the woman he had once held in his arms for seven hours.


Around four in the morning, Ludwig Winther woke with a start. He was sweating all over and had dreamt of a city where he was on holiday with his wife and daughter. Thousands of people were walking through the streets, there were shops and food stands everywhere, the cafe terraces were overflowing and they were turned away from every restaurant they tried to go to because there were never any free tables. When he noticed a pub that reminded him of one back home, he hurried inside and actually managed to find a place. Then he went right back outside but his wife and Esther had disappeared.

He walked back the way they had come but the buildings had changed, beneath the noonday sun the streets were empty and some of the shops even had their shutters down. He called after a young woman cycling past to ask if she could show him the way to the post office but she just rode away as quickly as possible.

Finally he came across a telephone booth in an alley-way; relieved, he reached for the receiver to dial his wife's number, as he knew she always had a mobile with her. But he could not remember it. After a number of tries where he never made it any further than the first two numbers, he walked dejectedly back to the main street and called out their names.

He hurried back and forth through the Mediterranean-like city which he, however, did not recognize, yelling out his wife and daughter's names. In the meantime, it had grown dark and insufferably hot, he was thirsty and was out of strength; he tried his best to remember his wife's number but was unsuccessful.

Where are you? he yelled. Have you seen my wife and my daughter? And he yelled four more times before waking up.

He slid on his knees to the side of the bed, almost losing his pyjama bottoms in the process, which he then had to pull back up, and that in turn caused a surge of pain—his back felt as if it had been stoned overnight—then he folded his hands in front of his stomach and looked at the framed photograph on the wall. His face was covered in sweat, and it ran into his eyes; he blinked, opened his mouth, could taste his salty misery and in a wheeze began to speak.

'I am letting you go, Doris . . . '

Afterwards he was not sure how many times he had repeated the phrase, maybe twenty-five.

Then, after a short, deep and dreamless sleep he got up early, washed and got dressed for work. First thing he was called in to see Reinhold, the acting boss, who was a good friend of Micha's, the bartender at Enzianstüberl. Reinhold—Winther had forgotten his surname—told him that his job would finish, not at some point, but at the end of that month, in January there'd be a new man with a full-time position; first of all, he'd have to learn the ropes and, second of all, company management had decided to get rid of all their part-time jobs as soon as possible.

The whole day Winther made his deliveries as if making his way through a universe which no longer made any sense.

CHAPTER SEVENTEEN

# He Who Is Yonder Will Be a Sage

Friday. I did not shake hands with a single person. I'm writing this down because I'm still ashamed. In my whole life I've never kept a diary, I never thought I was important enough. But now I don't know what to do with what I want to say any more because there's no one there I trust enough to listen.

I don't trust anyone. Isn't that terrible?

My daughter left me. False. Esther was murdered.

By her own father.

I know that, and that is the truth.

You cannot speak about something like that with anyone, certainly not with your own sister. Inge made an effort, I have to give her that, she made sure all the guests were taken care of and made sure there was always schnapps on the table. She also spoke with Ludwig a lot, they went outside together. Rather incredible because Inge never really liked him, she always liked feeling superior to him. And when I stay real quiet now and only pay attention to the lined paper, I have to say she was right. She saw through him, even if I didn't. So many years in the same house, in the same bed and nevertheless betrayed and lied to.

Buying this little notebook was a good idea. An exercise book! Just like the ones I used to buy for Esther, in the end that was a nice time. The first day of school we'd go to get all the things that were written down on the slip of paper that Esther had brought home. When she was at grammar school, I even made covers for all her books so they wouldn't get dirty and wrinkled. Just like my mother had done for mine. At some point, Esther forbade me from doing it any more. They feel sticky, she said.

Do you remember that, Esther?

What did my sister and Ludwig have to talk about there in front of the pub? That I didn't accept anyone's hand? That's my business and mine alone. How disgusting. Maybe at the moment people wondered why, but by the next day they'd already forgotten.

It's like someone has cut up all my thoughts and scattered them around my head and I can't put them together any more. I can't make out my own thoughts any more, they're all so confused, everything's been moved around, what day is it? I wrote Friday there, so it must be. It's good that I'm here alone and that no one calls. Ludwig and my sister are at the cemetery, they wanted me to come but I said that I felt dizzy and wanted to lie down. That was not a lie. I don't lie. It's better to stay quiet than to lie.

Esther grew quieter and quieter.

Ludwig talked like always, every day, completely normal. Now I also understand why. He had to act as if everything was normal. And Esther didn't show a thing. And I didn't understand a thing. I was the real idiot.

Until Sigrid made me see the light, that is.

I mustn't think about that.

Even the inspector was at the funeral.

I cannot write down what we experienced together here, no one would believe me, and I can hardly believe it myself. It seems as if it happened last year, but it was just four days ago when the man sat here in the kitchen and ate some of my fresh apple cake. Around four in the morning or so.

I would not have thought that I could stand up on my own after he let me go.

I have to stop, the murderer's coming back.


Saturday. In my dream, the ground was shaking and I thought the house was going to come crashing down and I wanted to run outside. Then it occurred to me that Esther was sleeping in her little bed, she was still a baby, so I walked back to the bedroom where her crib was. But it was empty and I was so frightened that I woke up and cried for help.

Ludwig was lying next to me, turned towards the wall, in a red T-shirt.

I hadn't screamed, that was actually in my dream. As if by remote control, I went to Esther's room and as I softly opened the door and looked inside, I saw her sitting up in bed, the blanket pulled up to her chin, watching her little TV on the desk. She put her index finger to her lips so that I wouldn't interrupt her while she was watching her favourite series. The TV didn't make a sound. Although I would've liked to say something, I just closed the door and turned around. I was in the stairwell of our hotel, on the third or fourth floor, and I was no longer sure which room number we were in, Ludwig and I. It wasn't next to Esther's, that much I remembered, the hotel management had made a mess of our reservation. And so I went from door to door, but most of them did not have any numbers. I was on the wrong floor, I thought, I have to go downstairs and was on my way. Before I made it to the next floor, I woke up.

Ludwig was snoring next to me, his upper body naked, lying on his back, as he usually did.

He doesn't have a red T-shirt.

From now on, I will only exchange essentials with him.

I will only say what's necessary with people. With the exception of Sigrid, my only friend.

At dinner, Ludwig and Inge asked me why I was so quiet. I said that I had a sore throat, for two days already.

Tomorrow my sister is finally leaving.

Today we went to the cemetery, and I didn't cry. Hundreds of roses, lilies and other flowers were laying there, and all the wreaths, and the photo of Esther on the small cross, squinting into the sun. Ludwig wanted to use a different one but I didn't allow it.

For some reason, I didn't want my sister to see me cry.

When we were young and I'd cry because I was sad or in pain, she'd talk down to me saying that I shouldn't act like a little girl. But I was a little girl. And I wasn't acting, I just couldn't do anything else. She thought I was putting her on, she and my mother too, she had no idea about me. I never understood why she was that way, and she's still like that today. At the cemetery, not only today but at the funeral too, she kept reaching for me, but I pulled away and folded both of my hands although I never fold my hands when I pray. What's it got to do with her?

No one will ever see me cry again.

Now they are sitting over in the living room and talking about me. The storage room with the old sofa and my parents' hand-carved country armoire has become my refuge. I sit at the square wooden table and write in my green notebook that I picked up especially at the department store. I should've done it sooner: just write everything down but stay silent.

I am slowly starting to understand my thoughts again.

When I think about my dream last night, I get scared. If the inspector comes back to ask how I'm doing, I'll answer: Arrest my husband, the bastard!

No.

I would never say something like that.

Why not?

Indeed, why not?

I don't feel well. Help me, Esther, say something.

I've got to hide this book.


Sunday. At the train station, alone. I sent Ludwig home and he didn't argue. He asked what I wanted to do and I said that I wanted to be around people without having to speak to them. Once he was gone, I sat down on a bench on the platform where Inge left for Berlin.

We hugged, and I didn't cry. She stroked my face and I felt like the little sister again who needed to be patted on the head because she looks so sad. At that moment, I hated her.

Don't look so idiotic, you stupid cow!

At the table next to me, a woman keeps looking over, observing me, but I'm just sitting here, drinking coffee and writing in my book. Go on and look somewhere else!

Why didn't I start keeping a diary a lot sooner? You can say everything and you don't have to feel ashamed and you don't need to worry about other people thinking you're an idiot.

I am sitting in one of the restaurants in the big hall and have the tracks in my sights. Earlier I was sitting on Track 22 and had to think of our mother who would ride to the station every Sunday morning on the tram and then get on the train to Salzburg. She knew someone there that we weren't allowed to meet. Then my sister would take care of me and treat me like a baby. I was already four or five. Sometimes our mother wouldn't come back until Monday, so Inge would have to make breakfast for us before she went to school and I went off to kindergarten.

If the old woman next to me knew what I was writing about! Or Ludwig. Or Inge.

If they only knew!

During that moment on the platform when Inge stroked my cheek, I not only hated her but everyone. I know that you're not supposed to say something like that because we just carried our daughter to her grave, the one who hung herself from a tree at seventeen, I know you have to be humble and quiet and can't send any bad thoughts out into the cosmos because they come back as curses, they say. But what if it's the truth? When what's in me and fills me and doesn't let any other thoughts in is nothing but hate? More than rage, more than anger, more than anything else: that is what I feel.

I don't want to. I haven't used the word for so long, and I never would've thought I'd feel it again. In the newspapers, every day they write about people's hate, hatred of foreigners, the Turks and the Vietnamese, about the East Germans after the fall of the Wall, about the capitalists and the socialists, everything and everyone is hated, but since I was a child I haven't hated anyone, that's the truth.

Until today. On the platform when Inge was leaving, the ground opened up under my feet and I fell back into my childhood where I never wanted to return.

Sundays my sister and I were alone in the tiny, third-floor flat and I was the loneliest girl on God's green earth. Inge would hang out in the kitchen painting—she was always scribbling something on some piece of paper or other, in hundreds of different colours because our mother always gave her new markers while I still had to play with the same old dolls. When I complained, no one listened, or my mother said that we didn't have enough money for new toys. Well what's with the coloured markers and the sketchbooks? I would ask her, and she'd say, the markers are really cheap and they give me the sketchbooks for free. I didn't believe that even back then.

I was lied to and betrayed and I didn't defend myself.

Hate was my only weapon.

Sometimes, at night, I'd stand next to Inge's bed and watch her sleep and stare at her with pure hate. It was beautiful. After that, I could always fall asleep. And I just had to take one look at my mother and she knew. Yes, she knew right away how I felt about her and today I know that she felt the same way about me.

She hated me for being born.

I had not been planned. Neither had my sister, actually, but my mother was still with our father at that time and thought that he would marry her, build a house and that they would start a normal family life.

For two years he lied to her and betrayed her, then I arrived and he took off. I was too much.

No one knew where he went. My mother didn't worry about it at all. She did not inform the police, she did not initiate any kind of search for him, she simply let him piss off.

If she had aborted me, I wouldn't have had to hate her.

And my sister with her coloured markers who, at barely eighteen, pissed off too.

I didn't cry at my mother's funeral. As opposed to Inge who could not control herself. What are you howling about? I asked her and she slapped me, right there in the bathroom of the pub. You're ill, she said, and that it served me right that I had to marry a trouser salesman because no other man was around. After that, I just stared at her and she understood immediately what I was thinking and how I felt about her.

Just like the old bag at the table next to me here, whose eyes I just looked into. As long as I stay here, she won't be looking back over.

And now it's my husband's turn.

I never would have believed that it could come to this.

Even when love dies a slow death or just changes and the physical side of things becomes secondary, you can't let it come to this, you cannot curse another person. That just cannot happen. It cannot be.

But now it's come to this.

Actually, I don't really want to talk about it.

I'm going to order a beer.

When she'd come back on Sunday nights, our mother would smell like white wine.

What did you do in Salzburg? Who did you screw? Was he so ugly that you couldn't introduce us to him? A clubfooted, fat-faced Austrian? Did he rub Mozart candies across your stomach and then lick them back off?

Not once did you even want to show us a photo of him. You said he was an acquaintance and that he was good for you.

He was good for you. And what did you do for us? Were you good for us? Weren't we good for you?

Why is all this occurring to me now?

Because of Inge. Because she patted me on the head. Because of her arrogance. Because of her whole personality. And because you were never there for me.

I don't remember for how long my mother would go to Salzburg almost every Sunday. Three, four years. Then it was over. And she never talked about it again.

I hated him. I imagined his face, his body, his hands, his hair, his voice, his phoney grin, his bloodless lips, his whole mouth, his watery eyes, his broken fingernails, his fat stomach. Everything about him was ugly and hateable. At the beginning, I wanted to talk with my sister about it. Because I was so afraid that our mother would not come home one day and that we'd have to go to a home, each of us to a different one, and that we'd be beaten if we weren't good, and that we would grow up in a strange family, with a mother who would be there but would treat us like strangers, with a father who was even more distant to us than our own who I had never seen and Inge herself for only two years. That we would be orphans and that no one would love us.

That's what I thought and wanted to talk about it with my sister.

But she just patted my face and said stupid things and sent me back to my little kid's room so that she could have her quiet to paint and scribble. And I'd sit at the window and outside the sun would be shining and I wanted so badly to eat a piece of apple cake because it was my favourite and my mother could bake it so well.

When I think about it, I want to kill myself.

No.

I'm not going to kill myself. I still have too much to take care of.

This beer tastes good.

Tomorrow I'm going to look for a headstone at Thalmeier's. And even though Ludwig got a week off because of a death in the family, I'm going to go alone.

From now on, I'm only going to be there for him on the outside.

A second beer can't hurt.


Wednesday. Many things taken care of. At Thalmeier's I already chose a nice stone of bright marble, a slightly frilled kind of script because she still was a child and had slightly frilled handwriting. I showed Ludwig a photo and he agreed.

We talk with each other, almost like always. He doesn't notice that I'm freezing him out, he keeps asking me why Esther did what she did, and I let him, and I always answer the same way: We should have looked after her more.

That's what the neighbours think too. They don't say so but I can see it when I meet them on the street or in the supermarket. The parents are always responsible when their child freely decides to die.

And what should you think?

And we are responsible.

When Sigrid told me what her daughter had told her, I should've done something and involved the police.

But then people would really have thought we were a mess, Ludwig and me and Esther too. Well-behaved homeowners who once the shutters were down did the most terrible things.

We would have been ruined.

Sigrid suggested I talk with Ludwig.

I did. I asked him whether he had something to tell me, and he wanted to know what I meant and I asked him if he'd had problems with our daughter that I didn't know about. No, he said. Then I asked him if he forced our daughter to do things she didn't want to do. He said that he was responsible for Esther doing well at school and not throwing her money out the window and constantly buying clothes like some of her girlfriends. Sometimes you have to be strong, he said.

I spoke with him.

Then I didn't.

I tried to speak with Esther too. It didn't work. She told me to leave her alone and not to come up with any idiotic worries.

Since when have there been idiotic worries?

Not even an idiot's worries are idiotic.

That's how it was and I thought: My whole life long I have been betrayed and lied to, why should it be any different now?

My sister thinks I've become bourgeois and conservative but I've just grown tired and old.

One morning I left the house, travelled to the East Station with the bus and from there took the Eurocity to Salzburg. What did I want to do there? No idea. I found my way to the river and wandered through the city. At a stand, I ate a bratwurst and drank a cola, the wind was cool and soft, and then I continued to wander around. After two hours, I returned to the station to wait for the next train back to Germany. I got home around six o'clock, Esther had already called Ludwig at work five times because she was so worried, she explained. Where had I been? I said that I had been in Nymphenburg Park, feeding the swans. Esther stared at me with her huge, dark eyes as if I were an escaped lunatic, creating disaster at every turn. Throughout dinner Ludwig shook his head. I thought he'd get dizzy.

I was in Salzburg and so what. That had nothing to do with anyone.

I was in Salzburg, where my mother's acquaintance was ready every Sunday.

I was in Salzburg, where my husband supposedly was while our daughter walked into the park and hung herself from a tree.

Goddamn Salzburg.

I'll never take another step in that city.

Maybe I'm crazy.

No.

I have to call Inge immediately.

Now.

It would've been better not to call her.

What did I really expect? That she'd say: I don't know. Or: What leads you to think something like that after all these years? Or: Leave me alone with the past. Or: Our mother has been dead for a long time, forget it.

What then?

I should have known that she knew. That she always knew. That they had a connection, my mother and my sister. That I was here and she was there.

I had to turn forty-one before I understood that I never existed for her.

Franz Teuschek.

All those years she knew his name.

Teuschek. Franz.

And not only did she know his name but she also knew what he looked like. Because she went there, with my mother. The two of them alone on the train to Salzburg. Where was I that day? I asked her on the telephone. She said that I had stayed with our neighbour, old *Frau* Griesbach, she had taken care of me. How old was I? I wanted to know and without missing a beat Inge said: Five. How can you be so sure? I asked and she said: Because I had just started second grade.

Understood.

And what lie did they use to get rid of me? She didn't know any more, she lied, after more than thirty-five years. I know that she's lying.

Franz Teuschek.

A fat guy, bushy eyebrows, narrow, shifty eyes, half-bald, red-cheeked, thick lips, hair growing out of his nose, big ears, and he wears Lederhosen and a sweaty linen shirt and stinks just like his flat, which he only airs out once a week, fifteen minutes before my mother climbs into his bed.

That's just the kind of guy she deserved.

And my sister had been there too. And on the way back, they didn't say one word about it.

That's how I grew up.

Are you all satisfied?

My daughter treated me like my sister did. My husband treated me like my mother.

I hate all of you.

Oh God.

No.

Stop weeping.

I can't.

Stop. Stop. Or else the murderer will know something's going on.

I have to go to bed immediately.

Tomorrow I can't forget to mow the grass.


Friday. Since I started sleeping in the storage room on the old sofa, I write in the green notebook early in the mornings.

The headstone looks really nice. I let the cross with Esther's photo stay but with a new, brighter photo, I had ten copies made. When I stand in front of it, I often have difficulty breathing. Out of pure cowardice. It became clear to me that my daughter had to die because I was too much of a coward.

Why was I such a coward? I could have called the inspector and told him: You must come and arrest my husband, the swine. I doubt he would have believed me. They never believe you. If a man denies having done something, he can just go back home.

And Esther said nothing. Nothing suggested that her father's presence frightened or disgusted her. I watched her, every day, and I never understood her. She always just said: Leave me alone, Don't worry. What should I have done? She was sixteen, then seventeen, and she proudly wore the red dress I'd given her for her birthday. She looked like an actress walking the red carpet. Like a woman, proud and unapproachable but at the same time in no way provocative or daring. When I saw her like that, I thought: I was never that pretty. She wanted to go to a dance at the Bayerischen Hof, but Ludwig didn't give her any money. And so she paid for the entrance and her drinks out of her allowance and didn't speak to her father for a week. She wanted to fly to America together with a girlfriend from school whose sister was studying on the East Coast. She wanted to buy herself a black leather jacket. She wanted to spend her entire summer holidays with her aunt in Berlin.

Ludwig always talked with her, and I was ashamed.

Now it occurs to me that we never spoke about these things, Esther and I. Whenever she wanted something, she went to her father.

Were you aware of that?

My hands are trembling.

Earlier, when you still were small, we'd talk about everything together, the three of us. That was wonderful.

Then we didn't. Since when?

Now I know why you always spoke with him about the important things and never with me, even when, at the end, almost every time you were upset and furious and would curse your father and lock yourself into your room without speaking to him for days.

Now I know.

You simply didn't expect anything from me. I wasn't important. Why go to the less important one and not straight to who's in charge? You thought that I wouldn't stick up for you, that I just let everything happen to me, that I wouldn't confront your father. Is that what you thought? Of course it was, I mean, what else could it have been? But that's not true! You just made them up in your head. How often I begged him and explained how important it was for young girls like you to go out, to have fun, to go eat and drink in chic restaurants and to not have to pay attention to every cent. I told him a hundred times. Yes, I tried very hard to turn him around, and you just ignored me and treated me like I was unnecessary.

That was cruel of you to do, and evil.

Evil and cruel.

I was there for you, but he wasn't.

He abused you, not me.

It was him, not me.

Why did you do that, Esther, my child?

And that you went and hung yourself, that was my punishment.

Dear God.

No.

You can't say something like that.

What kind of family did we become? Such a lovely house, and you were so beautiful, everyone liked you, and I loved you.

Today *Frau* Jordan from across the way didn't say hello to me. She blames me for what happened.

I don't trust myself to leave the house any more.


Thursday. Today my friend Sigrid came over for coffee. We sat in the garden and ate the cake she'd brought with her. She admired the beautifully growing box tree and both of my round Thuja plants. When Sigrid made a comment about the Rhododendron, I told her how Esther had often claimed it smelt like chewing gum. All of a sudden, Sigrid turned very serious.

She said: Your daughter told me something strange. Something that she had also heard from her classmate Sandra, Esther's best friend.

I listened and was afraid and didn't really know about what.

Sandra said that Esther had made up certain things in order to make her father angry and to make him look ridiculous.

What kind of things? I wanted to know, and my hands grew colder. Mischief, Sigrid said, her father had supposedly done something to her or tried.

At first, I didn't make any sound. Then I looked at her and she understood immediately what I was thinking. She knew what she had just told me, she said, but had only done so because Amanda had been so upset by what she'd heard at school.

But it's not true, Sigrid said simply. She was really sorry she had been so gullible and had trusted her daughter. But her daughter had also been misled. What had Esther been thinking? she added, and I sat there and felt betrayed. My left hand was shaking so much that Sigrid had to hold it and almost began to cry.

Esther died six months ago today.

Every day a humiliation.

Every day full of dead time.

Every night the return of hatred.

What should I do now? I wondered, sitting there in the garden. Sigrid also mentioned a chance meeting with Dr Jordan, whom Esther knew from Café Ludwig where she waited tables during her holidays and sometimes even on Sundays. He'd also heard the rumours and not believed a word. He'd even asked his foster son Patrick, who'd got along with Esther well, what he thought and he said that Esther could be mean and had come up with some sick ideas.

What does the boy know? He's ten or eleven. He comes by now and again and cleans out our refrigerator. I can't imagine that he has to go hungry at home. Esther liked him, that's true, she laughed a lot with him even though she wasn't really inclined to laughter.

Six months and now I'm learning that everything was a lie.

I must've had a stupid expression on my face because Sigrid asked me if I had really believed Ludwig to be capable of such a thing. I just sat there while my thoughts came apart in my head.

The sun was shining the whole day long. I should have watered the grass.

Did you really believe Ludwig would sexually abuse his own daughter?

Yes.

Really?

Yes.

Why didn't I confront him? Because I didn't think that it was possible? Because something in me said no?

No.

He did it, and Esther buried her shame inside until it destroyed her.

There's no other way to explain her death. Otherwise there'd be no way to measure our guilt, we would be the ones who'd done something wrong, something we didn't even have the slightest idea about.

What?

That just can't be.

What should I do? Go over there and tell Ludwig: I believed you were a criminal, and that was wrong. On the contrary: We are both criminals, we killed our daughter together.

What did you do, Esther?

Who were you in your room?

On your way to the dear Lord you're wearing the red dress I gave you for your sixteenth birthday.

What should I do?

Tuesday. One year ago, on the fourteenth of February Esther left the house in the morning and did not come back alive.

Her friend Sandra came over and said Esther had been depressed.

Clueless, self-important, presumptuous creature.

Standing in our living room in her black, low-necked dress spreading lies about our daughter.

I don't know what's going to happen.

Ludwig wants me to see a doctor, a psychologist or a psychiatrist. That's something I'm never going to do.

Last Saturday Inge called from Berlin, she wants to come to the one-year anniversary of Esther's death. I said no. Then she talked with Ludwig, and he tried to change my mind. He just doesn't learn. He still doesn't know me, but it doesn't matter any more. We were alone at the graveside. At least for a little while, before some of her classmates and a teacher showed up. Each of them placed a rose down on the grave. I wasn't in a position to speak with them.

Leaving the house, we ran into Dr Jordan. Ludwig told him we were on our way to the East Cemetery because it was the first anniversary of Esther's death, and he offered us his hand. As far as I've heard, he has sex with young girls, that kind of thing doesn't stay hidden. But he's careful, you can't prove anything, and the girls stay quiet.

Did you also have something going on with him?

It's got nothing to do with me. Nothing has anything to do with me any more.

I haven't changed a thing in your room, I air it out every day and once a month I change your bed linens. Your clothes are hanging in the wardrobe, your underwear has been washed. I vacuum too and clean the windows.

Your father has begun to drink. He does so in secret, but he's terrible at it. He tells me things, I listen, but then forget it all immediately. He seems to be happy about the World Cup in America in June. Germany's playing in the same group as Spain, I noticed that much. Why?

You wanted so badly to go to Madrid just once. In your desk drawer, there's a travel guide to Spain.

You never managed.

No more trips.

Not even to Salzburg.

I don't think he's still alive.

Franz Teuschek.

God judges cheats.

He betrayed and lied to our mother and she let him.

No.

God judges liars and cheats equally. She ended up in hospital, for two weeks she was in a room with two others and then died one night of heart failure.

There's no escape.

Look at yourself in the mirror, Doris Winther. You're an old woman who's almost forty-two. You married a man in whose name it snows without cease. You were never really there.

That is your destiny.

Thursday. Esther was right: the Rhodedendron does smell like chewing gum.

For a while I stood by the bush observing the grey apple tree. Where does it always get its lovely apples? I wondered and had to smile. I think.

Someone has to prune the box tree.

Friday. What are you waiting for?

Saturday. I'm going. I never want to see you again.

20–5

Franck stood up and went over to his desk. On it lay the book with the verses translated from the old Egyptian of a man who was tired of life and his soul.

*Verily, he who is yonder will be a living god,*
*Averting the ill of him who does it.*

*Verily, he who is yonder will be one who stands*
    *in the Bark of the Sun,*
*Causing choice things to be given therefrom for*
    *the temples.*
*Verily, he who is yonder will be a sage,*
*Who will not be prevented from appealing to Re*
    *when he speaks.*

# CHAPTER EIGHTEEN

# The Unfamiliar Child

The following morning, he read Doris Winther's diary a second time, even those pages where she described her daily work in the garden inside and out and made a list of how many things she always had to take care of. At certain points, Franck had the impression that she wrote down such insignificant things just to have a reason to retreat and take a moment for herself and enjoy her new-found habit of writing, her saying everything, her coming to terms with the ghosts of her life, of which she was one herself.

While in an act of desperate hopelessness her hus-band would tear the fourteenth of February out of his calendar, Doris Winther had decided to confront the inexpressible pain of the situation through words that she steadfastly refused to share with him. And yet, after she had made the decision to die, she did not destroy the green book—it was as if she wanted to give her husband the gift of one final, spiteful silence to accompany him on his way, a silence through which, as she would no longer be there, he would be unable to break.

Franck was certain that immediately after Doris' death, Winther had at least browsed through the notebook and had probably been overwhelmed by its contents. In any event, he had to know about the accusations that had been levelled at him, something he had wanted to keep quiet about when he came to Aubing and throughout his discussions, something he just was not able to do.

Silence—as was customary in that house with the lovely garden, a silence that stretched across generations: the grandmother who would go to meet her lover in another country but never say a word; the father of her daughter who disappeared without a sound; Doris, who, without making much of a fuss, almost unquestioningly, resigned herself to marrying a salesman thereby letting go of any academic future she might have had; her sister who disappeared to Berlin, thereafter the two of them only spoke to each other when absolutely necessary; and Esther, only child and heir to her ancestors' silence, who understood her parents' system and lives, or had at the latest since puberty, and lived in a world of soundproofed dreams.

So how else, Franck wondered, was Winther supposed to act today? Up in his little flat beneath the eaves he was the caretaker of the final legacy of that family he once had founded: a green, lined notebook filled with loneliness, a loneliness that reflected in his eyes.

On his way through the city on that windy, raw November afternoon, the inspector asked himself over and over again whether it was possible that Doris Winther had admired Esther's act and whether the night he was there she had already decided to follow her, and whether the diary was supposed to serve as a kind of Bible so that she would not lose her nerve.

He declined the coffee she offered him; he had other appointments planned and did not want to lose any time. But the former branch director of the city bank thought it was important to make her point of view as clear as possible; obviously—just as was the case with Esther's former best friend Sandra Horn—she was plagued by a guilty conscience. Franck was familiar with such behaviour from his time on the force but his understanding had its limits.

'That was a difficult time,' said Sigrid Nickl, a sixty-two-year old, slender woman who for their meeting had dressed in a dark suit, put on make-up and done up her hair, dressed like that, Franck thought, she must have been similar to the banker she once was. She had almost managed to erase all traces of her former Upper Palatinate dialect; all the same Franck noticed it, as his ex-wife was from there. 'And the girls were stubborn, moody, too, but I don't want to make any excuses.'

She smoothed out her skirt and tried to bring her uneasiness in the presence of an inspector under control. 'Naturally, I remember telling Doris about it, and I still remember how scared she was and how I had to calm her down. One or two days later, I asked Amanda about it again, whether what she had told me was true and she said that some of the girls at school weren't whispering about anything else. What was I supposed to have done? And what do you think? I was completely taken by surprise when my daughter came and said that, as far as anyone knew, Esther had made the whole thing up. Made the whole thing up? In this case? You tell me. How would you have reacted?'

'How did you react?' Franck sat in a high-backed chair with his legs crossed and wrote various words down on his notepad, words which had more to do with his thoughts than with what the woman had to say.

'Naturally, I was very straight with Amanda, I told her: You just don't spread those kinds of rumours. Full stop. I knew the Winthers well, they were clients of ours, we helped finance their house, Ludwig Winther would regularly come by to talk about his credit or some stocks.'

'He had stocks.'

'Only for a little while. He had bad luck and lost money. We helped him out of the situation, that wasn't a problem back then; today you need to complete a whole pile of safety measures before you can transfer someone money, it doesn't matter how well you know the person. Ludwig Winther was a frugal man and losses caused him pain, it could be that he was a little too cautious when it came to money.'

'Did you ever talk with Esther about the rumours?'

'You just don't get involved in other people's family life. No, I called Doris and hoped that she hadn't taken the whole thing too seriously. Please understand. The two of us, Doris and I, knew Ludwig, she knew him better than I did, of course, but neither of us would have ever thought he was capable of such a thing. On the other hand, every day you read in the newspapers about horrific cases of sexual abuse within families, you can never be too sure.

'On the telephone, Doris seemed calm and didn't seem angry at all. If I remember correctly, I was convinced that she had spoken with her husband and cleared everything up. What else is there to add? Like I said, the girls were going through a difficult phase, and Esther just had to come to an agreement with her father somehow whenever money was concerned, and he wasn't particularly generous. Who can hold that against him? He had to pay a mortgage, he had a car, he was the only one making money in the family and working as a salesman at Weinzirl's boutique brought him about ten thousand a month. He had every right to be concerned about money, don't you think?'

'Doris Winther told you that she had spoken with her husband and cleared up the whole situation with the rumours.'

'That's how I understood it at the time, I think.'

'You're not completely sure.'

'How long ago was that?' Sigrid Nickl bent forward, inconspicuously she thought, in order to try and see his notepad; at the same moment, Franck leant back as if by chance, laid his pen down across the paper and his hand on top of it, as if taking a rest.

'More than twenty years,' he said. The number had come up in their conversation on the phone when he had told her why he was calling and asked her if she would be free to meet.

'That's a long time.' Sigrid Nickl was silent for a while until the thought occurred to her that the inspector might think she wanted to keep something from him. 'Of course. I felt guilty afterwards. Maybe I shouldn't have said anything. It was a chain of events. I thought a lot about it after you called me yesterday. I remembered that Amanda had told me about it at breakfast and that that afternoon Doris had come by the bank to take care of something. I invited her to a coffee, we began to speak, and for some reason I felt that it was important to tell her about the rumours at school. As I said, she was completely taken aback which you can well understand; but later, when I called her and told her that Esther had greatly exaggerated, she acted like she hadn't believed it before whatsoever. That's how it was, and the reasons why Esther killed herself don't have anything to do with that at all, I'm quite sure about that.'

The reasons for Esther's suicide, Franck thought, likely lay in the darkness of her family history and remained, in spite of the green fossil in his pocket, as puzzling as ever.

'Do you know the dentist Dr Jordan?' he asked.

'One of the Winthers' neighbours.'

'You spoke with him about the subject back at the time.'

'I don't think so.'

'You did indeed.'

'I can't remember.'

'Doris wrote about it in her diary.'

'Doris kept a diary?' Sigrid Nickl asked, her voice rising. She cleared her throat and made a serious face. 'Excuse me, this is now a bit . . . I wouldn't have imagined Doris to keep a diary.'

'Why not?'

'Because . . . She was . . . I can't explain it to you.'

Of course not, Franck thought and said, 'Dr Jordan confirmed the rumours to you, but he felt them to be unfounded.'

'Aha.'

'And he talked with his foster son about them, whom Esther knew quite well.'

'I remember him, an energetic young boy. And what did he say?'

'That's not clear. Apparently, Esther could also be rather distant and cold when something didn't suit her.'

'Sadly, that's true. I had completely forgotten to ask you why you are even bothering with the whole thing. And on top of that, because you are retired. Is something not quite right with the suicides?'

'What shouldn't be right?'

'I don't know . . . I'm just a little bit confused.'

'Why do you think that Esther took her life at seventeen?'

'No one knows.'

'You never spoke with Doris Winther about that?'

'She didn't want to. I'm sorry that I almost laughed earlier when you mentioned the diary. It's clear to me now that, although we met each other regularly, I knew so little about her. And at the same time, she always had something to say about work around the house, her garden where she was so busy day and night, about Esther and school, about celebrities and their problems she'd read about in the paper. She always seemed good-humoured, talkative, open. After Esther's death she grew more closed, that's true, but we still got together; and the garden did not take care of itself, and the gutters were leaking again, and the front of their house should've been repainted already, you understand what I mean: she took care of all the everyday things. I thought that she'd manage, that she'd get herself back into life. She went to visit Esther's grave every day, took care of all the plantings; when she told me about it, she didn't seem dejected, she seemed to have accepted things as they were.'

'Did she talk about her husband too?'

'Rarely. He was back at work, she stayed at home and did what she'd always done.'

'Until the day she went into the garden and hung herself,' said Franck.

Sigrid Nickl sank her head, played with her fingers. 'You mean that I should've noticed something,' she said. 'Should've recognized the signs. But I have to tell you: You can't. Some people don't want to be understood; we sit across from them and think we know them but we only see what they're wearing and only hear what they say, we have no idea what they look like in the nude or whether they cry when they're alone. We gladly let ourselves be deceived; maybe because, otherwise, in the face of such total helplessness, we wouldn't be able to go on ourselves.'

Franck stuck his notepad into his bag, Sigrid Nickl stood up. When the inspector also stood, she reached out her hand, he took it and she held it tightly.

'The last time we saw each other she brought me two pieces of apple cake she'd just made,' she said. 'She apologized for having used store-bought apples because the ones in the garden weren't ripe yet. Why should they have been? It was only May.' She let go of Franck's hand. 'How was I supposed to sense that in a week's time she would no longer be there?'


As his office was closed just like every Wednesday afternoon, he invited the inspector to a restaurant near the East Station; there he ordered an Italian appetizer for two, a bottle of mineral water and a carafe of Tuscan white wine, which Franck did not touch. The alcohol-free wheat beer he drank instead evinced a pained look from Dr Paul Jordan.

'Really?' he asked. 'Esther and I met each other in a cafe by the university?' Dr Paul Jordan had a good appetite and after almost every bite wiped his mouth with the white linen napkin which reminded Franck of Winther's habit with the handkerchief, and, with his sixty-five years, exuded a youthful air in the carefree way he spoke and gesticulated; with his orderly, shoulder-length hair, his oval-shaped designer glasses, chequered shirt and jeans, Jordan could have passed for a continuing student or as someone who worked in the Internet industry or in TV, but not someone who made their money as a dentist.

'It's possible, I used to frequent the student area regularly in the past, always felt comfortable there. You were saying that you were going through the old files regarding Esther's death and that you had discovered some inconsistencies? How did you come to me? I was curious, that's why I wanted to meet you and today was convenient.'

Franck—notepad and pen next to his plate with the rest of his oddly-tasting spinach—returned the dentist's bright look with, as his ex-wife used to say, an inscrutable, policeman-like one. 'Some months before Esther's death, there was a rumour going around saying that her father had sexually abused her and you heard it.'

After taking a drink of his wine, Jordan pursed his lips, tilted his head and wrinkled his forehead. 'It's a bit too acidic. Could be the fault of the marinated onions. Are you a wine connoisseur? I'm not. When I used to go to congresses, I always acted like I was when colleagues went a bit overboard with it all. At some point, it became clear to me that I liked to drink wine, sometimes one litre after another but I don't really need to be an expert, my palate tells me all I need to know. Sorry, I didn't mean to get distracted. I remember. Terrible thing. I confronted Esther about it, I think, I wanted to know why she was saying such things. I don't remember any longer what she said exactly, I could imagine that she stuck with her story. I didn't believe a word. Yes, Esther could be rather odd at times, my little nephew had even noticed it back then, even though he was the one who usually bothered other kids and tried to outsmart us.'

'Did you have a relationship with Esther?'

For a moment, the relaxed dentist's neck grew stiff, then he went back to his usual mood. 'That's an interesting question, twenty years on. Does who I might have an affair with have anything to do with you? You aren't a private detective my wife hired to test my faithfulness, are you?'

'No,' said Franck.

'Of course not. May I give you an honest answer?' He actually waited for a reaction, but when he did not receive one, finished off his glass of wine and filled it again. 'She wanted something with me but I didn't want anything with her. And that was that.' He drank, wiped his mouth with his napkin, and shrugged his shoulders.

'You rejected the girl,' said Franck, the sentence immediately struck him as inappropriate.

'If you want to put it that way.'

Franck wanted to write something down but his thoughts distracted him, pulled his notes away from beneath his fingers; he stared at the man across from him as if he were a living fossil from the Palaeozoic era of humanity on Bernauer Straße in east Munich.

'What's the matter?' Jordan asked. 'Did the meal disagree with you? Should I order an Averna for us?'

'Yes,' said Franck although he meant to say no. Jordan gestured to the waiter, called the name of the drink out across the restaurant—in the meantime they were the only guests—and looked at the inspector with concern.

'I beg you,' said Jordan. 'At this point in time, you won't be able to find out why the girl hung herself. It wasn't because of heartache. And certainly not because of me. A lot of boys were going after Esther, she had her own ideas about the world and those ideas didn't always fit reality. But that's not all that abnormal.'

The waiter placed two glasses filled with herb liqueur, ice cubes and lemon down on the table and cleared away their plates. Jordan raised his glass. 'Let's drink to the sad girl from across the way. Believe me, none of us could have ever imagined something like that happening.' He emptied his glass in one go, Franck raised his glass and put it back down.

'Did Esther threaten you?' he asked, sensing the answer.

'I'm not really sure about that now. She was persistent, that's for sure. Maybe she was also a little bit jealous of her friend or one or the other girls at school. No, I didn't allow myself to be threatened, please.'

'You had a relationship with Sandra Horn.'

'Excuse me?'

'With Esther's best friend.'

'Sandra. Yes. Those were just adventures, nothing important. What do you think? I was . . . in my mid-thirties and the girls were sixteen, seventeen, eighteen. I liked to go out, I danced, flirted, had fun. I was married, true, and we had taken custody of my brother's son. But was I supposed to stay home every night just because of that?

'I worked hard, I was already a partner of a group practice, business was going well, we had a house, like the Winthers, like many others in the neighbourhood. My life was just beginning to get going. And the girls were by no means nuns, they knew exactly what they wanted and where the boundaries were. And I never, *Herr* Franck, overstepped the boundary. That was an unwritten rule: everything had to be voluntary or not at all. The girls accepted that and when one of them became too pushy, I sent them home.

'And Esther, I knew it right away, wanted something special; no, not what you're thinking; she wanted to possess me, she wanted us to be together. That's how she was and that's why I had to make it clear to her, quickly and ruthlessly, what was acceptable and what wasn't. She agreed, but it wasn't easy for me.

'There were nightly telephone calls, she'd call me from a phone booth, she wanted to talk, wanted to see me, go out with me. Why are you looking at me like that? What are you thinking? That I'm guilty? Because I rejected her? You can forget about that. That's not how it was. She'd understood, really. I still remember her coming to the office one day, supposedly because she had a toothache, and when the assistant was away she told me not to worry, that she had understood that it was all crazy, what she wanted from me, and that things were over. Case closed.'

For the second time that day the circumstances surrounding Esther's death were referred to as a case. 'The case,' said Franck, 'was closed. And what happened then?'

'Nothing else.' Jordan looked at the empty carafe. 'She never called again. Everything was over. Drink your

Averna! Or would you rather have ice-water with an aftertaste of herbs?'

'How much time passed between Esther's visit to your office and her death?'

Jordan ran his hand across his stomach, shrugged his shoulders. 'Hard to say. One year? Ten months? Eight? I can't say for certain any more. There's no connection— why can't you understand that? The causes are in her family, I've always been convinced of that.'

The one, thought Franck, did not cancel out the other whatsoever. He said that he would like to ask Jordan's nephew some questions, which seemed to cause the dentist to fall into quiet contemplation before he was able to answer.

'That will be difficult,' he said. 'You can try, naturally, but the boy's catapulted himself out of the normal world. Before you find out on your own: He has a record, assault and battery, robbery . . . he's out on parole and, for the most part, has kept straight. At the moment, as far as I know, he's a bouncer.'

'You have little contact with him.'

'Little to none. My wife and I really made an effort, and where else could he have gone? Of course we took him into our care after the thing with his mother. You must know about all that . . . Nils . . . They'd been fighting again, he lost the plot, punches back and forth, then Nils just completely lost it.' Jordan shook his head. 'I liked his Liese, she was a good-natured woman, we often went bowling together, Patrick was there too, at that point he was four or five.'

'How many years did your brother get?' Franck asked.

'The district court of Munich thought eight years would be appropriate. That was a shock to all of us; of course we thought his lawyer would make an appeal. I don't know what he had in mind, but Nils kept him from doing it. He'd decided to take the punishment and sit it out, he accepted his guilt. It didn't change a thing for the kid, his mother was dead, his father was sitting in prison, he was utterly alone, and that's how he came to be with us. He stayed with us for six years, he'd just started primary school in Lohfeld where my brother had lived. Nils ran a car dealership there, people knew him, no one thought he would've been capable of such a thing.'

'What's he doing today?'

'He works at a nursery here in the city. He only travels to Lohfeld to visit Liese's grave, he's quite involved with it, always pays for its upkeep one year in advance. He's turned into a quiet man, my brother. Sometimes we meet and try to talk. Brother to brother, you see, you know what I mean. He's always friendly, asks how I'm doing, how everything's going at home and at the office, those kinds of things. But he ... sometimes I think I need to pay more attention to him, so that one day he doesn't do something stupid. But then he seems happy with his life again. We know each other so little, and it's never been otherwise.'

'What's the relationship between your brother and his son like?'

Jordan hesitated. 'May I tell you something?' He almost did not trust himself to look at Franck. 'I think that my brother stays away from him; he doesn't want to get sucked into Patrick's chaotic, criminal lifestyle. That's my opinion, and it doesn't make me feel very good, but every time the subject comes up, Nils avoids it and loses himself in small talk. Maybe he feels guilty and imagines that Patrick has inherited some kind of violent gene; he let something like that slip out once. In the meantime, we have a silent agreement not to mention Patrick's name other than if he's up to something or, as so often, he needs his lawyer's help, whom I happen to be friends with.'

For a while the two men were silent.

'So, Patrick moved from a village to the city,' said Franck. 'And had difficulty adapting.'

'A lot of difficulty. After just one week we had to take him out of class, he'd thrown books on the ground and interrupted lessons numerous times; any kid who said something to him that he didn't like could count on getting a beating; it was a tough time for all of us. The following year Patrick was sent back to school, he'd quieted down a bit, had got to know some kids from the neighbourhood, had become friends with the Winthers; I think he was happiest when he was over there. He loved Doris' apple cake. Who didn't?'

'He also became friends with Esther,' Franck said. As with many murder investigations in the past, he could now—after all the discussions and observations and the evaluation of his notes and misgivings—see a hidden door opening up but was still unable to recognize what was behind it: the crystal-clear solution to a case or the eternal eclipse that was the fate of thousands who would never see justice done.

In the case of Esther Winter—which was no case at all, as Franck knew, but the nearly hopeless attempt of two men to ease their guilty consciences—there would likely not be any new charges, at least not in a legal sense. Franck could feel an old unease as his investigator's veins once again began to throb.

Jordan thoughtfully sipped at the rest of his mineral water. 'Patrick and Esther had a similar way of disregarding other children they didn't like or who had made them angry; they ignored them, no longer talked with them, froze them out almost to death. It was quite odd. How old was Patrick when Esther died? Eleven. And she was? Eighteen?'

'Seventeen.'

'You're right. What does a seventeen-year-old want from an eleven-year-old? And vice versa. Although I have to say that Patrick was always very direct with older children, with adults too, he got along with them better than with kids his own age for some reason.'

'Where can I find him?' Franck asked, thinking of a phrase he had noted down during his first talk with Ludwig Winter; apparently Esther had mentioned someone to her father who she said she did not like but who was nice. After various indications pointed to the local dentist who was known to have affairs with half-grown schoolgirls, Franck thought that Esther had been referring to Paul Jordan; but, in the end, it was quite possible she had been referring to eleven-year-old Patrick.

Jordan gave the waiter a sign that he wanted to pay. 'I can give you his mobile number,' he said. 'Maybe you'll get lucky and he'll answer. He lives in a flat on Daiser-straße.'

It took Franck thirty minutes to find a parking spot, in the end, he squeezed his fifteen-year-old Ford into a space near the Am Harras underground station and was just arriving at the building he had been looking for when a wide-shouldered man in his early thirties wearing a black suit and a black leather coat that hung down to his ankles stepped out on the street. He had an angular face with a thin beard, light-blue, watery eyes and closely cropped, dark hair. His fingers were decorated with four massive silver rings.

Franck spoke to him on the off chance that he would respond but their conversation simply remained off.

'Are you Patrick Jordan?'

'And?'

'My name is Jakob Franck, I'm an ex-police officer investigating the suicide of Esther Winter.'

'Man, you're really on the ball. *Servus.*'

'You knew the girl, I'd like to speak with you briefly.'

'Cool.' He crossed the street to a metallic-orange BMW Z4, pressed the electronic door-opener, let himself fall into the black leather seat, waved in the direction of the inspector with two fingers on his temple, closed the door, revved the engine and slowly drove down Daiser-straße.

Franck felt the pressing need to be around someone who had not completely lost all sense of compassion.

CHAPTER NINETEEN

# The Short-Sighted Witness

Through the glass door he saw that his ex-wife was busy with two customers; she had not seen him, so he decided to make a call that he had not found the time for in two days from the cafe across the street.

He sat down outside by the serving window, ordered a double espresso, leafed through his notepad, read what he had written about the dentist and his nephew/foster son and tried to put the images that came to his mind in some kind of order. Then he called his former colleague.

'You've got to be kidding,' André Block said after telling Franck that there was no match between the traces of DNA found on the spoon he had stolen from Café Ludwig, the plastic bag in the park or the rope Esther had hung herself with. 'And now you want me to follow another vague clue? This Jan Roland's out of the game but you have a new suspect that might've committed a murder? No, Jakob. I'm not going to look into anyone else, and you're not either. Put the files down in the base-ment, relax, dedicate yourself to your free existence as a pensioner, go hiking or get down to reading the collected works of that writer you've been meaning to for a hun-dred years now, Padura or whatever his name was . . . '

'Pavese,' said Franck. 'He was an Italian, Padura's Cuban.'

'Then read his collected works too while you're at it. Why else do you have a bookseller for an ex-wife? You'll always get a discount.'

'Just one more comparison,' said Franck. Two women came out of the shop across the street with bags full of books. 'The young boy knew her well, I'm going to speak with him again and just want to be able to exclude something.' He waited for a response; most likely Block had to shake his head first.

'Let me guess,' he said. 'Just like in the good old days you're suffering from your intuition.'

'I'm not suffering, I'm establishing connections.'

'What else?'

'His data is saved, he has a record.'

'Got it. Have you spoken with Marion in the meanwhile?'

'I'm about to.'

'About to? You need someone you can talk to, Jakob, someone who understands what makes you tick. Who will remind you that you're no longer a police officer.'

Franck stood up and brought his cup to the window. 'Call me as soon as you have the results,' he said into his mobile; Block made an unintelligible sound and hung up.

As soon as Franck entered the bookshop, his phone rang; he left it in his shoulder bag, kissed his ex-wife on both cheeks and, as if it were the most natural thing in the world, held on to her hand for a few seconds. She looked at him—even eighteen years after their divorce, he imagined that her eyes still saw the man he once had been before the ghosts of the dead began to haunt him and he began to serve them while, at the same time, neglecting his own life's guest of honour.

'Take a look at you,' she said and straightened out the collar of his leather jacket. 'I was worried because you haven't been in contact. Is everything all right? You look pale, are you eating well? Your face is thin, and you look stressed. You look like you're back on the job and just back from a crime scene. What's wrong with you, Hannes?'

She had called him that since the early days, and their divorce had not changed a thing; he also still called her by a name from the same film; for years, they went to the cinema regularly and at the weekends watched films at home on video, some of them so often they knew the dialogue by heart and, lounging around on the couch animated by wine, they would move their hands and talk just like the characters on screen.

'I'm a bit uneasy,' he said. 'It's true, I'm working on an old case.'

'Ah,' said Marion Siedler. 'That explains the trusty old shoulder bag and the policeman's gaze.'

She was five years younger than he was; but the fact that, in her eyes—above all when he was working, but not only then—he was a model of correctness and his daily choice of clothing would have honoured the branch manager of a rural Raiffeisen bank, did not keep her from indulging, as she always had, in her own, unique way of dressing.

Her trademarks were her vibrantly, but by no means garish, coloured blouses, skirts and floor-length clothes; her unruly and, at times, surprisingly bleach-blonde, at times dark and chestnut-coloured, hair that, in spite of all the clips and pins, seemed to explode; her bright, nearly make-up free and open face with its green eyes; and her voice, which was untarnished by any impatience or frustration.

When Franck had first got to know Marion—convinced that, as a boring patrol cop, he would soon have to find a new girlfriend—he found her voice to be an acoustical embrace. He had never met anyone he could listen to for so long without ever longing for a moment of silence. That too had not changed after eighteen years of being divorced.

'What kind of case is it?' she asked.

'Esther Winther, the girl who hung herself in the park in Ramersdorf.'

She was putting the books customers had left on the table back on the shelf but, having grown reflective, turned to Franck. 'I remember that one. You'd had to deliver the news of someone's death again.'

'That's right.'

She observed her ex-husband as if slowly beginning to understand why he was dressed the way he was, why he was acting the way he was, why he was even there. In a few sentences, he told her about the job Esther's father had asked him to do and all the bewildering conversations he had had since then.

'If it was a crime,' said Marion Siedler, 'then your colleagues would have declared it one back then. But it says a lot about you that you continue to stand by the father. Do you want a coffee?'

The bell above the door rang, and a customer came inside.

'No,' said Franck. 'I'd like to clear up a few more things. Maybe I'll get in touch at the weekend.'

'I'll be at home reading. Just give me a call.'

He wanted to say something but the words just did not come to him. He kissed her cheeks, nodded to her once more and left.

Once he was outside, he turned around again and through the glass door saw that Marion was looking at him over her customer's shoulders. The image of her blazing, pitch-black hair accompanied him on his drive through town.

He thought about Marion's decision, half a year after the day of their divorce, to quit her job at a large bookstore to open up her own on a not particularly busy side-street, not far from a competitor and without any office stationary, newspapers or school supplies; but, instead, shelves full of non-mainstream, not particularly best-sellers and—in an ironic but sweet nod to his profession, as she had explained to him—at least three hundred, constantly changing crime novels from around the world whose authors, up until then, had only been known by initiates.

In the meantime, Marion had been running her shop for almost two decades; Franck knew that she had had to make it through some financial crises which had ruined others; Marion did not talk about it, she just held out and pushed her clients the books that were closest to her heart. And the times got better again, almost as if—Franck thought as he parked his car on Ungsteiner-straße—all the books from Marion's bright present formed a clearing in the middle of the 'Egyptian darkness of trash and low-end commerce', as she liked to describe the market.

Getting out of the car, he thought about the call he had not answered when he was in front of the bookshop; he listened to his mailbox.

Adriana Waldt—the woman from the airport who had also kept a diary since the day her sister drowned herself in the sea—asked him how he was doing and whether he was interested and had the time to go eat a soup; she suggested a restaurant near the main train station that had images of the North Sea on its walls; furthermore, she thanked him once again for his invitation and for having listened to her. Franck intended to call her back later or the following day.

Franck did not expect any fundamentally new information from the woman he had called after his short meeting with Patrick Jordan but hoped to get a few useful statements from a witness who, in his opinion, his former colleagues had not questioned intensively enough.

Hobbling in front of him, she made her way into the living room and dropped into one of the two massive easy chairs; her right foot was in a cast. She'd had a fall, she explained upon greeting him, one night in the stairwell because the light was out again.

Linda Schelling—wearing a light-blue, billowing woollen dress and in the habit of scrunching up her eyes before she said anything—was in her mid-sixties and clearly a good friend of white wine. On the table were two half-full bottles, an empty water glass and a crystal glass, from which she slurped her wine with abandon; Franck first had to get used to the sound.

He sat across from her, sunk deep into the chair, and refused a drink. After taking a look around the room decorated with simple, practical furniture and waiting for her to put down her glass, which she did not do, he made an effort to stretch his back. 'In the files, I read that you have a dog. Where is he?'

'In doggy-heaven.' Her eyes were tiny slits. 'Has been for ever. He was a she, Frieda. The two of us, we were a team. I never stumbled when she was with me, Frieda looked after me. She was reliable and loyal. There, can you see it? There's a photo of her.'

Down on a low bookshelf that, once Franck had a good look, was filled with Alpine-themed dime novels, was an ostentatious silver frame with a picture of a wire-haired dachshund in a green meadow. 'Frieda,' Franck said.

'For fourteen years we were together.' Linda Schelling sipped noisily at her glass. 'That she made it to be that old is almost a miracle. She had difficulties with her discs and, in the end, was almost lame, but she was brave. A real fighter through and through. An animal like a human being, sensitive, tough, trustworthy, reliable, everything a person needs when they're alone. Do you have a pet?'

'No.'

'It'd be good for you. Do you live alone?'

'Yes.'

'You'll see, you'll become a better person. I don't want to be too personal, you understand, you are a police officer, that's not bad at all, you belong to the good ones. But for your inner life a pet like that can be a blessing, believe me.'

Franck was afraid of sliding off the chair, he had come to be sitting so close to its edge. 'You don't have a pet any longer.'

'Frieda was it. Before her, I'd had Elsa and Lissi, then Frieda came and she stayed by me the longest. Then I said to myself: You're never going to find a sweeter one. Perhaps that was a mistake. But now I'm used to it. Are you sure you wouldn't like a sip of wine? It's a Franconian Riesling, absolutely lovely.'

'Thank you, no. You remember the day you were in the park and you found the dead girl.'

'I spoke with Frieda about it often. You don't forget something like that. The poor girl was hanging from the tree, there was no saving her by that point. I recognized her immediately, I knew her, her parents lived over there, on the other side of Balanstraße. She came to the park often, often with her girlfriends, they'd secretly smoke cigarettes or drink beer. What you do at that age. She always greeted me in a friendly way.'

'On that day, from the time you left your house with your dog to go for a walk and the moment in the park when you found the girl, you didn't encounter anyone.'

'It was a spooky afternoon and neither of us wanted to go out, Frieda or me, and if it hadn't been necessary, we would've stayed at home. Far and wide, we were almost the only ones out. How late was it? Around five.'

'In my colleagues' report, it says that you discovered the body around seven.'

'Were we out so late? That sounds dubious. But if that's what's in their report, that must have been when it was.'

'You called the police from your mobile phone.'

'Luckily, I already had one of those things. Back then, it wasn't as common as it is now; I dialled one-one-two immediately.'

She poured wine into her glass from one of the two bottles, took a sip and leant on the armrest. 'Later on, the police officers assured me she was already dead by the time I got there. I never would have forgiven myself if I'd failed to notice she was still alive. I literally froze with fear. Frieda didn't make a sound, she normally barked and enjoyed herself and ran around like a world champion; she was as shocked as I was. Then a patrol car arrived and two officers checked her pulse. It was all just so sad. Little Esther. People said she was depressed, is that true?'

'We're not entirely sure,' said Franck. 'And you really did not see anyone there around Esther? Another person on a walk, perhaps, someone, kids playing.'

'At that time of day there weren't any kids playing. Maybe nowadays they do, but not back then.' She straightened herself up, squinted and looked at the inspector or at least in his direction. 'Otherwise there were always children around, all day long; that park is a wonderful place to play, lots of green, no cars, they can play football and the real little ones have a sandbox. All the kids from the neighbourhood used to go play in the park after school and the two of us used to like to watch them, Frieda and I.'

'Do you remember the young boy Patrick Jordan? He was friends with Esther and lived on the same street.'

'Patrick?' She stretched out her arm and stared at the built-in wardrobe while reaching for her wine glass, she took hold of it, guided it to her mouth, took a sip and put it back down on the table, a frown still on her face. 'Sure, sure, Patrick. A real hoodlum that kid. But he was a lot younger than Esther, no?'

'He was eleven,' said Franck.

'He was always hanging around the park. Difficult boy. Skipped school a lot, everyone knew that, played on his own a lot, even football, would kick the ball across the field and run after it. An unpredictable lad. Yes, Patrick, he practically lived in the park. It's quite possible that he was somewhere around there that afternoon. Back then already I didn't see too well.'

'You didn't say a word about that to my colleagues.'

'No? It's also not important.'

Franck considered standing up not just because of his stiff back but to pressure the drunk woman a little bit by his presence; he decided against it. 'Please think about it,' he said, trying to use a soft tone. 'Was Patrick in the park that evening? Did you see him? Did you possibly speak with him?'

'By no means.' Linda Schelling shut her eyes and kept them closed for so long that Franck was afraid she had fallen asleep. Then her eyes snapped back open and she blinked violently. 'I never spoke with him, he was always just running around, he wasn't talkative. No, no, how did you come up with something like that?'

'Was he there, *Frau* Schelling?'

'Probably. He was always running around there, then running off, probably home, it was already late. That doesn't mean all that much, I'm saying he was there all the time, every day, I forgot that kid as soon as I saw Esther hanging there, the poor, poor girl. Why did she go and do that? That was such a creepy sight, the beautiful girl with the black hair and the white sweater, those cowboy boots; she was hanging on the tree and I thought, I can't be seeing this, you understand? I had to go all the way up to her to be sure. I couldn't believe it, and Frieda was also so afraid. Everything was quiet. The park, everything. As if the trees and the shrubs and the birds had gone silent out of respect. I will never forget that, that should never have been allowed to happen.'

With a sudden movement, Franck stood up. 'What you told me was important, thank you for your time.'

She reached for her glass again. 'I have a lot of time. I sit here, have a sip, turn on the TV in between, watch half an hour of trash, turn it back off, take a walk around the block. Sometimes I call an old girlfriend or we agree to go play cards at the pub. You're welcome to come by again some time, do you play cards?'

'Now and again some poker.'

'I'm a bit short on money for that, we play *Watten*, I played it as a child with my father. Wait a moment, I'll walk you to the door.' She pressed her arms into the armrests and mentally got herself ready.

'Please stay seated.'

As if relieved, she plumped back down on to the cushion, stretched out her legs, sighed and peeked in the inspector's direction. 'What ever became of the boy? At some point, he disappeared and never came back.'

'He had a few problems with the law.'

'Who'd be surprised? His father was a murderer, what could you expect?'


Back at home, Franck sat down on his couch in his office and for an hour did nothing at all. He was patiently waiting for a phone call; he saw faces, listened to the voices from the day, held his notepad in his hands but did not open it up. Little by little, his thoughts began to take shape.

Then his colleague André Block called and explained that the fingerprints on the plastic bag found near Esther's corpse did in fact match those of the thirty-two-year-old, previously convicted Patrick Jordan, which had been saved in the computer.

'And that tells us what?' he asked.

Franck did not move, the result surprised him only slightly—perhaps because by then he had come to think the most far-fetched and unlikely things in relation to Esther's death were possible; and he might as well have asked himself the same question his colleague did.

If the eleven-year-old had been directly involved in the schoolgirl's suicide, the investigators would have found clear signs on the rope or on the corpse; Franck excluded the possibility that he had worn gloves; in addition, the autopsy report had been unambiguous in spite of the indication of a minute, incongruous trace, which nevertheless—Block had cleared that up too—had definitively not belonged to Patrick.

Which meant that the boy had to have been nearby—and Linda Schelling's claims seemed to confirm the suspicion—and likely saw what happened but never spoke a word of it to anyone.

Even more silence, Franck thought, and another person casting a double shadow.

'I'm going to have a word with him.'

'I'll come with you,' said Block.

'No.'

'Why not?'

'The case is closed,' said Franck. 'You're no longer responsible.'

Explain to me why I didn't stay in the room, why I just had to find my Porsche Carrera again, why I am guilty of everything that happened? You've got to at least know that.

# CHAPTER TWENTY

# The Wave from Behind the Wall, III

'You don't have a thing on me,' said Patrick Jordan. 'You filled me up with vodka and got me to tell you all about my life. What's it to you? It's all in your files.'

He groaned, tipped over onto the side of the cracked, black leather couch, crossed his arms behind his head and tapped his stomach—his crumpled, black silk shirt hung out of his pants—then shot back up. On the round glass table in front of him stood a bottle of vodka, two glasses and a full ashtray, next to it a pack of cigarettes and a gold-coloured Zippo; as Jordan stretched out his arm to reach for it, the lighter slipped away from his hand.

'You can go, big man.' With an awkward movement, he picked up the lighter from the floor, took the pack, leant back and lit a cigarette, then cast his guest a cloudy glance and waved his hand—whatever that was supposed to mean.

Franck had been calling him for one and a half days; he had received the files on Elisabeth Jordan's death from his friend and former colleague Block, but had only discovered the six-year-old boy two pages on. Apparently,

Patrick had been so convincing that none of the investigators had doubted his testimony, he had been in his room the entire time and had not been aware of the dramatic fight at all; it was only once he heard the front door slam that he had left his room, afraid, and seen his mother lying motionless on the living room floor; after that, he had walked over to his neighbour's, *Frau* Endres, and continuously rang the doorbell and, when she opened, taken her by the hand and led her to his dead mother. Klara Endres notified the police.

That same night, according to the report, Patrick's uncle, Dr Paul Jordan, and his wife Lydia had brought the terrified boy to their home in Ramersdorf where he would live from then on. Patrick did not have to appear in court.

In the questioning with a female inspector, Patrick explained that his parents sometimes argued but 'never so badly', his mother worked with his father at the shop and in the summer they would fly to Mallorca where his parents would meet up with friends 'and it was real nice there with Mom and Dad.'

As to his motive for committing the crime, Nils Jordan explained that he had completely lost control that night after having argued with his wife yet another time over her, in his opinion, improper behaviour with clients and she had accused him of promising people things when they purchased their cars that he could not provide. She, on the contrary, was open and direct in her approach, even if in so doing there was always the risk that they might lose a potential customer.

What is more, Nils Jordan told the police, she pampered the boy and would immediately stay at home whenever he had a cold or, as on that fateful day, had to go to school later than usual. She neglected the shop but put on airs of being the boss and took the liberty of telling the other employees to do things though it was not her position.

On top of all that, Nils Jordan maintained that he had recently seen his Liese walking around with his head salesman; for a while already he had suspected her of having an affair, which she vehemently denied. 'One thing led to another,' Franck read in the report. 'We got into an argument in the kitchen, then she slapped me and I lost my mind.'

He could not explain how he suddenly found the silk shawl in his hand, everything had happened as if he were delirious. Furthermore, the cries coming from the TV had annoyed and encouraged him, he did not know why. Again and again he declared he could no longer remember the course of events: it was only once he was kneeling in front of his wife and he understood that he had killed her that he became aware of what he had done and had to vomit. Then he fled in panic and 'downed three or four beers and three or four fruit schnapps' at his local bar—up until the police came to take him away.

'Thank God,' Nils Jordan had added in his statement, his son had not had to see what he had done.

Both the prosecuting attorney and the judge were extremely doubtful about the perpetrator's claim of being unconscious. Nils Jordan was sentenced to eight years in prison.

After learning his hours from the owner of the strip-club where Patrick Jordan worked as a bouncer and security guard, Franck had parked his car in front of the building on Daiserstraße and transformed himself—just like in the early years on the force—into the beast of patience that a stake-out requires. He had brought coffee with sugar and milk in a thermos, a package of butter cookies and two dried pretzels; the gift for his host was lying next to it all.

He got out of his car every hour to ring the bell, from the third time on, a number of times in a row; there was no answer. Patrick's orange-coloured BMW was parked in a row of other cars just a few metres away. Maybe he was not at home but at a gym nearby, but Franck wasn't convinced; in his experience, bouncers and the members of like professions would always take their pumped-up partners with them to go and work out.

Around evening, Franck left another message on Patrick's phone saying that he was the one at the door and that he would like to drink a few rounds of the vodka he had brought with him; by chance, he had learnt the night before that, after a raid, the strip-club would be closed for the foreseeable future and that Patrick would therefore have an hour to spare for a conversation about Esther Winther. The leaseholder overseeing a cleaning crew had told Franck about the search.

Until around eleven o'clock, Franck had had just enough coffee that he would not have to go to the toilet—

a technique that had also become an advantage to him on tedious and long investigations. Out on the pavement, he took a breath of the cool, damp air before his thumb once again took up the familiar rhythm on the bell.

After about a minute, the intercom crackled.

'At your age shouldn't you already be in bed?' a grating voice boomed.

'I'd like to talk to you about your mother's death,' said Franck. 'A few things that I don't understand came up in the old files. I don't think you told the whole truth back then and I think that, if you trust me more than you did my colleagues, I might understand Esther's suicide better too.'

'Why are you coming up with these old stories now?'

'Someone has alleged that Esther could possibly have been murdered.'

'Who would allege something like that?'

'Could we discuss it further in your flat? I have a good Belarusian vodka with me.'

'Be careful, Inspector, when I hear the word "Belarus" my muscles automatically tense up. I have colleagues from Belarus, they don't make life any better in this city, you can bet on that.'

'Can I come in?'

'Before you annoy me even more.' Patrick Jordan buzzed him in.


Essentially the flat consisted of a thirty-square-metre room—furnished with an eighty-inch flatscreen TV, a worn, black leather couch, a plain, round table with two Plexiglas chairs, a white, ceiling-high shelf full of DVDs, a parquet floor covered with black streaks and a black floor lamp with LED-bulbs whose light had been lowered.

Patrick Jordan sniffed at the open bottle, poured a bit into a bulbous glass, swished the vodka around in his mouth and swallowed it down with a disgusted face.

'What's this shit taste of?' he asked.

'Of vodka,' said Franck.

'And what else?'

'Birch sap.'

'Birch sap?'

'Belarusian birch sap.'

'You're a terrible comedian.' Patrick Jordan was drunk—next to the couch were four empty beer bottles and half a bottle of Jägermeister—he swayed, poured himself another glass and drank it down.

'It's all written on the bottle,' said Franck.

'It's too dark in here. Why didn't you bring any Polish starka, fifty per cent.'

'Forty should be enough.'

Patrick filled his glass a third time, placed the bottle back down on the glass table and fell onto the couch without spilling a drop.

Without a word, Franck went to the table, took a chair, sat down in front of him, laid the files on the floor and poured vodka into the second glass that Patrick had grabbed from the kitchen unit; he raised it and drank.

Shoes and boots lay everywhere, on the door hook hung a leather jacket with an imitation fur hood, next to the door there were at least ten pizza boxes. A smell of alcohol, sweat and cigarette smoke hung in the air of the unkempt and unlovingly decorated flat—the ashtray on the table was full—while on the TV behind Franck, an American football game played on mute.

The bouncer lit another cigarette, blew the smoke into the vodka glass, took a sip, put the glass down on the floor and the ashtray next to him on the couch.

'You lied to the police after your mother's death,' Franck said suddenly. 'I don't blame you, you were a child, six years old, you were in shock, you were alone, you had experienced something no child should ever experience: your mother being murdered by your father.'

Patrick Jordan looked at the inspector with a cold and at the same time startled glance. For a while, Franck returned his gaze, then he said, 'I know that you were nearby on the day of Esther's death, your fingerprints were on the plastic bag.'

'That's all over now.' Patrick's voice was apathetic. 'What do you want? Why are you bothering? You can't change anything, the dead are dead and buried and aren't coming back.'

'That's not true,' said Franck. 'The dead do come back, whenever they want, they sit at the table with us and talk. We can't walk away, we have to listen, hour after hour, the whole night. Then they disappear but we know that they'll keep coming back, over and over again.

How often does your mother come to see you, Patrick, and talk with you and tell you about how she died?'

'Everyone thinks I didn't see anything,' said Patrick. 'That was fine. I wanted it that way. It wouldn't have worked otherwise. I had to find the car, the car, don't you get it? I had to finally find the car, I'd already been looking the whole afternoon, and Willy just squawking away because he could feel that something wasn't right. And then I was behind the couch, and there was the Porsche. And the TV was running. A woman kept saying my name, over and over . . . '

Two hours went by, half a lifetime. Patrick Jordan—having become a child, a stammering adult—would not stop talking.

'You can go, big man.'

Franck had not taken any notes; in between he had almost got up a few times to go sit next to the young man, put his arm around him and share in his imploding proximity. It seemed to him as if Patrick's well-trained, muscular upper body would shrivel up under the tight, black, wrinkled shirt and the only thing left would be his face, turned a stone-grey by the dim light and unexpected force of his voice, with its feverish eyes that strayed through the times and broke apart on the granite horrors of his childhood.

With a trembling hand, he held on to his cigarette and looked at Franck, then patted his stomach again and waved.

Franck leant forward. 'Did you bring the rope that Esther hung herself with in the plastic bag?'

As if trying to ease various points of tension in his body, Patrick moved his head from side to side, raised and dropped his shoulders and stretched his back; he stamped out his cigarette in the overflowing ashtray, wiped his mouth and placed his hands on his hips.

'And if I did?' he said. 'And if it's not got anything to do with you? If there was something between Esther and me? Then what? I didn't hang her from the tree, that wasn't me.'

He stood up, kicking the vodka glass with his naked foot, it rolled across the floor. He went into the hall then into the bathroom and, leaving the door ajar, began to urinate; the toilet flushed, he washed his hands and came back into the room. With his arms outstretched, he shook his hands and rubbed them dry against his trousers.

Franck looked at him; when Patrick noticed, he turned towards the TV where the football match continued. 'Did Esther ask you to bring the rope?' the inspector asked.

Patrick shook his head absentmindedly. 'Would you like a soft drink too?' Without waiting for an answer, he left the room; Franck could hear the sound of glasses in the refrigerator door. Patrick came back with two open beer bottles, one of which he held out to his guest; he raised his bottle and took a long drink.

'That birch sap's really done me in,' he said on the way to the couch; he sat down, stuck out his legs, held the bottle with both hands on his stomach. 'She really didn't want to hang herself,' he said. 'Who's been saying that?'

'You know the answer to that,' said Franck. 'The people around her were convinced that Esther suffered from depression, her parents had no doubt about the declaration of suicide.'

'Fitting phrase.' Patrick raised the bottle but did not take a drink, put it down on the ground and bent forward, just like the inspector. 'Suicide! That was a test, and I got it. What is that supposed to mean: the people around her? People had no clue what was going on with the girl, I was eleven, I got it. The people. That father of hers. That subservient mother. Her stupid girlfriends. She liked me because I didn't pretend with her; all the others laughed at her because she hung around with a kid like me; she understood what was going on with me. And, big man, she was the only person who'd ask about my mother; the others were scared shitless, they thought I'd start crying immediately and would get depressed if the topic came up. Esther was the only one, I could even tell her what I dreamt at night and that I always saw my mother and that she'd ask me where I was. Where I was as she died.

'I've told you everything but still don't know why. Why you won't leave. Why you're sitting here and making me vomit everything up in front of you instead of throwing you out and telling you that if you ring my bell one more time, I'll give you something to think about that you'll still be thinking about next year, bet on it. But no, I'm not. I'm sitting here and we're talking about old times.

'What do you think then . . . Franck? Franck. What do you think, Franck, that was like for me? Do you think it was a game? I didn't get it. But naturally I didn't chicken out. For her it was probably supposed to be a game, but that only occurred to me later on, a lot later on. She said: Can you bring me a rope from my garage, I've got an idea. I've got an idea, she said.

'She always had ideas. I don't know what they were any more, she never talked about them, and why should she have, there wasn't anyone around who understood her. She was completely misunderstood. And I was eleven and the others thought I was just a kid; a bad past, that's for sure, but still a kid. But I wasn't, it was just my age. Esther believed that and I understood her and that's why I was there when she needed me.

'We smoked together, I helped her steal from the department store because her best friend Sandra, of course, was too scared; at least she'd hide Esther's stolen clothes at her house afterwards. I was there for her, I saw how she cried. She never did that, no one was allowed to see her cry, only me. And the other way around too. When I'd had another fucked up dream and was totally out of it at school, I'd wait for her and ask her to go with me to the park. And then. Then.

'People had no clue about any of that. I asked her if she could hold me, she knew why and did. We stood there and she wrapped her arms around me. She was a lot taller than me. I could hear her heart beat and smell her perfume; I could have stayed like that the whole afternoon and the night and always. You can't understand that. That's how she was. Esther.

'And when one day she said: Can you bring me a rope, I want to try something. I said, yes. Then we met in the park, as always, it was almost dark, shit weather, not a soul walking around. She took the plastic bag out of my hand, there was a can of cola in it too, just for her, but she said she wasn't thirsty; I didn't say anything, just looked. She took the rope, threw it over a thick branch, made a perfect noose and knotted it. The whole time we didn't say a word; that was tough for me, I wanted to ask her what it was all about 'cause I'd seen a lot of Westerns, people were always getting strung up. But it was Esther and you couldn't see through her and I thought she was playing a game and I was the first that was allowed to be there.

'Then she looked at me and said: Don't be afraid.

'But I became afraid, because of her voice, because of the voice inside the voice. She undid the zipper of her parka and smiled and I thought, she's not smiling because something's beautiful but because she can't do anything else she's so sad. Probably because I often thought the same thing about my mother when she smiled, but she didn't have those eyes.

'Don't be afraid, Esther said a second time, and I nodded and she said: It's just a game, I'm just trying something out. And I couldn't stay still and asked: And what's that? And she said: Scaring people to death so that they finally understand they can't treat me like they do.

'They can't treat me like they do. Later that sentence wouldn't stop haunting me; that night I'd only half heard it. Does that make any sense to you?'

'Yes,' said Franck. 'What happened next, Patrick?'

'You know what happened next.' Waving his hand through the air, he leant back and shook his head. 'She hung herself, what else is there?'

'But she didn't mean to hang herself, she just wanted to try something out.'

'Who knows?' Patrick tilted his head back and stared at the ceiling.

Franck could not allow him to fall silent. 'What did you do then?' he asked.

'Stop being so formal with me, it's annoying.'

'What else did Esther say to you?'

He spoke to the ceiling, 'The real game would take place in her parents' garden. I'm going to hang myself from the apple tree and dangle there, and then they'll never treat me this way again.' He dropped his head; his expression, Franck thought, was that of a child who had been frightened too many times. 'Then she said that I should go hide in the bushes so that no one would see me in case they walked by. And that's what I did, with the cola in my hand, I ran to the bushes and hid. And then. And then . . .

'She climbed up on to the branch, it wasn't too high up, I'd have got up there easily myself. She put the noose around her neck and then carefully slid down the trunk. She was paying attention and was real careful. I saw everything.'

He jumped up from the couch, breathing heavily through his nose and wheezing as if he had been running;

his words tumbled over one another; he did not notice that Franck had also stood up to allow him room to move back-and-forth and punch the air.

'She slipped some'ow, what the fuck. How was I supposed to know? All of a sudden her legs jerked and kicked and she tried to get air. And I ran away. I couldn't watch. I saw my mother there at the tree. Can'ya understand that? Everyone can understand that!

'I took off but always in a circle, the can of cola in my hand, but to where? I've never known. I've never known. Goddamn. She just hung there, I didn't look. Fucking game. Why don't you understand that? How come no one understood? In the garden from the apple tree. Why? She didn't like apples. She was allergic to any fruit with seeds. Everyone knows that.'

Patrick ran through the room yelling. 'And before that, she'd been to a bookshop. Did'ya know that? No one knew that. She told everyone she had an appointment. And she did: with a book. Don't know what kind of book, but a book—probably about how to hang yourself, how to do it, she just told me to bring the rope and she learnt all about it beforehand. I didn't get it at all. What's that supposed to mean: I'll learn about it. Never'd heard that before, that way of putting it. So, she knew all she needed to know by the time she came in the park. But I didn't, not a thing; I was just a dumb fuck.

'And stayed one. But I didn't show anyone how much of one I was. I never said a word. And people thought Esther was depressed and that's why she hung herself from the tree. Don't know. I don't know—we're born dark. Or not? My mother was that way, Esther too. And so am I, but no one sees that. Do you see that? Take a look at me. Do you see any depression anywhere? I bet you don't.

'I took off. In a circle. And she. And she.

'And she'd had me come there so that I could help her out in an emergency. Wasn't that the deal? So I could hold her if something went wrong with the knot or the game. Something like that, right?

'But I couldn't watch that happen. Her dying.

'Watching Esther die, that was just impossible. The dead always come back, you're right, they come and come and come, and every single time I want to beat them off and throw them out the window. But, goddamn it, it just doesn't work.

'And I thought everything was behind me. And then you show up. What's going to happen to me now?'

Patrick Jordan was too worn out, too lost within himself, to return the embrace. Secretly, however, he hoped that, though it did not look like it, the inspector had a few hidden muscles and would not let him go again right away.


He watches her go and climb up the tree, then he runs off for the bushes, one hand around the can, the other in his face, ducks behind a wall of leaves and holds the kiss tight to his cheek.

CHAPTER TWENTY-ONE

# The Next Morning

She asked him why, in his opinion, after all those years Patrick Jordan had made a confession. He did not answer; neither the events nor his feelings about them seemed like a confession to him.

What had Patrick done? He had been more of an earwitness than an eyewitness to his mother's death and an overwhelmed minor at Esther's.

Franck considered his encounter with the previously convicted bouncer who tumbled from job to job, the one he had shamefully brought forty per cent alcohol to get him to talk, to have been an act of mutual self-defence.

On the search for a potential murderer of Esther Winther, Franck had opened up the hidden door of the family as well as a handful of those they knew and found a series of dungeons made up of nothing but dusty silence and a massive tangle of lies—almost like any other terribly average murder case. But Esther had not been murdered, even if her father had convinced himself otherwise to the extent that it almost seemed to console him. Through his inquiries, Franck was supposed to finally grant him release.

Instead—he talked with Marion about it before the two of them watched their favourite film together with some wine and beer—Franck had returned to the catacombs of his own past, to that night that refused to end and to that woman who just one year later bid farewell to life as if his presence had never had any point.

'Don't talk yourself into things, Hannes,' said Marion Siedler when greeting him, she had called him that and as if the most natural thing in the world he had responded, 'Hello, Gisa.'

'That was humiliating for me,' said Franck.

'You didn't know the family, the parents weren't honest with you or your colleagues, you had no opportunity to get to know their real faces and no reason to have to recognize them. The girl hung herself, now it's been confirmed. What's the father had to say?'

Franck still had not been able to reach Ludwig Winther; he had left a generic message on his voicemail and on the answering machine at his flat numerous times but had not received any call. At the beverage shop, he learnt that Winther—most likely because he knew that he would be let go at the end of the month, as the manager explained to him—had taken his remaining holidays. At the building on Ellinger Way, he only encountered the wife of the flat's owner; she said that Winther had told her he would be travelling for a few days, something she found 'brutally' surprising. 'He doesn't have enough money to travel.' In any event, over the last three nights the attic flat had remained dark.

When Marion Siedler asked him whether he would tell Esther's father about the boy's presence in the park that evening and his fingerprints on the plastic bag, Franck grew silent. He still had not made any decision; but it would probably be best to inform those who had remained behind that, according to the sole witness' statement, Esther's death had been an accident, even if how it occurred—despite Patrick's description—would remain as mysterious as the reasons why. Esther had wanted to try out the act of committing suicide which she intended to imitate perfectly later on in her parents' garden in order to shock her father and rip her mother out of her impassivity—or were there other reasons?

'I believe the boy,' said Marion Siedler. 'I mean, the young man that he is today.'

'I believe him too, even though he was hiding in the bushes and couldn't have seen too much. And what do you think about the girl?'

She thought about it for a while, her hands hidden in the sleeves of her red-chequered lumberjack's shirt. 'She didn't want to kill herself, she wanted to play a cruel trick on her parents and girlfriends and everyone who made her feel misunderstood, ignored and small. She couldn't speak with anyone, she had to figure everything out on her own, just like her mother was to do later on by writing in her diary and ceasing to speak with her husband. Esther slid out of the world and began to enjoy that state, began to make herself comfortable there. That's how I see her. A lonely girl on an uninhabited piece of earth. Like so many at her age; they don't understand life any more, they look up at the sky and think that maybe it would be better up there, simpler, clearer. Esther had never heard anyone say: Thank you for being.

'She told her best friend that she had an appointment in the city, and then she left, but not because she was going to see a man; instead, she wanted obtain information in some bookstores on how to hang herself. She wanted to know how you tied a knot, fashioned a noose, she needed the exact details so that nothing would go wrong later on. No, this girl had lost her means of speech; speaking was no longer possible, she could only act. Show something, demonstrate something, do something unheard of. Look over here, I'm hanging here and it's your fault. Take a good look at me, you murderers, this is what you've done to me.

'And then, once everyone was crying and screaming and walking over to hold her—finally, finally someone would hold her, finally, finally she would be able to touch someone, finally, finally she would be the one they meant, she alone—then she would snap open her eyes and live, and something new would begin, life, just the way she wanted it to be.

'She died during the dress rehearsal for her new life and the young boy had to watch, as if it hadn't been enough to have been near his mother when she died. What do you want to tell the father? Would he understand? I don't know, Hannes, I just don't know.

'The boy, the young man, opened up to you on the one night, after twenty years, he found the courage, you can't accomplish any more than that. You're free, Hannes, you are neither guilty of *Frau* Winther's death nor *Herr* Winther's condition. You won't get any closer to the truth, and you don't have to.

'In the end, as suits your profession, you always want to have a confession. But it seems to me that sometimes there's nothing to be confessed, only understood.

'And don't look like such a cop. You've got a beer, I've got my wine, the DVD's set up, let's get ready for *Great Freedom No. 7.*'

'Let's go,' said Franck. 'But I've got to tell you one more thing about the night I told Doris Winther about her daughter's death.'

Ludwig Winther stood at his window in the dark. He looked down at the street and took a step back whenever someone walked past. He had listened to Franck's messages and sensed what he had to tell him. Nothing new. He had not yet decided whether, in the end, he would take the pills he had carefully been piling up; what he did want to do—if he was still around the following year—was no longer tear the fourteenth of February out of his calendar.

That's a good idea, he thought, and continued to stare outside.

The next morning they hugged each other at the front door but decided not to say anything. Out on the sidewalk, Franck turned around once more, looked up towards the first floor and waved to Marion Siedler before she closed the window. He stopped and listened. The birds were singing; for a few moments, he did not know what day it was. Then it came to him.

Sunday.

# TRANSLATOR'S NOTES

**Page 113.** *You turn people back to dust* . . . Psalm 90:3, New International Version.

**Page 167.** *Death is in my sight today* . . . Quoted from 'The Man Who Was Tired of Life' in William K. Simpson (ed.), *The Literature of Ancient Egypt: An Anthology of Stories, Instructions, and Poetry* (Raymond O. Faulkner trans.) (New Haven: Yale University Press, 1973), pp. 201–9; here, pp. 207–8.

**Page 264.** *Verily, he who is yonder will be a living god* . . . 'The Man Who Was Tired of Life', p. 208.